THE GRIMOIRE
OF KINGS

Book #1 of The Tales of Bramoria

Blake R. Wolfe

ISBN-13: 9798411298352

Cover design by: Get Covers
Library of Congress Control Number: 2018675309
Printed in the United States of America

It's funny, isn't it? I had to get lost on my own in a strange new world to realize that I never knew myself to begin with.

ONE

Tyler Wilson was doodling in the corners of his notebook completely ignoring the droning raspy voice of his social studies teacher. It was the last day of school and he'd be damned if he was going to spend any more time listening to what that old duff had to say. Besides, who the hell cared about another war? They were all the same, lots of dead people for no good reason except to claim land, oil, or dominance.

"Mr. Wilson," the teacher called in his condescending tone across the quiet classroom. "I don't care if it's your last day, this isn't art class. Put it away."

Tyler looked up from his notebook, ready to argue. He'd put up with the bullshit for long enough. As he opened his mouth to retort, the shrill clattering of the school bell interrupted him. The shuffling of chairs and feet filled the room as everyone headed out into the hallway and Tyler realized he'd missed his last chance to tell off that stubborn old asshole. He shook his head. It was probably for the better anyway. His mom wouldn't like it if he got in trouble, even if it was his last day. If he couldn't walk at graduation, she'd be heartbroken.

The bell was the final of the day and the last of his high school 'career' as his teachers liked to call it. While they liked to use professional terms to make public school sound more important than it was, he preferred the term 'federally mandated boredom'. It had been years since he felt challenged in his classes and had therefore lost all interest in them. Most of the time he was mulling over new ways to improve the video game he was building, doodling designs and maps in lieu of notetaking. Even though he was bored with school and ready to be done for good, he wasn't looking forward to college and the challenges it would bring. Leaving home and the world he'd always known was a terrifying thought and one he really didn't want to pursue. That and there was so much he didn't know about himself yet, like what he wanted to do with his life. He wasn't sure if going to college was really a good idea for him. At least not yet.

According to his mom, however, he didn't have a choice. As he walked down the hall he glanced at the edge of a letter peeking out from the pages of his notebook and felt the unease swell in his chest. It had come in the mail three weeks ago and he didn't know how much longer he'd be able to keep it a secret, especially from his mother.

Tyler stepped up to his locker, reaching out a hand to grab the handle, but stopped halfway. There was a condom slipped over the lock.

"Ew..." he said under his breath.

For some reason, the senior jocks didn't understand that senior pranks only lasted for one or two days, not every single day of the year. With the corner of his notebook, he worked the floppy piece of latex off the handle. Pulling his hoodie sleeve over his hand he lifted the lock, trying to avoid the greasy lube smeared over the metal. His locker was mostly empty, cleaned out the days before to make his last day as quick and easy as possible. He slipped the notebook and the few remaining items into his bag, pulled it over his shoulder, and slammed the door shut for the last time.

"Hey dickhead!" a boy shouted to his right, nearly causing him to jump out of his skin.

"Hi Clay..." Tyler sighed, a hand placed over his chest in fright.

"Glad to be out of this hellhole once and for all?" Clay grinned, leaning his shoulder against the lockers with his arms crossed. He always had that cocky smile on his face.

"We still have to come back for graduation."

"You're coming back for that shit?" Clay scoffed, lifting an eyebrow.

"You know how my mom is, she's gotta have photos and souvenirs for every menial task I accomplish."

"Must be nice. My old man couldn't give a fuck less," Clay replied, turning his gaze away.

Tyler saw his expression shift to one of envy, but it was quickly driven out of his mind by a mark peeking out from under Clay's collar.

"What's that?" Tyler asked, pulling the neck of Clay's shirt aside to reveal a deep purple bruise across his clavicle.

"Nothin'," Clay lied, taking a step back.

Tyler reached out again."Is it broken?"

"I said leave it alone," Clay batting his hand away.

Placing a hand on Clay's opposite shoulder, Tyler lowered his voice. "Again? Are you okay?"

"It's not a big deal–"

"Yeah, it is!"

Clay laughed. "Yeah? Well, you're the only one that seems to give a shit." He raised his voice, "Nobody around here gives a flying fuck! Especially the teachers!"

Tyler didn't break eye contact. "You need to get out of there," he said seriously. "You're eighteen now. Get a job and get the hell out. Come live with me if you have to."

Clay cast his eyes downward and ran a hand through his dark hair. He always did that when Tyler got serious with him.

"Dude believe me if there was a way to get out of here I'd do it and spend the rest of my life doing everything I could to never come back. But nobody our age can afford to live on their own, you know that." He shifted nervously. "I appreciate the offer but my dad would come looking for me, he always does. I don't want to bring trouble to your place. Besides, it's not like I can keep living there after you go to college."

"Then come to school with me! I could use the company

and it'll get you away from all this," Tyler replied, gesturing to the bruise on his neck. Having Clay at his side would make the transition to college much easier and it would be good for him. "Give yourself a fresh start!"

"Right, sure," he chuckled. "I'm sure they'll take a fuck up like me at your fancy school, especially on short notice."

Nobody, especially the teachers, believed Clay was a smart guy. But Tyler knew better. Clay had read more books in the past four years than most people read in a lifetime. He knew something about everything and what he didn't know he'd learn in a matter of hours. However, his favorite genre was fantasy, an obsession that they shared. It wasn't uncommon for him to blaze through a thousand pages every couple of days, especially when his father was on another drunken tirade. Tyler knew it was a form of escapism and he couldn't blame Clay, not with the kind of home life he had. His grades and manner of speaking didn't reflect his intelligence, but then again, who had time for tests when you're worried about having your arm broken *again* because your dad had a bad shift at work? Clay had other things to focus on.

"Maybe I didn't get in," Tyler replied with a shrug. "Maybe I don't want to go."

Clay looked back up at him, a smile spread across his face. "Yeah right. I'm sure they looked at your four-point GPA and decided you weren't smart enough."

"It's a public university, Clay. They'll let almost anyone in as long as they can get you to sign the loan paperwork."

Clay pulled away and Tyler knew he was finished with the topic. So much for taking a buddy to school with him.

"Any big plans for the summer?" Clay asked, crossing his arms again and leaning against the lockers. "Drugs? Girls? Boys? Maybe a sudden fascination with knitting? Hell, maybe you'll even start to exercise a little. This teenager's metabolism isn't gonna keep you skinny forever."

Tyler sighed. Clay always liked to bully him when he was feeling too exposed. "No, not really. I'm just working on that game and getting ready to leave I guess."

"Ah-ha! I knew you got in," Clay smiled, punching him in the shoulder. "Well, since you aren't doing anything *productive* this summer, we should probably hang out as much as possible before you leave. It's our last summer, after all, we gotta make the most of it." He glanced around the hallway, making sure nobody was nearby. "Maybe we can start a cult or something? Take over a small country? That would be pretty fun."

Tyler ignored those last comments. "You know you can come over at any time. My mother, for some unknown reason, loves you to pieces."

"Your mom is pretty hot..."

"I swear to god, Clay."

"Don't swear on stuff you don't believe in," he chuckled, lifting an eyebrow. "It's not my fault your mom is single and attractive."

"Maybe I'll just go to school *now* so I don't have to listen to any more of this," Tyler huffed. "Seems it would make both you and my mom happy to have me out of the house for good. Obviously, I'm not wanted."

Clay wrapped his arm around Tyler's shoulders, leading him toward the exit. "First of all, I'm charming as fuck, so your mom wouldn't stand a chance if you were gone. Second, you know I love you, dude. And third, quit being such a pussy. It's just college. Just think of all the chicks you'll get to bang between classes."

Tyler shook his head. Clay didn't understand. "Right..."

Together they walked out of the school and across the parking lot to Tyler's rusted SUV. Pulling the driver's door open he tossed his bag into the backseat. Clay climbed in the passenger side without warning and kicked his feet up on the dash.

"So, what's our first stop for the summer?" he asked, nearly bouncing with excitement.

"Shit!" Tyler swore, palming himself on the forehead as he remembered something. "I totally forgot about Danny's stuff!" He turned back to Clay. "I promised the secretary I'd take him the last of his paperwork for the year."

"No worries, dude," Clay said, his excitement deflating into a grimace. He pulled his feet down and stepped out of the car. "I can walk."

"Are you sure? It'll only take me a minute."

"Nah. No way I'm going back in that building ever again." His expression turned grave as he glanced at the ground. "I'm uh... not really fond of seeing Danny. In his current state, I mean."

Tyler knew Clay didn't like hospitals, especially after his mom had died a few years back. She'd been in the hospital for over a year before she passed away, hooked up to all sorts of machines and things. That was before his father started drinking.

"He's been doing better," Tyler replied, trying to smile. It was hard to do when thinking about Danny. "Last time I was there he was off most of the machines. They were pretty hopeful he'd be off them completely soon."

"That's good to hear," Clay said flatly. He stuffed his hands in his pockets, still staring at the ground. "I thought we were gonna hang, but I guess I can find something to do."

"I'm sorry, Clay." Tyler came around the car to meet him. "Are you sure you don't wanna go with me?"

He took a deep breath and paused. Tyler could see the fight happening in his head. Clay never wanted to go home because of his dad, but seeing Danny reminded him of his mom too much. But there was something else there too, jealousy that Tyler had seen many times. He and Danny were close and Clay got left out when they were together.

"Not this time, dude," he replied, finally letting the breath out.

"I understand."

"Tell him I'm sorry and that I miss him."

"Of course."

Tyler reached out and pulled Clay into a hug. He was

reluctant for a moment, but eventually, he took his hands out of his pockets and hugged Tyler back. It had been years since Clay's mom died and he still couldn't stand the sight or the sounds of the machines. The constant beep of a heart monitor would send him over the edge and Tyler couldn't blame him. Everything in Clay's life fell apart the day she died and he was left to pick up the pieces at only thirteen years old. Ever since then he'd been a troublemaker, fighting anyone who stood in his way as a cry for help. But nobody listened. After all that time the only thing he had left was his books and the fantasy worlds he buried himself in over and over to forget the grief and pain that filled his every waking moment.

"Look, dude, I know you really like me, but this is getting a little gay for my tastes," Clay chuckled, still holding tightly to Tyler. He put his head on Tyler's shoulder, muttering into his ear. "Actually, I think I've seen this porno before. Where's the teacher eating a salad that's going to catch us in the act?"

"You're an impossible person," Tyler sighed, pushing him away. "You know that?"

"Thanks, cutie." Clay gave him a wink.

"Seriously, get out of my sight before I run you over with my car."

"Oooh, BDSM! I'm into that."

Tyler squeezed his eyes shut, pinching the bridge of his nose. "Oh... my god."

TWO

T yler's SUV pulled into the half-circle driveway in front of an imposing white house. Perfectly trimmed hedges outlined the driveway with a gap leading up to four sparkling white columns. Between them was a large arched entryway, the door set inside made of heavy wood and stained glass. Everything from top to bottom was decorated in white and black, the door glass acting as the only splash of color to draw attention. Danny's parents were the richest people in town and it showed in their immaculately curated landscaping and catalog-worthy home. Despite that, they were some of the most generous and kind people Tyler had ever met. He wasn't sure if it was because of their son or if that's just who they were, but everyone in town knew their name because of their charity. It wasn't uncommon for them to sponsor the arts in the area or donate a large sum of money to a local fundraiser for people in need. They were always smiling, always happy, and always the first to get involved when the town needed something.

As Tyler stepped out of his car, a cardboard box full of papers and books in his arms, he noticed another vehicle in the driveway. It was a white van bearing the emblem of the local hospital, which was odd. Usually, a nurse would come to see Danny every day, but they drove sedans with a nurse logo on the side. Tyler felt his heart lighten as he put the pieces together. Maybe Danny really was getting better and they'd finally taken him off the machines completely. That was the only reason the van could be there, to take them back to the hospital they'd been rented from. It was a relief to think that Danny had come so far in the past few weeks. Although Tyler had to admit he hadn't been great about visiting him for the past semester. He said it was because of exams and applying for college, but in reality, he was having a hard time dealing with Danny's deteriorating condition too. Like Clay, he'd begun to hate the sound of the machines and would make almost any excuse to avoid being near them, preferring the safety of his own bedroom and the quiet solitude it contained. But all that was behind him now. He was elated to know that Danny had finally made some progress. Maybe this time he'd go into remission permanently and he could start to actually live for the first time.

With a smile on his face, he marched up to the door, ringing the bell nestled between frosted glass panes. The deep bells chimed inside the house, like the old church down the road on Sunday mornings. A few seconds passed by before he heard the latch click and the stained glass door swing inward. Standing in the doorway was Danny's mother, but something was wrong. Her hair was frazzled and her makeup smeared under her swollen red eyes. She'd always been the kind of person that took a lot of pride in being picture-perfect at any given moment. For her to look less than her best was nearly unheard of.

"T-Tyler," she sniffed, standing in the center of the doorway holding a handful of tissue under her chin. She glanced down at the box. "Are those f-for Daniel?"

"Yeah," Tyler muttered, suddenly feeling like he was intruding on something immensely private. "It's the rest of his stuff for the end of the year and graduation." He shifted the box, glancing inside. "It looks like they put his cap and gown in here too."

A choking sound came from her throat as she lifted her hand to her mouth, tears forming at the corners of her eyes.

"Excuse me, ma'am," a man said from behind her, his approach unnoticed by them both.

"S-Sorry," she sputtered, stepping out of the way.

The man pushed past her and Tyler. He was wearing a hospital-branded hoodie and carrying a large monitor of some kind in his arms. Tyler didn't understand why Danny's mom was so upset that the machines were being taken away. Wasn't that good news since Danny didn't need them anymore? What was bothering her?

"Why d-don't you take those upstairs," she said through sniffles, beckoning Tyler inside. "Daniel's in his r-room. I'm sure he'll w-want to speak with you."

Tyler nodded without a sound. He stepped inside and kicked off his shoes, leaving Danny's mom standing in the doorway, staring out at the yard like a zombie. As he headed across the large living room stuffed with black leather furniture he saw Danny's father sitting in one of their overstuffed chairs near the fireplace. He was stiffly perched on the edge of the shiny cushion, staring toward the wall with unblinking eyes. A crystal whiskey glass full of amber liquid was held loosely in his hand. There was no reaction from him as Tyler walked by, heading for the stairwell.

He felt a weight begin to form in his stomach, like a stone dragging him down as he ascended the stairs. He'd never seen Danny's parents without a smile on their faces, but today they looked like corpses, all their previous vibrancy completely gone. The air didn't feel right, the house was stuffy, and it was too quiet. At the landing, he saw Danny's room at the far end of the hall, the door standing ajar. Every step he took toward it made the weight grow heavier and heavier in his belly until he could barely breathe. He stopped just outside it, terrified of what he'd find inside.

For a long moment, he stood there, too scared to go any further, terrified of what waited on the other side of the door. His parents would have said something if he'd died, right? Tyler's heart rate doubled. They wouldn't have let him up there if that were true. It couldn't be. He'd know if his best friend in the whole world was dead, wouldn't he? Finally, he shook his head, forcing himself to take a deep breath, and knocked lightly.

"Come in," Danny's familiar baritone called.

Breathing a sigh of relief, Tyler pushed the door open and saw the room he'd visited so many times in his life. For the first time in four years, it was completely free of machines. Instead of a hospital bed and monitors, there was just Danny's twin bed and a desk filled with papers. Pencils and notes were strewn over it although the textbooks from school looked mostly abandoned in a dusty stack on the floor. Against the walls were shelves of books, posters of various punk bands, and random knick-knacks from all over the world his parents got him when they had to travel for work. One, in particular, a hand-forged sword from a blacksmith in Romania was his favorite and hung on a handmade mahogany plaque over his bed. He, like Clay and Tyler, had a fondness for fantasy and the worlds he could visit when his body made it impossible for him to leave the house.

Danny was sitting in his office chair, one elbow on the desk as he scribbled a few things down on a page. His dark unkempt hair was ruffled a bit, his fingers laced through it as he wrote. He was pale, too skinny, and dressed in baggy clothes as always. Nothing about him seemed different except for his eyes as he turned to look at Tyler. For the first time in a long while, he looked truly happy.

A smile pulled at his gaunt features, his pale blue eyes lighting up. "Hey Tyler!" he said, pushing himself up from the desk. He walked over and glanced inside the box. Realizing it was school stuff he took it away and threw it to the ground before he wrapped his arms around Tyler. "How are you doing? I haven't seen you in quite a while!"

"I'm okay," Tyler replied anxiously, hugging him back lightly so as to not hurt him. He'd been worried Danny would be mad at him for not visiting, but he seemed fine. He pulled back and looked Danny in the eyes, his voice suddenly serious. "What's going on?"

"What do you mean?"

"Danny," Tyler said seriously. "I'm not an idiot. Your parents look like zombies and the hospital was just here." He gestured around the room. "Why is everything gone? What happened?"

"Only good things," Danny replied, with a smile on his face. He went back to his desk and sat down, shuffling some of the papers aside. "Did you know I started writing a book recently? Fantasy of course! You'll have to read it once it's done. I made myself the main character, because well... why not, right? I've always wanted to be a hero..." His gaze wandered off and out the window for a long silent moment. Suddenly he laughed, realizing he'd spaced out and pulled all the papers into a neat stack before setting them aside. "But enough of that, I want to hear about you! You said you had something to tell me over the phone? You didn't seem very excited though."

Tyler sighed. Danny was the master of redirection. Knowing he had no choice but to indulge him he pulled his backpack around to his chest and opened the top flap. From between the pages of his notebook, he produced a letter with an embossed gold seal on the front. It was the same one he'd been carrying around for the past three weeks. He handed it to Danny.

"You heard back from them? What did they say?"

"Read it."

Danny pulled open the letter and unfolded it carefully, making sure not to crinkle or bend a single corner. His face burst into a smile as he read the first paragraph.

"You got in!" he exclaimed, continuing to read. "And... holy fuck Tyler! A full ride? Are you kidding?!"

Tyler turned his gaze to the floor.

"This is amazing! Congratulations!" Danny got back up from the desk and pulled him into another hug. Tyler could feel every rib through his baggy shirt. "They must have been really impressed! That's a hard program to get into, much less a full ride!"

It was obvious Danny wanted him to be excited. Forcing a smile he tried to think of something clever to say. "And I didn't even have to play sports to do it," he chuckled. "Just had to be the world's biggest fucking nerd."

"Second biggest," Danny quipped. "Although if we include Clay, you might actually come in third."

Tyler's smile faded a little. "He… uh… wanted me to say hi for him by the way. You know how he is… the machines kinda freak him out."

"I understand," he nodded, not letting his smile fade. He gestured around the room. "But you can tell him it's safe to come over now. Those machines won't be coming back." He was beaming. "I'm free of them at last."

"You're… You're in remission then?"

It was Tyler's turn to genuinely smile, happy to hear some good news at last. He'd been so worried and with the state of Danny's parents, he'd expected the worst. Maybe they were just overwhelmed with the news. After all, they'd been in a constant battle with hospitals and doctors since high school started.

Danny's smile didn't falter. "Nope, but I'm done with them anyhow."

The breath caught in Tyler's throat. "What… What does that mean?"

"Come sit down. I've got something to tell you," Danny said, gesturing for him to sit on the bed.

Tyler felt the anxiety building in his chest. If Danny wasn't in remission, why were the machines going away? Did they find some new kind of treatment or something? Had something gone wrong? Was he moving to another country with better treatments? Thousands of thoughts and feelings were racing through his mind as he took a seat on the chevron patterned bedspread, the mattress creaking slightly under his weight. Danny sat down next to him, his shoulder pressing up against Tyler's. Both of them sat there in silence for a long moment, neither wanting to be the one to speak first.

"Well, I guess I might as well say it," Danny sighed, turning to Tyler. "The doctors gave us some news last week that could be considered not the greatest." He stopped there, waiting for a question, but Tyler stayed silent. "It looks like my leukemia is back and it's worse than ever. Nothing is working anymore, not even the chemo."

Tyler felt his heart stop in his chest, his breath catching once more as he tried to inhale.

"But it's not the end of the world," Danny said, noticing his reaction. "They said they could put me on a higher dose and give me six months to a year if they kept me hooked up all the time."

"But… why did they take the machines away then?" Tyler asked. None of it made any sense. "Are you getting new ones?"

"I turn eighteen in a couple of days." He paused for a long moment. "And I've decided to refuse treatment."

Tyler opened his mouth to argue immediately, tears forming in his eyes, but Danny cut him off.

"Listen," Danny urged, suddenly serious. "You've watched me faithfully for these past four years. You were always there during the good and the bad, bringing me school stuff, keeping me company, and making my life more normal than it would have been otherwise." Danny reached out a hand and wrapped it over Tyler's. His palm was dry and cold. "You know what I go through when they put me on chemo. I get *so* sick Tyler, and I'm tired of being sick. I don't want to spend the last months of my life in a hospital bed being pumped full of poison."

Tyler glanced down at Danny's hand covered in red splotches, a symptom of his illness. "But… won't it help? Even a little bit?"

"No." Danny shook his head. "There's no way out of this one, buddy. Even if we do the chemo, I won't make it this time."

The world seemed to stop spinning.

"That can't be true!" Tyler cried, losing control of himself completely as the emotions consumed him. "You've been doing so well for so long! You even came back to school at the beginning of the year! I don't understand how it could have gotten so bad so fast!"

"It just did," Danny replied with a shrug, fixing those pale blue eyes on him. "And there's no way out of it." He squeezed Tyler's hand. "I have a big favor to ask you and I know it's a lot, but I need your support on this. My parents are really upset with me and I think most people will be. You're my best friend in the whole world and… it would mean a lot to me to have your support in this decision."

Tyler could barely breathe. "Of course, I'm on your side," he managed to choke out, tears rolling down his cheeks. He hesitated for a moment, afraid to ask what he really wanted to know. He knew he'd have to learn it eventually. "How… How long without the chemo?"

"Three months," Danny shrugged again. "Maybe four."

"That's it?!"

"That's it."

Tyler pushed himself up from the bed, letting go of Danny's hand. He marched over to the window seat and leaned against the cushion, staring out over the yard. It was late May and the leaves had finally opened all the way, the trees full to bursting. Everything in the world was turning green and coming alive. Daffodils and tulips were unfurling in the sunlight, the professionally designed landscaping around the house full of color. Birds sang, children were laughing in the street on their way home from school, and the air was full of sweetness as summer drew close. All of that was in harsh contrast to what was going on inside the house where the veil of death close at hand hung heavy across everything. And in that small room, Tyler felt his heart break at the thought of losing his best friend, the one he'd had since kindergarten. It wasn't fair, but as the anger began to rise in his chest he knew he wasn't going to let that stop him.

"We're getting out of here," Tyler said, still staring out the window.

"We are?" Danny asked, his voice full of surprise and intrigue.

"Yes. I'm gonna make sure you have the best fucking summer you've ever had." Tyler turned around, glaring at Danny with bloodshot eyes. "We're going to go on an adventure, almost get arrested, and do a bunch of shit we'd be too scared to do otherwise."

Danny smiled. "I like the sound of that."

"Good. Pack a fucking bag because we're leaving. I'm not gonna sit here and watch you live your..." he swallowed hard, "*last* summer here in this room. You've spent enough time in here."

"My parents aren't gonna like this..."

"Then I'll kidnap you! I don't give a fuck!"

"I don't think I've ever seen you be so passionate," Danny laughed.

"I'm coming to get you tomorrow," Tyler said with finality. "We're going to spend your birthday out in the real world, wherever you want to go."

Danny cocked his head to the side, a wide smile on his face. "Let's get lost, like the adventurers in the books we love. No maps, no plans, just wandering in search of something exciting."

"Anything you want," Tyler replied, walking over and pulling him into another hug. "This is *your* summer. I'll follow your lead."

"You're really the best friend I've ever had," Danny muttered against his shoulder. "Thank you."

Tyler felt the tears well up again as he squeezed Danny back. One summer left, that was all. But it was going to be the best they'd ever had, Tyler would make sure of it, even if they had to run away and abandon their parents in the process. College wouldn't start until fall anyway and he hoped his mom would understand. Even if she didn't, she was going to get everything she wanted anyway, so she could grant him this one selfishness.

Tears fell down his cheeks as he held his friend close. At that moment all that was left was Danny and the clock ticking in the back of Tyler's head.

THREE

Tyler stood in the tiny wallpapered kitchen with his mother, her hand over her mouth in surprise. She was holding his acceptance letter.

"A full ride?!" she gasped, still staring at the page, unable to pull her eyes away.

"Yeah," Tyler replied, his voice lacking emotion.

"Oh my god!" she yelled, pulling him into a hug. "That's amazing! To think my child is that talented and smart!" She leaned back, her hands on his shoulders. "I told you I was good at this parenting thing. I was worried after your bastard of a father ran off that I wouldn't be able to do it, but here you are! Barely an adult and already accomplishing amazing things. Soon you'll be making more money than me and being the man I always knew you could be!" She stared at him for a moment. "Aren't... Aren't you excited?"

"Yeah, no, I am..."

"But?"

"Well," he glanced up at her, the guilt building in the pit of his stomach for holding back the truth of how he felt about school. But he didn't have time for that now, he had to find a way to get away with Danny. That was more pressing. "The school called me today... and they want me to come up to the college right away for a couple of weeks." The lie felt like nails in his throat. "It's a special orientation of some kind. I have to leave tomorrow morning."

"Well then you better go!" she replied without hesitation. "I'm so glad to hear that you're finally taking this college thing seriously! I was getting worried, you know, but I'm glad you're taking responsibility and stepping up." She paused for a moment. "Do you need anything for the trip? Money? Food?"

"A little cash would help," he sighed, feeling worse by the moment. He never lied to his mom, but this time there was no other choice. No matter what he told her about Danny or about not wanting to go to college, he knew she wouldn't understand. All she ever saw were her dreams for him. "Just enough for food and stuff. Nothing crazy."

She reached into her purse and pulled out her wallet. She took a card from one of the sleeves and handed it to him. "Just take this," she said. "Put whatever you need on it. I was going to give it to you to go to school with, in case of emergencies, but since you got the whole thing paid for, it's the least I can do."

"Are you sure?" he asked, looking around the dingy kitchen with random items stacked all over the counters. Their lives weren't exactly plentiful when it came to money and his mother worked herself to the bone keeping a roof over their head. He did his best to keep the house clean, but even so, it was still falling apart. Their lives have always been paycheck to paycheck. That's why she put a lot of pressure on him to build a better life than she had. "I don't want to make things hard on you."

"Believe me, you've made everything a lot easier just by getting that scholarship and by proving to me you really want this." She reached out and touched the side of his face, smiling at him. "I'm *so* proud of you, honey. You've done an amazing job."

The pit in his stomach twisted painfully. "Thanks, Mom…"

"Now, you better go upstairs and get a bag packed! Make sure you don't forget your toothbrush or clean underwear."

"I know how to dress myself…"

"And I know how gross boys are," she laughed, patting him on the shoulder. "I've got to work an early first tomorrow, so

I won't be able to see you off..." She looked down at the wallet in her hand. "How about we get pizza to celebrate?"

"You don't have to do that."

She was already on her phone, the local pizza restaurants number on her quick contacts. "Too late! It's the least I can do for my college-bound boy!"

Tyler smiled back at her, trying to cover up the guilt he was feeling. He knew she'd be disappointed in him when she found out what he was really doing, but it didn't matter. He and Danny had been friends forever and he hoped she'd understand. Asking permission wasn't a choice, that was a given. Besides, he'd make it up to her one day. After all, it wasn't like he had a choice about going to college, especially now. He'd pay four years of his life for this transgression, but Danny was worth it.

Clay was knocking on Tyler's front door at the crack of dawn, just like they'd planned the night before. When Tyler answered it he didn't notice the large rucksack or the extra camping supplies Clay had brought. Instead, all he could focus on was the new black eye he was sporting and the cut across his cheek.

"What the fuck happened to you?" Tyler asked, pulling the door wide.

Clay grunted and pushed his way inside the house without a word. It could only mean one thing. His dad had been drinking again.

"Are you okay?" Tyler shut the door and chased him into the kitchen. "Do you need some ice?"

"It's fine."

Tyler reached out for his arm. "Are you s–"

"I said it's fine!" Clay snapped, tearing his arm away and raising a fist as if to strike.

Both of them froze for a moment, Tyler taken aback by the sudden outburst. Clay sighed, running his fingers through his greasy hair. It looked like he hadn't gotten a chance to shower or sleep. He'd probably been up all night defending himself from the drunk asshole that liked to beat him regularly.

"Sorry, dude," he said, his voice gravelly with fatigue. "I just… I don't want to talk about it."

Tyler nodded. He understood, even if killed him to stay silent about the entire situation. He wished he could save Clay, to take him away from the terrible life he'd been dealt, but he was a seventeen-year-old kid. Even if he wanted to do something about it, he was neither old enough nor strong enough to help. If he couldn't convince Clay to help himself, there wasn't much else he could do.

"Danny isn't expecting us until eight," Tyler muttered, keeping his voice soft. "Why don't you go grab a shower and I'll get the car packed up."

"Thanks…" Clay croaked, clapping him on the shoulder as he headed for the bathroom.

Tyler listened to the sound of the door closing behind him and sighed. He was glad they were getting out of town for a while. Maybe, if they played their cards right, they could find a place for Clay to go and get him out from under his father's thumb once and for all. Hell, maybe Tyler would stay with him just to avoid telling his mother that he wasn't ready to leave home yet. Both of them could be runaways together.

"Dude, I can't believe your parents fell for that," Clay giggled as they pulled out of Danny's driveway, his bags tucked safely in the back of the vehicle. "Tossing the bags out the window for me to grab, then telling them you were just going out to lunch? Genius." He sat back in the seat, but then leaned forward again. "Wait… your parents believed you two were going to lunch at eight in the morning?"

"They've got other things on their minds right now," Danny smiled, his blue eyes sparkling in the sunlight as they drove along. He rolled down the window and closed his eyes, letting the wind ruffle his dark hair, making it even more unruly than usual. "The air smells so much better out here." He turned to Tyler. "It's not the same as opening a window, you know? I miss feeling the breeze on my skin."

Tyler forced a smile despite the lump in his throat. He'd forgotten how many small things Danny never got to experience. Feeling a breeze, sunlight, or even just stepping foot outside were things he only got to do once in a while. He glanced over to Danny who'd turned his face back to the open window. The sun highlighted the small red spots peppered across his skin. They could be easily mistaken for freckles, but he knew better. Tyler's heart fell slightly, but he coerced the smile on his lips to widen.

"Where do you want to go first?" he asked, both hands on the wheel. "This is your trip. You make the calls. We'll go anywhere you want to go."

Danny laughed. "I thought you were taking me to lunch?"

"If you think I'm gonna pay for your rich ass, you've got another thing coming," Tyler laughed. "You should be taking *me* to lunch."

"Oooh, I've seen this porno too," Clay interjected. "This is what they call a *Sugar Daddy*, right?"

"Dude, how much gay porn do you watch?" Tyler joked, glancing back at him. "I thought you said you were straight?"

"Do you have any idea how stupid some of those bimbos in straight porn sound?"
He leaned forward between the seats breathing heavily and imitating a sound that resembled a pterodactyl being mauled by a bear. Tyler had never heard anything so ridiculous in his entire life. It was less than five seconds before he and Danny were both laughing so hard that they could barely breathe.

"Seriously!" Clay exclaimed. "That's what they sound like! How the hell am I supposed to jerk off to that?!"

"Oh... my god..." Danny wheezed, clutching at his chest. "That's the most accurate impression I think I've ever heard!"

Clay put his elbows on the center console, resting his chin in his hands, a coy look on his face. "So Danny, serious question."

"Oh boy..."

"Fuck off, Tyler," Clay snarked, turning back to Danny. "So... you ever get lucky with one of the nurses? Ya know, they were scrubbing you down and suddenly, *whoops*, handjob?"

Danny burst out laughing, but Clay looked serious, wanting to know the answer.

"How many people do you know that just get a handjob by accident?" Danny laughed, leaning close to Clay. "Is that how you get yours?"

"Nah, chicks can't keep their hands off me. I have to beat 'em away with a stick!"

"You're so full of shit..." Tyler sighed.

"Sounds like something a virgin would say."

"Tell you what Tyler," Danny cut in. "If this trip goes well and you're really nice to me, I'll give you one. Same goes for you, Clay."

Clay laughed as Tyler felt his face flush red immediately. "W-What?"

"What?" Danny said nonchalantly, shrugging his shoulders. "Bros before hoes." He leaned down to Clay, a hand on the side of his mouth. "That's what that means, right?"

Clay looked away from Tyler who was still bright red, a huge smile on his face. "This is gonna be a fun trip, I can just tell."

Danny glanced back at Tyler, noticing how uncomfortable he was. "Where's the music?" he asked, changing the subject. "Aren't road trips supposed to be full of musical montages?"

"Oh thank god..." Tyler breathed, punching the button on his dash computer.

Suddenly the car was filled with the sound of electric guitars and drums. It was one of Danny's favorite punk rock bands. He reached over and cranked the knob to the right, blasting it loud enough for the whole neighborhood to hear. Without a care in the world, they headed off on their adventure, singing at the top of their lungs with the windows down.

FOUR

They'd been on the road for two days, heading toward the northern end of the state. The trees whizzing by were slowly shifting to pine as they made their way toward the white dunes and big lakes. The past days had been filled with restaurants, roadside parks, and any stupid-looking tourist trap they could find. More than once they'd spent several hours on a beach, just laying in the sun and enjoying the onset of summer. The lakes were still too cold to swim in, but that didn't stop them from going in anyway.

Danny was mostly glued to the window as they drove, watching the landscape slip by. Occasionally he'd look down at his phone and sigh. The previous day had been punctuated by an extremely uncomfortable phone conversation with his parents. Tyler had been able to hear them shouting from the other end of the phone, but Danny weathered it all with a smile. He told them he'd be back in a couple of weeks. His mother had tried to guilt him into coming home, using his birthday as an excuse, but he brushed it away. Instead, he told them that he didn't have much life left to live, so they were going to allow him that one infringement. They didn't seem happy, but it was enough to stop them from starting a manhunt with the local authorities. However, all through the day and night, his phone buzzed, texts from his mother coming through in an endless stream.

"Man, she's really good at this guilt-tripping thing," Danny sighed, quickly typing out a response to her most recent message. "Listen to this. *Wish we could be there to celebrate your eighteenth birthday like we planned. Hope you're enjoying adulthood without us.*"

"Your mom needs to take a chill pill," Clay chuckled from the back, his feet propped up on the center console. "Or get a hobby."

"Both would probably be good," Danny nodded. "But I get it. She's spent her whole life taking care of me, making sure I was safe from everything except my own body." He paused for a moment, staring out at the trees along the highway. "I don't know what she's going to do when I'm gone."

Tyler grimaced. He really wished Danny would stop talking like that. To him, it was no big deal, but to Tyler, it was a constant reminder that his best friend would soon be gone forever, that he'd no longer be able to send silly texts or share dumb pictures with someone he trusted and understood. It broke his heart to think about it. He tried to hide how he felt, but his reactions hadn't gone unnoticed.

"Sorry," Danny said with a sad smile. "I keep forgetting."

"It's okay," Tyler replied. The last thing he wanted was a dying person apologizing to him for anything. "Everyone deals in their own way I guess."

"You are definitely a morbid motherfucker," Clay added. He pulled his feet off the center console and leaned forward between the two of them. "By the way, where are we going next?"

"Danny said he wanted to get lost in the woods, so I was heading for the bridge," Tyler replied, glancing at them both. "Where do you want to go?"

"I'm cool with wherever as long as it's not home," Clay said, looking at Danny. "I'll do anything to never go back to that place."

Danny was staring out the window as a large exit sign zoomed by with lots of businesses listed. "Why don't we stop here for the night?" he suggested. "We've been on the road a lot and I'm getting tired of sitting. We can wander around town and see what we can find. I've got my dad's credit card, so we can do whatever we want." His smile turned mischievous. "Besides, it's my birthday. I need to get a present or five for myself."

Clay pulled out his phone and scrolled through a couple of screens. "Looks like there's a lot of shops and stuff here. Tourist things mostly." He paused at one, gasping. "Holy shit, dude! There's a medieval shop in town! They've got swords and shit!"

"I guess we're going there then," Tyler smiled, clicking on the blinker to take the exit on the right. "Two hundred miles from home and we're buying swords. Why not?"

"Can we camp tonight too?!" Danny asked excitedly as a brown sign with a tent icon on it zoomed by. "Swords and camping go together!"

"I mean, I didn't drag all this tent shit out here for no reason," Clay said, gesturing to the bags in the back of the SUV.

"Fine," Tyler acquiesced. "But tomorrow we stay someplace with a shower. Both of you stink."

An hour later the boys found themselves wandering around the densely packed downtown area. The buildings were original from when the town was founded, but they'd been resurfaced and decorated to look like an upper-class seaside village. Most were shops filled to the brim with postcards, shot glasses, stupid knick-knacks, and sweets, their windows stuffed with colorful garbage. But that's not what they were there for. Clay and Danny had both gotten it in their head that they were going to buy themselves swords, claiming they would come in handy while they were getting lost in the woods. Tyler could only shake his head, wondering what kind of trouble they'd get in if they were caught attacking local flora by a forest ranger.

The road they were on ended in a small turnaround-style loop with shops lining the entire edge of the circle. Several people milled about, most of them drifting towards the shop selling fudge. The smell of hot sugar and chocolate wafted over the street, turning most of their heads. Tyler wanted to stop there after the swords. The other shops had a steady stream of people going in and out. The tourist season hadn't officially started yet and most of the people there were retirees. The families would be along in a few weeks once school was out for the summer. Then the streets would be filled with screaming children, crying about not getting their fourteenth helping of sugar for the morning.

Tyler ignored the shops mostly, following quietly behind Danny and Clay. However, one small shop caught his attention. It was wedged between two others and was completely empty, the glass panes of its thin window broken, and a large chain looped through the door handle. The paint was peeling off the weather and graying wood. It looked completely abandoned. Tyler thought it was a bit odd that such a popular place would have an empty shop, much less allow it to look so terrible. As he moved closer he noticed a freshly installed sign to the right of it. It was slated for demolition. Passing it off with a shrug, he followed the others into the medieval shop that had a large red paper mache dragon hanging in the window with tissue paper flames extending from its open jaws.

A half-hour later they emerged, large rectangular boxes in each of their hands. The boxes all contained a weapon of their choice that Danny had insisted on paying for, citing his birthday as the reason for the gifts. Clay was happy to accept since he had little money of his own, but Tyler felt a bit guilty. The plan had been to treat Danny on his birthday and for the whole trip, not let him buy everything just because his parents were wealthy. However, he was happy to be spending as little as possible on his mom's card, absolving him from a small portion of the terrible guilt he felt. After all, he'd lied to her about going away to orientation, the least he could do was not be unwise with her charity. One less thing to explain when he got home.

Danny and Clay cried out as they smacked each other with their boxes, carrying on nearly into the street itself. The geriatric tourists were staring, disapproving looks on their wrinkly faces. Tyler was about to call them back to avoid having the cops called on them when something caught his eye.

The abandoned shop had a light on inside. He took a few steps closer, noticing the panes of glass were no longer missing or broken and the chain on the door was gone. Across the window was a small wooden sign with peeling letters. It read *The Lone Phoenix* in flaking red and gold paint. Just behind the dusty glass were stacks of leather-bound books and a dark figure moving in the center of the shop.

It didn't make any sense. Just a half-hour ago it had been broken, derelict, and completely abandoned. How had the repairs been done so quickly? Not to mention the entire store had been stocked, cleaned, and unchained. Tyler glanced to the side of the building, noticing the sign for demolition was gone, the dirt looking as if it had never been touched. He continued to stare in confusion. Had he imagined all of it? He didn't notice the others coming up beside him.

"What's up Tyler?" Danny asked, stepping to his left.

"Did you guys see this shop before we went in?" he asked, not breaking his gaze for fear the shop would revert back.

Danny and Clay both glanced at it for a moment, shaking their heads.

"I didn't even notice it," Danny replied.

"Is this a bookstore?" Clay asked, stepping up to the window, the excitement clear in his voice. He pressed his face against the glass, cupping his hands around his face to see better. "We should go inside!"

"Sounds good to me," Danny agreed, stepping up to the glass as well.

But Tyler hesitated, still staring at the dark figure inside moving about. Something was wrong, he just couldn't tell what. "I don't know you guys. I've got a weird feeling about this place."

"About a bookstore?" Clay said, jabbing at him with his finger. "Don't tell me you're too chicken shit to go inside."

"No, I just—"

"Sure, sure," he laughed, making chicken noises at Tyler. He reached behind him and grabbed the door handle, pulling it open. A bell tinkled deep within the shop. "Ain't no way I'm passing up a creepy old bookstore. You two can sit out here and be lame on your own."

He disappeared inside, the heavy door shutting loudly behind him.

"Come on Tyler," Danny urged, pulling him by the sleeve.

He couldn't shake the eerie feeling. "I don't know..."

"Tyler," he said seriously. "What could happen? It's just books. You'd be in more danger in the fudge shop across the street."

He shook his head, suddenly realizing how silly it all sounded, even to himself. "Yeah... you're right. Sorry."

Danny wrapped an arm around his shoulders and pulled the door open, the bell ringing inside the shop again. "It's all good. Our brains can be weird sometimes."

"Can't argue with tha–"

Tyler stopped mid-sentence as his eyes fell on the interior of the shop, the door closing hard behind them. Every wall from floor to ceiling was composed of bookshelves, most of them bowing under the weight of the massive tomes placed upon them. Tables and any odd piece of furniture with a flat surface were covered in books as well, most of them with a layer of dust settled on their covers. But that wasn't what surprised him, it was the books themselves. Every single one of them was bound in leather and most were decorated with jewels or ornate carvings across their covers. Immediately he wondered if they'd wandered into a collector's shop. If that was the case, everything in the place would be far too expensive for any of them to purchase except for maybe Danny.

Clay was a few feet ahead, already bent over one of the dusty tomes. Both Danny and Tyler stepped up beside him, glancing down at what he was examining. The book was covered in ornate filigree and strange runes that had been carved into the leather, none of them Tyler recognized. In the center sat a hexagonal faceted jewel the color of honey. Above it was the embossed title that read *The Grimoire of Kings*. Clay was rubbing his fingers over it, leaving streaks in the dust. A gold latch adorned the right side, a small brown piece of paper hanging from it, which he assumed was the price tag.

"What's this?" a raspy voice said from behind one of the bookcases. "Three customers at once!" An ancient man-made of nothing but wrinkles stepped out from behind a case, his skinny frame leaning heavily on a gnarled wooden cane with a dark blue gem set into the top. For some reason, he was dressed in a double-breasted vest made of reds and golds, a long gold pocket watch chain hanging from the pocket. On his left lapel was a stylized gold pin featuring some sort of bird with red eyes. "What brings young lads like you in today?"

"We're just looking," Tyler replied automatically, feeling suddenly out of place, almost like he was intruding.

"Nobody finds *The Lone Phoenix* without a reason," he smiled, his deep brown eyes wrinkling at the edges. "So I'll ask again, why are you here?"

"We're looking for adventure," Danny replied nonchalantly as if it was a completely normal thing to say. "And we're all fond of reading."

"Adventure, huh?" the old man said, scratching his chin. "Many who come into the shop find that their lives are inexplicably changed by what they find here. So maybe adventure is what you'll get."

Danny tilted his head to the side. "How can a book change someone's life?" he asked. "I mean, they are fun but I'm not sure about life-changing."

"How many books have you read?"

Danny shrugged. "Hundreds. Thousands probably."

"And they never changed you?" He stared at Danny, waiting for a reply, but when none came he continued. "Readers devour books every day searching for something missing from their own lives. A way to escape the drudgery." He paused for a moment. "But the books in this shop do something else. They devour their readers."

Danny and Clay both laughed, thinking the man was telling some sort of joke.

"You should put that in the book you're writing Danny," Clay said. "Some mystical mumbo jumbo a wizard would say."

The owner of the shop didn't look impressed with them. "I see you're not open to what I have to offer," the man replied, his smile fading instantly. "You'll find plenty of *fake* adventure in that section over there." He lifted a bony finger and pointed toward the right-hand wall lined with a shelf of mass-market paperbacks that Tyler could have sworn weren't there a moment ago. "Be quick about it. I'm a busy man," he added, a tone of impatience suddenly in his voice. "Pick what you want and get out of here. You're wasting my time."

The sudden change in tone caught Tyler off guard, but the others didn't seem to notice or really care. Both Clay and Danny hustled over to the shelf, searching for anything that caught their eye. But Tyler made his way slowly around the opposite side of the shop, looking at the leatherbound books on the walls and tables. Their spines were completely unreadable, although a rare few had geometric patterns on the covers that intrigued him. In a way, they reminded him of the spell circles in the fantasy games he'd played, but he knew they were probably collector's editions of famous stories or something. However, the price tags didn't make any sense to him. Each had a single brown paper tag hanging from the binding with a dollar sign, but no numbers. Instead, he saw prices like "All the wisdom of your teeth", "The silence of a cat's paws", and his favorite "The memory of losing your virginity". Tyler chuckled to himself, reaching up to pull the last one from the shelf, wondering what could possibly be worth a memory he didn't possess. He heard a sound like an angry cat spitting from behind him.

"No touching!" the man yelled, whacking him in the back of the thigh hard with his cane. "If you're not going to buy, you don't get to touch!"

The other two looked over from their shelf.

"S-Sorry," Tyler sputtered, rubbing his thigh. The man tore the book from his hands and put it back on the shelf. Tyler looked at the others with an eagerness on his face. "Are you ready to go?"

"Yeah," Danny replied, a look of confusion and surprise

that the old man had attacked his friend. "There's nothing good here anyway," he said, his tone turning surprisingly confrontational.

"My store not good enough for you, boy?" the man accused, his lips curling back in a snarl. He'd gone from looking like a kind old man to a worn-out possum. "You young people wouldn't recognize adventure if it was staring you in the face! All you want is phones and apps, a cheap thrill to get you off so you can go back to your mundane little lives." He took a step closer to Danny, his voice shaking. "Even *you* who has the least time left."

Clay was already crossing the shop, stopping for a moment at the table next to Tyler. Danny held his hands up in mock defeat, making his way toward the door, not reacting to the man's comments.

"Sorry old-timer," he said, his voice missing much of its usual cheer as he neared the door. "I don't care what you think, but there's no reason for you to be a dick to us."

The old man's eyes bulged in anger. "Get the hell out!" he snapped, lunging after them with his cane.

All three of them skittered toward the door, pushing their way out into the street. They jogged to the other side and rounded a corner, putting some distance between them and the old man who'd suddenly gone crazy.

"And don't come back!" the man hollered from out of sight.

"Dude… should we call the cops or something?" Danny asked, looking at Tyler. "That old bastard attacked you for no reason! Since when are you not allowed to touch books in a bookstore?!"

"It's not a big deal," Tyler replied, still rubbing his thigh. "I don't want to put up with the hassle. He was kind of a dick though… I wonder why?" He paused for a moment, meeting Danny's gaze. "He said some of the oddest things.."

"He was just some crazy old coot, don't read into it," Danny smiled, waving the concern away. "I still have half a mind to call the cops on him though."

Danny turned his attention to Clay who was a few feet ahead, giggling to himself with his hands unnaturally crossed over his stomach.

"What's up with you? Get some sort of sick pleasure out of watching me get hit by a stranger?" Tyler asked, annoyed that Clay always seemed to have fun at his expense. Little bits of it during school weren't so bad, but with Danny around Clay had a new audience. He'd been ruthless over the past couple of days and it was getting on Tyler's nerves.

"I mean… yes, but that's not it." He reached in his jacket and pulled out the dusty leather tome with the honey-colored gem set into the cover. "You think that'll teach him?"

"What the fuck!?" Tyler cried, not believing what he saw. "You need to take that back!"

"No way," Clay smirked, hugging it to his chest. "You want me to go back there and get arrested? Besides, if you ask me, the old asshole deserved it."

"Fine, then I'll take it back." Tyler reached for the book, getting his fingers around the edge of it. For a moment they fought over it, but he managed to wrestle it out of Clay's grasp and turned around, heading back toward the shop.

"We're gonna get fucking arrested if you do that!" Clay called, not moving from his spot. Danny stood nearby with a worried look on his face. "Don't say I didn't fucking warn you!"

Tyler ignored him. He had to take the book back, mostly for his own conscience. Even if the old man had attacked him, it didn't feel right to steal from him. Besides, he was getting tired of Clay doing that kind of shit all the time. Just because he had a hard time at home didn't mean he had to be an asshole or get into trouble as often as possible. As far as Tyler was concerned, it was a one-way ticket to fucking up his life for good. Even if Clay wanted that for himself, he wasn't going to take Tyler down with him, or Danny for that matter.

Standing at the door to the shop, Tyler hesitated for a moment. He really didn't want to deal with the backlash from the old man. He thought he could maybe leave the book out front for him to find but quickly dismissed it. If it was half as valuable as it looked, it was not something that should be left outside. Besides, he was already going to be in enough trouble when he got home. Shoplifting and damage of private property were not things he wanted to add to that growing shitstorm.

Grabbing the door handle, Tyler gave it a pull. But it stopped short, the chain rattling against it. He glanced down, not believing his ears. There was a chain wrapped through the handle once more, the window papered over from the inside. Taking a few steps back he glanced over the storefront. It was dark on the inside, there were no books in the window, and the panes of glass were broken once again, with a few shards laying on the sidewalk. The sign with the peeling letters was gone. Even the demolition notice had returned, fresh dirt overturned where it had been installed. He couldn't believe what he was seeing. They'd just been in the store less than two minutes ago.

Tyler walked back and forth, trying to wrap his mind around what had happened. But all he could find was a small piece of paper taped to the inside of the window. It read "All Sales are Final" in bold red lettering. Tyler turned the book over in his hands, searching for the tag. Maybe it wasn't as expensive as he first thought. Ripping it free of the book he saw the price scrawled across the tag in loopy golden ink.

"Your Integrity" was what he read.

FIVE

The night had grown chilly as the three of them huddled around a campfire with their sleeping bags laid out on the bare ground. Stars shone brightly overhead, filling the sky with millions of tiny pinpricks of light. Tyler had his hands laced behind his head, staring up at them as he let his thoughts drift by. He was trying to figure out a way to tell his mom that he didn't want to go to college without her flipping out. It seemed like an impossible task. Each new scenario that ran through his head had the same outcome, him going whether he liked it or not because he knew he couldn't say no to her. Not after she'd spent so many years taking care of him all by herself and placing all her bets on his future.

Beyond that, he was thinking about Danny and what would become of him after the summer ended and his time ran out. Where would he go when he died? Would he just slip into a black void or would there be somewhere else to go? Maybe some sort of adventure like he'd read about in all his books. He thought Danny would like that. Something full of dragons, magic, and intrigue, that always seemed to be his favorite. Tyler didn't know if he believed in an afterlife or souls, but he hoped, for Danny's sake, that there was such a thing. He didn't want to think of him just ceasing to exist, forgotten by everyone eventually and lost to time. Maybe he'd incorporate Danny into his video game, that way he'd live on in some capacity and be remembered by all who played it. Or maybe he'd finish his book and Tyler could get it published for him as a memento of his legacy.

Tyler felt the tears welling up in his eyes and he reached a hand up to wipe them away. He didn't want to be crying in front of the guys, especially Danny. If this was to be one of his last trips, he wanted it to be full of laughter, not tears. He pulled his gaze away from the stars, the vastness of space above him leaving too much room to think. Instead, he leaned on his side and gazed at the fire. The warmth washed over him, flames dancing over the logs. It was closer, palpable, and full of life, unlike the endless darkness above. He let the feeling roll over him, trying to force away the despair building in his chest. Danny was sitting on the other side, smiling and talking with Clay.

"If you really think about it," Clay said, gesticulating grandly. "There's really no such thing as right and wrong because it's based on perception and it's subjective. Sure there are socially accepted norms, but those change all the time. What's okay today is not okay tomorrow and vice versa. Morality and ethics are an ever-shifting narrative spun by society. And those in power are the ones that get to decide what's acceptable."

"I've never thought about it like that," Danny nodded.

"I feel like it's one of the universal truths people are starting to accept. For better or worse they are waking up to reality," he sighed. "Not to sound like a shitbag, but I'd give anything to be one of those people in power."

"Why's that?"

"Are you kidding, dude?" he laughed. "That would be amazing! You could make all the rules yourself and you don't even have to follow them! I'd basically be a god. And I wouldn't have to go home again…" His voice grew quiet and dark. "I wish I didn't have to go back ever…"

"So is this what you're sitting around thinking about while *not* doing your homework?" Danny asked, driving the conversation back to something less dire.

"You say that like it's a bad thing, dude," Clay smirked,

snapping out of his thoughts. "Look at it this way, I don't need good grades to get started in a trade and we all know college is a crock of shit." He glanced over to Tyler. "No offense."

"None taken."

"I just don't see the point of moving away, going into a ton of debt, and learning something that I'm not even gonna get to use." Clay gestured back to Tyler. "This ass got a full-ride and he's gonna be someone. In reality, he doesn't even need school because he already knows how to make those games he loves. He just needs some shitty piece of paper and a transcript to prove to some rich asshole he's not a moron."

"So what are you going to do? With your life I mean," Danny asked, gazing earnestly at Clay. "What's the plan?"

"Dude... I don't fuckin' know." Clay slumped back on his sleeping bag, leaning on one elbow. "I mean, I could go learn a trade I guess. That makes decent money." He paused for a moment. "But I mean, what's the point? I'm going to go learn something so I can do it for forty years until my body is too wrecked to do anything else, then I die. What a great life."

"It doesn't sound so bad to me," Danny replied.

"Yeah, well, you won't have to do it, will you?"

The entire camp went silent. Clay's eyes grew wide as he realized what he'd said.

"Dude... I didn't mean... I'm sorry."

Danny held up a hand, a half-smile still on his face. "No. You're right. I won't have to go through all that or make those decisions." He glanced at Tyler, then back to Clay. "I wish I could go to college and experience it for myself, but I don't envy the work and the *real world* that comes after." He paused for a moment. "I guess I'm just jealous of the beauty both of you are going to see without me. Those little moments filled with passion, love, and excitement. That's what I wish I could have more of."

"I'm sorry..." Clay said, shaking his head.

"Don't be," Danny chuckled, patting him on the leg. "We can't sit around and pretend that we don't know the truth of the situation. Delusions may be easy to accept, but eventually, they always fall apart."

All three of them were silent for a long while, their gazes returning to the fire. There they stayed for a long while, each of them lost in their own private thoughts. For Tyler, it was mostly about Danny and what he'd do after he was gone. He didn't know how he'd be able to handle the loss of his best friend. And then to be forced to start college at the same time. He wondered how he'd bear the weight of it all. He already felt like he was about to break from the strain.

"Hey Tyler," Danny said, pulling him from his thoughts. "Where's that book?"

"Oh yeah," Clay piped up. "Where is *my* book?"

"You mean the one you *stole*?" Tyler snarked back.

"Hey, finders keepers, right?"

Tyler pushed himself up from his sleeping bag, knowing better than to argue. He stomped over to the car and pulled the book out of the back seat. Clay's cavalier attitude about getting them in trouble was wearing on his nerves more and more and Danny was starting to pick up some of Clay's attitude. Tyler wasn't looking forward to both of them being a pain in the ass for the entire trip. He turned the book over in his hands, wondering where the shop and its owner had gone. Neither of the guys seemed to care about what he'd seen, all they wanted was the stupid book. Walking back to the fire he tossed it over to Clay, not trying to be careful.

"Alright, let's see what we've got," Clay smiled, rubbing his hands together.

He tore the tag from the book, snorted at the price, and tossed it in the fire without care. Danny scooched in close as he undid the gold clasp holding it shut. Running his fingers over the jewel once more he looked up at Tyler.

"You gonna join us, grump ass?"

Tyler rolled his eyes with a sigh, crawling over to where the other two were sitting. He sat on the opposite side of Clay and crossed his arms.

"Hold onto your butts," Clay muttered, quoting a favorite movie of his.

He flipped the book open with a flourish, exposing the colorful swirled end pages that held the binding to the cover. On the edges of the cover was a series of tiny tacks that held the leather to the book, the corners cut neatly to leave almost no seam showing. Clay turned the first page, the thick cream-colored paper making a satisfying sound as it bent. The title page was decorated in looping letters written in blood-red ink.

"The Grimoire of Kings," Clay said as if it were a spell of some kind.

"Interesting," Danny commented, looking for the page. "It looks pretty old. I wonder if it's got some references to the Key of Solomon or maybe the Greek Papyri."

"Bro… How do you know that shit?"

"Living in a tiny room for years leaves a lot of time for reading."

"Fair enough."

Clay turned to the next page. Written in the same beautiful calligraphy was what looked like an inscription. All of them leaned in to get a better look.

"Those who seek the power of the kings of old," Clay read aloud, "do so at their own peril. For those who open this grimoire are transported to worlds unknown and in doing so they are forever changed. There is no going back." Clay paused for a moment, wrinkling his nose. "Weird… almost sounds like a warning doesn't it?"

"Or like a great opening to an even better book," Danny murmured, pulling at the next page. "I want to see what's in it." At the top of the next page, it said simply "Welcome to Bramoria" and nothing more. Danny turned to the next, but it was blank. He grabbed another. Blank again. Page after page he turned, taking the book from Clay and flipping through all the pages at once. But there was nothing. The entire book was completely blank from front to back except for the title and the strange warning.

"Huh," Clay mumbled, holding a page up to the firelight as if the book was written in invisible ink. "That's weird. Do you think it's just a fancy journal or something?" He flipped it back to the cover, running his fingers over the jewel again. "It kinda looks like half a d20. Maybe it's meant for a tabletop game or something?"

"Man," Danny sighed, leaning back on his elbows. "I was really hoping for an epic adventure story. Maybe something I've never read before."

Tyler actually felt a little better seeing that the book was blank. Stealing a priceless collector's item could land them in jail if the old man turned them in. But a journal wasn't so bad, even if it was rather fancy.

"Did... did you two see the store after we left?" Tyler asked again, pulling his eyes away from the blank book.

"No, like I said, I stayed with Clay," Danny replied, staring back at the fire. "I didn't want to get yelled at or beaten by the crazy old asshat."

"Something was... different about that store," Tyler began, trying to find a way to word it that didn't make him sound crazy. "The lights were out, the door locked, and the books were gone. Almost like it had never existed." He wrapped his arms around his knees nervously. "Did either of you see the shop before we went inside?"

"I was too focused on the swords," Clay smiled.

"Me too," Danny added.

"How could it have disappeared so fast?"

Clay and Danny exchanged knowing glances. It didn't go unnoticed by Tyler. They had already made it clear they didn't believe him. But even without their support, he couldn't shake the feeling that something extremely odd had happened, that he wasn't making it up.

The camp was quiet for a few moments, all of them staring into the fire. Tyler was glad they'd been able to find a place so empty. Only a couple of families were staying at the far end near the lake and he was glad Danny's first time camping wasn't full of screaming children and obnoxious drunks. All of them had been happy to keep to themselves inside the trees and away from the lakeshore where the other campers were. From their site, they could still hear the eerie calls of the loons on the lake at sunset, their melancholy sounds filling the air. But now that night had come, the world was full of insect sounds and the first faint flashes of lightning bugs.

Danny picked up the blade he'd gotten in town, a falchion, and turned it over in his hand. "That store was weird, but no more than any other old bookshop I've been in."

"Same," Clay agreed, running a finger over the blade of his rapier that Danny had bought for him. "That old bastard was nuts though."

Tyler glanced at his own shortsword. It was a simple blade without much decoration, but he liked the look of it. He wasn't much of a collector when it came to such things, but it seemed like a good keepsake to remember their trip. Besides, in Danny's mind leaving without one wasn't an option. It was his birthday after all.

"I wish we could go on a real adventure. A quest to slay the dragon, be heroes of the realm and all that," Danny mused, holding his blade up so it flashed in the firelight. "What I wouldn't give for a life full of brave crusades."

"You and me both," Clay agreed, picking up his rapier. He pressed the blade against Danny's, the metallic clang echoing through the trees. "Off fighting pirates or leading an army to war. Coming home with mounds of gold and living like kings! That would be the life."

"It sounds okay, I guess," Tyler added.

"You guess?" Danny asked, giving him an incredulous look. "Don't you want to go on an adventure like that? That's what your games are about after all."

"It sounds lame, but I like keeping it in the game," Tyler sighed, running a finger over the sword in front of him. "There's nothing to lose in a game, you can just start over from your last save point. But in the real world, everything is on the line whether it's swords and dragons or jobs and family." He thought of his mom and how devastated she was when his father walked out on them, never to be heard from again. Now she'd be devastated by him too when he finally told her the truth about school. *If* he ever told her. "Honestly, I think it's best to just keep your head down and not get involved. If you aren't risking as much, it's harder to get hurt."

The other two stared at him for a long moment, the firelight dancing across their faces. They looked surprised by his words. After all, he was the one with a full ride, the one going out in the world to do all the things he claimed to not want to be involved in. But if he was honest with himself, he wasn't going because he wanted those things. He was going because it took a burden off his mother's shoulders and would make her happy. The more he thought about it, the more he realized he didn't have a choice. If only there was a way he could disappear and avoid the real world that terrified him down to his core.

"No offense, but you're really fucking lame," Clay finally said, cocking an eyebrow.

"Saying 'no offense' doesn't make it less offensive, asshole," Tyler quipped, shooting him a dirty look. "It's not like you're facing up to your problems either."

Clay's face darkened.

"I didn't mean…"

"No, it's fine. I understand," Clay said, waving him off, although his expression stayed the same.

Danny, sensing the tension, clashed his blade against Clay's, pushing himself up from the sleeping bag. "Fight me you dirty scum!"

"Aye!" Clay yelled back, taking the bait immediately, the metal ringing through the trees. "Avast! Or whatever!"

Tyler moved away, watching the two swing at one another wildly. He leaned back and threw a couple more logs on the fire, keeping well away from their joust. It was a relief to have Clay distracted and Danny looked like he was having the time of his life. Even though he knew their time was short, he was happy to see them smiling. Danny needed the distraction and Clay needed the time away from his father. There was so much turmoil going on in both of their lives that Tyler found himself feeling ashamed that he was so worked up about leaving home. Clay would have given anything to leave and Danny would never get the chance. Who was he to complain when they had it so much worse? Still, he couldn't shake the anxiety that ate away at his belly, reminding him of all the future fears that would eventually come to pass.

A few minutes later a roasting stick and a bag of marshmallows were dropped in his lap by Clay, pulling him from his thoughts. He hadn't even noticed they'd stopped fighting.

"A knight's got to eat," Clay said, plopping down and wiping the sweat from his brow. "Get cooking, wench!"

"When did I turn into the bitch of the group?" Tyler asked, cocking an eyebrow.

"Bro, I hate to tell you this," Clay replied, glancing at Danny for a moment. "But you were born a bitch. Sorry."

Tyler punched him in the shoulder, their laughter ringing through the trees. Together they talked into the night, eating and carrying on until the wee hours of the morning. Eventually, the exhaustion overtook them. Too tired to set up their tents in the dark, they each crawled into their sleeping bags, staring up at the stars on a cloudless night until they drifted off into dreamworld.

SIX

T yler woke up with a start. He'd been dreaming. The sounds of birds echoed through the trees and he threw an arm over his eyes, blocking out the light. Still half asleep, he could recall almost everything that had transpired.

The dream started with him getting up from their campsite in the dark and walking through the woods until the sun rose, the night passing in an instant. Eventually, he came to a giant field full of rolling hills as the sky turned blue. The trees were sparse and tall grass grew everywhere. At first, everything had been fine, the land around him quiet and serene. But the longer he stood there the more he noticed a strange sound. It was a deep beating, like a drum in the distance but with more force behind it. Finally, realizing it was coming from above, he looked up, spotting five massive figures zooming through the sky in his direction. Roars filled the air along with jets of blue and orange flame. He recognized them immediately.
Dragons.

The hills were suddenly full of people as they rushed out of the woods on all sides, their battle cries echoing over the land. Medieval siege weapons were drawn onto the field as soldiers dressed in leather armor came rushing in. In less than a minute ballista bolts were shot into the sky at the creatures bearing down on them. A few key figures in different colored cloaks stood alone leaning on great staves, their eyes turned toward the sky. He knew they were wizards immediately, their pointed hats and long beards giving them away.

With strange incantations they summoned huge balls of fire and energy, firing them toward the dragons at an astounding speed. Some of the beasts were barely able to dodge the attacks, but not all. Tyler watched as a giant ball of flame collided with one, punching a massive hole in its wing, and the creature began to plummet. At breakneck speed, it collided with the earth, dirt and rubble flying in all directions. Tyler could feel the rumble under his feet as the dragon struck and skidded, eventually flipping over and onto his back before it came to rest, no longer moving.

Gouts of flame swallowed up whole battalions of soldiers and siege weapons were turned to ash in seconds as the dragons remaining continued to attack. But they were no match for the mages. One by one the beasts were shot from the sky and Tyler didn't know whether to feel bad for them or terrified that they seemed hellbent on destroying everyone in the hills regardless of the cost. One by one they crashed into the ground, their impacts echoing like thunder. The soldiers rushed on them, quickly slaying those that survived as they were rendered nearly helpless.

A vicious roar filled the air and Tyler turned his attention back to the sky. He watched as the very last dragon, a massive metallic monster, set its sights on the mages. It leaned back, flaring its wings out as energy began to coalesce around it, sucking into its mouth. Shouts echoed across the field, hands pointing up toward the sky. The mages began their incantations once more, all of them focusing on the creature preparing to destroy them all with its one final attack. Balls of fire and lightning flashed through the air before the great beast could release the built-up energy. Several collided with it at once, the elemental flames wrapping around its body. Tyler thought it would be completely consumed, but a moment later the air cleared and he saw it was hurtling toward the hills, straight for where Tyler was standing. Realizing it would hit him if he didn't move, he ran toward the top ridge of the hill, heels digging into the loose soil.

On its way down the dragon, somehow still alive and conscious, began to breathe fire across its attackers, mowing them down in a last attempt at victory. The fire hit the ground first and Tyler could feel the heat on his back as he ran. He glanced over his shoulder only for a moment to watch the dragon strike the ground and skid, cutting a deep path in the dirt. The flames stopped only a few feet from Tyler's position, lighting the grass and singing his eyebrows. At that moment he felt another deep rumble, vibrating his entire body so hard that he woke up.

"So intense... and weird..." Tyler whispered to himself, his arm still over his eyes. He could still feel the rumble in his body and the heat on his skin as if it had really happened. "I'll have to work that into the game somehow, a final battle or something." He pulled his arm away and sat up, rubbing his eyes. "Danny, you're not gonna believe the dream I ju–"

Tyler stopped mid-sentence. He rubbed his eyes again, not believing what he was seeing. The campsite was gone. He pushed his sleeping bag aside and stood up, turning on the spot. There was no sign of the campfire, friends, the car, or his shoes, just a never-ending sea of trees in all directions.

"Danny?" Tyler called out. "Clay?"

Could he still be dreaming? Tyler held out his forearm and pinched the skin as hard as he could, wincing at the pain.

"Okay, maybe not dreaming," he said to himself. "Did I sleepwalk again?"

It had been years since he'd done that. As a kid, he would go to sleep in his room and wake up on the couch or in the basement. Once he even managed to wake up in the yard. He glanced down at the sleeping bag still lying on the ground. It would have been the first time he'd ever brought something along with him that wasn't a teddy bear. Was it possible the guys were messing with him?

"Alright, very funny you guys!" he called into the trees. "You can come out now!"

There was no answer.

"I'm really not kidding, assholes!"

Still nothing. Tyler sighed, reaching down he picked up the sleeping bag and rolled it up, brushing as much of the dirt and leaves off it as he could. If he had started sleepwalking, the guys might have thought it was funny to lead him off into the woods to freak him out, but the joke was on them. They were in a tiny peninsula-shaped campground just outside the city. There was only one way in or out and water on three sides. Getting lost was next to impossible. He'd just walk in a straight line until he found water or the road, both of which would lead him back to camp. It seemed odd that Danny would agree to play pranks on him, but he knew how convincing Clay could be when he wanted something. He could charm the pants off anyone if he wanted to and he had a habit of getting everyone into trouble. Besides, Danny had been picking up some of his bad habits the past couple of days.

Shaking his head Tyler tucked the sleeping bag under his arm and headed off in a random direction, his socks soaking through with moisture almost instantly. As soon as he found Clay he planned on punching him square in the mouth for leaving him out there with nothing, not even his shoes. He was more upset than he expected, a seething anger twisting at his guts. After all, it had been his idea to take Danny on this trip and Clay had been dominating most of their time with his stealing and thoughtless comments about the future. Not to mention he'd been convincing Danny to go along with him on his stupid decisions. The trip was supposed to be about giving Danny a chance to see the world and if Tyler was being honest with himself, making up for the lost time. He felt guilty that he'd been working on his game and school projects instead of hanging out with Danny for the past few months. Now to find out that Danny didn't have much time left, he felt even worse because his reasons had been entirely selfish. He wondered if that made him a terrible friend.

Tyler forced himself to focus on the task at hand,

brushing away his thoughts. The woods were dense, more so than seemed possible, with tree trunks so thick it would have taken three people to wrap their arms around it. As he leaned back to stare at the sunlight drenched canopy high above he wondered how he never knew trees like this existed in his own state. For how big they were, he was surprised they weren't some sort of tourist trap. The underbrush was minimal, although he'd already scraped his bare legs against the bramble more than once and the pine cones kept stabbing through his socks.

There were game trails crossing over one another, but to his dismay, no footpaths to be found. He thought it was odd. Usually, when he went anywhere that people frequented, especially parks, there were always footpaths leading down to the lake or to other attractions. He knew he'd run into something eventually, but his feet were getting cold and the mosquitos were growing thicker by the moment. It was impossible to get lost in the world nowadays, wasn't it? After all, GPS was on everyone's phones.

His phone.

Tyler nearly punched himself for being so stupid. He'd completely forgotten about his fucking phone. A quick ping from a satellite would give him a direct path back to the campground. Here he'd be wandering around the woods for fifteen minutes like an idiot, looking for landmarks like it was some boy scout orientation. Cursing under his breath he tossed the sleeping bag to the ground and dug through his pockets, hoping it still had enough charge to get him back. He pulled it out and immediately swiped the screen to open it before his brain could register what was in his hand.

"What the fuck?" he breathed, turning it over.

It was a rock. But it was shaped like his phone. He checked all his pockets again, finding nothing in them. Another mosquito bit into his neck and he slapped it away, growling in frustration. Looking back at the stone he saw it was mostly clear, like a piece of quartz, although perfectly rectangular and thin. He didn't understand what was going on and his irritation with the entire situation reached a boiling point.

"Are you fucking kidding me!" he shouted into the trees, his voice echoing off the trunks. "This isn't fucking funny, Clay! Come out you asshole!" He honestly couldn't believe Danny or Clay would have left him stranded in the woods like that or for so long. "I've had enough of this bullshit!"

He turned on the spot, looking for any sign of the other boys as he jammed the rock back in his pocket. But there was no response. In fact, there was nothing. His ears began to ring and goosebumps erupted across his skin. It was at that moment that Tyler realized the woods around him had gone totally silent. The hairs on the back of his neck stood up, the familiar feeling of being watched creeping through his system. His breath slowed and his heart pounded in his ears as he turned on the spot. Nothing moved. Even the air was unnaturally still as he searched the woods with his eyes, doing everything he could to not make a sound.

A small shifting of light caught his attention in the distance. There was a dark shape moving through the underbrush. At first, he thought it might be Clay or Danny coming to save him, finally realizing that they'd fucked up. But as the shape drew closer, stepping out from between the trees, Tyler realized it was too big and too dark to be either of them. His heart leapt into his throat as he saw the hunched back and rippling shoulder muscles behind a square head and massive jaws filled with sharp teeth. The body was long and sleek like a panther, but the front half was much taller with a sloping back, like a hyena. Two beady black eyes stared in his direction, the beast crouching down and wiggling its shoulders like a cat as if it was about to pounce.

Before he could even form a thought, Tyler bolted in the opposite direction, running as fast as he could. He ignored the brambles that tore across his bare legs and the forest debris stabbing at his feet. The monster had to be some sort of bear, but definitely bigger and more ferocious than any he'd ever heard of. He tried to think back to school and what he knew about bears. All he realized was that there was a definitive lack of bear avoidance training. He needed to get away, to climb a tree or find someplace small to hide where the beast couldn't get at him. But all the trees were too big to climb with no low hanging branches and the forest was flat for as far as he could see. The pounding of massive paws and the snapping of twigs was all he could hear above the blood throbbing in his head. For a moment he wondered if this was how he was going to die. Being killed by rabid wildlife on a camping trip definitely wasn't what he'd expected.

The growling was getting closer and Tyler swore he could feel the hot stinking breath on the back of his neck. He suddenly darted to the left, hooking around a massive tree to put some space between him and the monster bear. Glancing over his shoulder he watched the creature slip in the dry leaves, its feet coming out from under it. He caught a glimpse of the long thin body and a whip-like tail trailing behind it as it crashed to the ground. Whatever it was, it sure as fuck wasn't a bear.

"Fuck fuck fuck!" Tyler cried, grinding the balls of his feet into the ground.

His calves were burning and his breath was coming in ragged gasps. He wasn't exactly the athletic type and now he was regretting it. Talking his teachers into letting him skip gym classes was going to be the reason he was eaten alive in the middle of nowhere. Behind him, he heard a roar of frustration as the creature got back to its feet and doubled its efforts to catch him. The footfalls were close together and gaining fast, thundering through the forest. His brain was so filled with fear he couldn't think.

Suddenly, from a cluster of bushes, another smaller figure emerged ahead of him.

"Duck!" it yelled, pulling up a bow with two arrows nocked on the string.

Tyler didn't get a chance to react as his foot caught a root, tearing him off his feet and throwing him to the ground with enough force to knock the wind out of him. A small pop and a sharp pain shot through his leg as he landed. At the same moment, the bowstring twanged above him, the arrows whistling through the air. There was the briefest moment of silence before a yelp followed by a thunderous boom shuddered the ground, vibrating through Tyler's body. He looked back to see the heavy creature fall, sliding to a stop only a few inches from his feet. He crawled away on his hands and knees ignoring the pain in his leg, the monster still thrashing in the underbrush. Two arrows were lodged in its throat, black blood pouring from the wounds. As it dripped onto the leaves they began to smoke and burn away as if it were made of acid. Tyler felt a strong hand on his collar and he was jerked backward, out of the reach of flailing claws and blood splatter.

"Get out of the way!" the masculine voice ordered in a strange accent, lifting him off the ground and tossing him to the side with ease.

The figure stepped in front of him, pulling the bow up once more. He fired arrow after arrow into the creature until its face resembled the rear end of a porcupine. Tyler watched in horror as more and more blood spilled to the ground, the entire clearing slowly filling with smoke. At last, after nearly a dozen arrows, the monster sank to the ground, its tongue lolled out in the dirt. A final rattling breath escaped its lips and it went silent.

It was dead.

SEVEN

Tyler could barely breathe. He was still laying in the dirt, his elbows propping him up in the leaves with a leg stretched awkwardly behind him. His lungs were burning along with almost every muscle in his body. He'd never been so terrified in his entire life. It was his first brush with death and he was surprised by the sheer exhilaration of it all. But it was quickly fading into exhaustion as the adrenaline started to wane from his system. He glanced up as a pair of leather boots stepped in front of his face.

"You alright?" the man asked, crouching down in front of him.

"Thanks," Tyler wheezed, still trying to catch his breath, his head slumping down nearly into the dirt. "What the fuck was that thing?"

"The locals call it the Silent Death, apparently it's been attacking the farmers and their livestock. There's been a bounty on it for weeks, but I couldn't seem to find it. Until you came along that is." Tyler could hear the smile in his voice through the thick accent. "Thanks for being the bait."

"Are you with the DNR or something?" he huffed. "They allow people to camp here with something like *that* roaming the woods? Seems like a good way to get sued."

"What's a DNR?"

For the first time, Tyler looked up at the man he was speaking to, opening his mouth to reply. But nothing came out.

Instead, he stared with his jaw hanging slack. The man had fuzzy ears sprouting from the sides of his head like a cat. He was lithe and muscular with dark hair and bright green eyes with slitted pupils. He noticed the hand that clutched the bow at his side ended in sharp nails, almost like claws. A long dark tail swished in the dry leaves behind him, filling the silence.

"What... what *are* you?" Tyler stuttered.

"A person." The man seemed surprised and slightly annoyed by the question. "What are you?"

Tyler pushed himself backward, suddenly losing all sense of thankfulness to the cat-man in front of him. "You have cat ears and a... a *tail!*"

The man cocked his head to one side, a crooked grin showing his elongated canines. "Have you never seen a Veordya before?"

"A what?"

"I'll take that as a no." He held out a hand, but Tyler didn't take it. "We're people, just like you humans, except we have a few extra parts and better senses." Tyler pushed himself back another foot and the man's face fell. "Now really. I know we're not common, but this is verging on extraordinarily rude."

"Sorry," Tyler responded automatically before he could stop himself.

"Don't worry, I understand. It's not every day you see one of my kind out and about. Especially on the outskirts of Bramoria."

Tyler's heart skipped a beat at that name. "What... What did you say?"

"Sorry, it's the accent. I said it's not every day you see a Veordya."

"No, the other part."

"On the outskirts of Bramoria?" The man looked thoroughly confused. "What's weird about that?"

Tyler felt a smile come to his lips as he realized what was going on. "Clay put you up to this, didn't he?" He looked the man over. "Is there a local furry convention going on or something?"

"I don't understand."

"This is a pretty elaborate prank to pull off and I'm not sure how you did the monster thing," Tyler chuckled. "First I wake up in the middle of the woods all by myself, my phone is gone, and now there's a cat-boy talking to me."

The man's face suddenly fell into a scowl as he reached out and snatched Tyler up by the collar. "Do *not* call me that," he growled, inches away from his face.

"Sure, okay, fine!" Tyler cried, holding his hands up. "Don't get your fur in a twist!"

The claws released and Tyler slumped back to the ground. He glanced over his shoulder to the monster, the blood still burning away at the leaves and acrid smoke filling his nostrils. That was the only part that didn't really make any sense. The more Tyler stared at the beast the more he began to worry it was real. It was easy to put on a costume and fake an accent, but fabricating a larger-than-life monster with fur, teeth, saliva, and blood was something they didn't even do well in the movies, much less in the middle of nowhere. Maybe he'd gotten sick and was having one of those crazy dreams that he couldn't seem to wake up from. It had happened before. But then again, he couldn't recall a dream that even came close to this level of lucidity.

The feline man stood back to his full height and walked over to the monster, a grimace darkening his features. Tyler had obviously insulted him, but he was too shocked by the situation to do anything about it. The man knelt down, pulling a knife from his belt, and began to slice off claws and place them in a leather pouch, completely ignoring Tyler.

"What are you doing?" Tyler asked, wrinkling his nose in disgust at the sound of cracking bone and tendons.

"Collecting the proof for my bounty and getting out of here," he replied without looking up. "Being stuck with *another* shitty human isn't my idea of a good day. I've had enough of that to last me a lifetime."

Tyler felt a surge of guilt at the venom in his voice. The

man had saved his life after all. He couldn't be all bad, right? Even if it was some crazy fever dream, he didn't seem to be waking up just yet. Better to play along and maybe get some content for his game, a research mission of sorts. That was the only way he could make sense of the situation.

"Look," Tyler began, cringing as he shifted his hurt leg. "I'm sorry. I didn't mean to insult you." The man turned toward him, blood dripping from his knife. "My friends are missing, I have no idea where I am, I think my leg might be broken, and all of this," he gestured to the beast, "is a lot to deal with at once."

The man sighed, cinching the pouch shut and cleaning his blade. He pushed it back into the sheath at his side and walked over to Tyler, crouching down in front of him. "Where does it hurt?"

"You don't have to help me..."

"Right, sure. I'll just leave you out here to be eaten," he looked up, the slitted pupils constricting. "I really want that on my conscience." Tyler winced as he pulled the leg of his shorts up to get a better look at his leg. "Why do you have no shoes? And what is this odd clothing you're wearing?"

"My shoes were missing when I woke up. All I had was my sleeping bag until that thing showed up." He gestured to the smoldering creature. "And my phone is missing too."

"You sleep in a bag?" the man asked, slowly feeling over the bones in Tyler's leg, a smile curling over his lips. "And I don't know what a *phone* is. Is it important?"

Tyler wasn't sure what to say. How could the man not know what a phone was? "Yeah... I guess it's important. It could have led me home."

"Well, your leg isn't broken," the man replied, pulling the fabric back down. "But you'll need to take it easy. I'm heading to the village over the hill to collect my bounty. You can come with me and we'll see if there's a coach that can take you home from there or something." He looked Tyler up and down. "You probably don't have any money either..."

"I left my wallet in my car."

The man sighed, pinching the bridge of his nose. "Charity cases… that's all I get. And a drunk one at that," he whispered to himself. Tyler wanted to retort, but he kept his mouth shut. Looking back up the man held out a hand. "The name's Koto."

"Tyler," he replied, taking his hand and giving it a shake.

"Odd name, but who am I to judge?" Koto pulled Tyler to his feet, helping him over to a tree for support. "Let's find you something to lean on. We've got a bit of a walk ahead of us. The next village is at least an hour away."

"Thanks…" Tyler began, but Koto had already headed off into the trees.

It had to all be a dream. That's the only thing he could wrap his brain around. The only place a cat-man, monsters, and bounties could exist was in a book or video game. Koto didn't even know what a phone was. As Tyler stood there, waiting for him to return, he allowed himself to let go of his fear, something he'd practiced many times in his nightmares as a child. Even if the dream felt too real, he knew he'd wake up if anything bad happened, so there was no reason to be worried. Instead, he'd take mental notes along the way. At the very least it would make the main plot of his game more interesting or a great story to tell his friends when he finally woke up. Besides, it was kind of nice to take a break from the real world, its problems, and the sorrow that seemed to work itself into every nook and cranny of his life. He smiled despite the dull ache in his leg. Maybe this would be fun.

Nearly two hours later Tyler and Koto crested a ridge and the trees fell away sharply, revealing a village not far below. A small river wound its way around the clearing, running through the center of the town that comprised no more than fifty buildings. A large mill was stationed at the far end, using the rush of the water from the hills to turn the wooden water wheel. The houses were simply constructed and if Tyler was being honest with himself, looked like they were straight out of a computer game, further solidifying the realization that he was dreaming. And the people were no different. Those who milled about were dressed in pale-colored linens and simple garb. It almost looked like a renaissance fair except without the raging drunks and public nudity. Then again, they were still a ways off, so his imagination had time to throw that in before they arrived to complete the scene.

"Keep close to me and your head down," Koto said as they started down the ridge. "We don't need to draw any unnecessary attention." He glanced over Tyler's clothing once more before taking off his cloak and throwing it over his shoulders. "There, keep that on. Maybe we can get you some *normal* clothing in town."

"This is normal," Tyler said, pulling the cloak around himself. He shifted the forked branch he was leaning on as a makeshift crutch.

Koto cocked an eyebrow. "I don't know where you're from, but *that* is about as far from normal as you can get. And believe me, you're going to want as little attention as possible."

"Why is that?"

"Attention only leads to trouble. The more people see you, the harder it is to avoid detection." He paused for a moment. "Better to be a helping hand without a face."

Tyler laughed at the ridiculous line. "Are you trying to tell me my stealth level isn't high enough?"

"What?"

Tyler shook his head, smiling at his own joke. "Nevermind. It's nothing."

"I'm serious. Even a town of this size will have its own guard outpost. The last thing you want is to be brought in for questioning just for looking suspicious. The king doesn't exactly keep his dogs on a short leash and on the outskirts they're even less friendly. Danger is everywhere."

"Doesn't sound like a very nice place to live."

"That's why I don't live here."

"Oh?" Tyler said, suddenly curious. "Where are you from?"

"The less you know, the better. Believe me."

"Ooh, mysterious," Tyler cooed. "You must be the main character."

Koto stopped and stared at him for a moment, a look of utter confusion on his face. "Did... did you hit your head or something? You're being awfully strange." He stopped, realization spreading across his features. Lowering his voice he said, "Are you a Muze user?"

"No head injuries," Tyler chuckled, rapping his knuckles on his skull. "And I have no idea what Muze is." He looked at the fluffy ears and tail. It couldn't hurt to tell Koto the truth, especially since he wasn't real anyway. "I've just decided that this is a dream, that's all. None of this makes any sense, so I'm accepting the only logical answer there is. I'm dreaming."

Koto was silent for a long moment. He walked up and put his face near Tyler's, getting uncomfortably close as he took a few deep sniffs. "I don't smell any Muze on you. Odd. And you seem fairly healthy except for the leg injury obviously." He looked hard into Tyler's eyes. "I can't tell if you're messing with me or not. You seem perfectly average by all means except the words spilling from your mouth are utter insanity."

Tyler smiled, patting Koto on the shoulder. "Don't worry about it, dude. I should have known that getting too meta would throw everything off."

"Dude?"

Tyler leaned back on his crutch and took a few steps. "Come on. Lead me on this grand adventure you're taking me on. I'm curious to see what's next. Maybe there's treasure or a dragon to slay!"

Koto stayed back for a moment. Tyler assumed it was because of his comments, but he knew it didn't really matter. The dream would fix itself and go back to normal. They always did. He didn't have anything to worry about. After a moment Koto caught up, keeping mostly to himself.

At the bottom of the hill, they stopped for a moment just outside of town. Koto tucked his tail into his belt and pulled his hood up to hide his ears. He gave Tyler a quiet nod and took the lead, winding them through the streets of the small village. Koto kept mostly to the small paths and alleys outside the main street of town. There wasn't much else besides the main road, so Tyler found himself having to hop over low garden walls and dodge piles of pig manure. He nearly kicked a chicken by accident, getting a glare from an older woman working in her garden. He just smiled and waved, struggling over the wall to catch up. Eventually, Koto led him to a two-story building, one of the few in town.

"Wait here," Koto said, putting his hand on the latch to the back entrance. "I'll be right back." He paused. "Don't... Don't do anything weird okay?"

"Sure thing," Tyler smiled, leaning against the wall. His leg was feeling much better already. He assumed it was because he'd been actively convincing himself it didn't hurt so the dream would just fix it. "I'll wait right here while you do your sneaky business."

Koto gave him an odd look, shook his head, and slipped inside. Tyler had to laugh to himself. He almost felt bad for Koto even though he was just a figment of his imagination. The poor guy was doing everything he could to help Tyler and be a good main protagonist, but the dialogue was really throwing him off. Tyler was honestly surprised he hadn't woken up yet, especially since the walk had taken so long. Usually in dreams things would just fast forward to the next event, leaving the impression that the walking had been done, like in his dragon dream the night before. But in this one, he could remember experiencing almost every single step and time had definitely *not* sped up. It was odd, but not enough to cause Tyler any worry. After all, he was safe and warm in his sleeping bag near the fire with his friends nearby. Nothing could happen to him.

"Hey! What are you doing back there?" a gruff voice called from the street.

Tyler looked up to see a tall person in leather plate armor staring at him. Except, he wasn't really sure if it was a person. They had wide shoulders and an impossibly thin waist, their slim legs ending in bare clawed feet. Their skin was a mottled green and brown with what looked like scales covering every available surface. But the face was what Tyler noticed the most. A long snout with sharp rows of teeth jutted out in front of bright ice blue eyes, both ringed with hard scales. There was no hair to speak of, but dark horns curled back from their head, framing the imposing visage. He almost looked like a dragon.

"Yeah, you!" the man-creature called, stomping in his direction and drawing a thick-bladed sword from his back. He held it out, the tip only inches from Tyler's face. "I said, what are you doing back here? Who was that cloaked guy?"

Tyler just smiled, knowing none of it was real. "Just waiting for my friend. He's doing sneaky things." He looked the man up and down, noticing a couple of others like him waiting at the edge of the alley, watching their interaction. "Are you a dragon or something? Maybe a lizard?"

"What the fuck did you just say to me?!"

Tyler felt the tip of the blade press against his chest painfully, cutting through the fabric with ease. He ignored it. It was just a dream. "Just asking a question. I've never seen one of you before."

"I ain't no fuckin' dragon," the man spat. "Don't you dare compare me to those monsters."

"Sure thing, buddy." Tyler felt like he was almost drunk with a lack of fear. "Whatever you say."

The tip of the blade sank into his skin and he gasped, a shot of pain preceding the warmth of blood spilling down his shirt.

"I don't like your tone," the dragon-man hissed. "And I don't like you."

Pain caused Tyler's fight or flight responses to kick in finally and adrenaline rushed through his system. Before he had a chance to correct his error or convince his brain to change the scenario, the door swung open and out stepped Koto.

"All taken care of," he said, pushing the door closed behind him. "Now we can find a place for you to sta–"

His eyes fell on the dragon-man and the blade pressed against Tyler's chest. His hood was back, the tall ears going flat against his head. The dragon-man pulled the blade away from Tyler and smiled.

"Koto," he cooed. "I was hoping I'd run into you." The blade shifted over to him as the man gestured for his friends to join him. "There's quite a bounty on your head, you know."

Koto glanced nervously at Tyler. "Fuck…" he whispered.

EIGHT

The other two dragon people came up behind the first, their weapons drawn. Both of them held wickedly curved scimitars pointed in Tyler and Koto's direction. Things had gone from bad to worse and Tyler was having a hard time keeping his panic down now that blood was running down his chest. It felt so real, he could barely believe it. His brain had really gone all out on this dream.

"So Koto," the first said, a malicious smile curving across his snout. "You left your cushy life to travel with idiots who have a death wish. Sounds very noble. Your father would be so *proud*?"

"And it looks like you're still going the same old thing," Koto replied with a sigh. "Being an asshole who hunts down innocent people for money. Tell me, have you sold your soul already? Because I know you already sold your *balls* to the king."

The blade pressed harder against Koto's throat. "We all have to make a living, don't we? You can say whatever you want, but you and I both know that the crown guard will pay more than any other bounty in the kingdom if I return you alive." He licked his lips with a thick pink tongue. "But they didn't say you had to be *unharmed*." He leaned in a little closer, the blade indenting Koto's dark skin. "I've been *so* looking forward to this, Koto."

"As much as I love our little chats Liran, I really have other things to be doing."

"You're not going anywhere. Not this time." He turned

the blade back to Tyler, pressing the tip against his throat. "Especially if you want your little idiot friend to live. I know you don't care about yourself, but you can't help being a goody fucking two-shoes."

Koto burst out laughing, his hands on his belly. "Kill him. I don't care. I just found him in the woods." He glanced at Tyler, seeing the fear in his eyes. "One less charity case I have to take care of. Not to mention he's so buzzed up on Muze that he's absolutely insane."

"But… I thought… I thought you were the good guy," Tyler stuttered, wondering how his dream was suddenly turning into a nightmare. He stared at Koto, trying to remind himself that he was in control. All he needed to do was wake up.

"Then you don't know *shit* about me," Koto scoffed, smirking in Tyler's direction.

"Enough of this!" Liran roared, giving Tyler a hard shove in the chest and knocking him off his feet, the crutch clattering across the ground. "You're coming with us, Koto. Whether you like it or not!"

With astounding speed Koto dove under the sword and out of Liran's reach. "Then come get me you overgrown lizard!" With that he ran down the alley, dodging the other two bounty hunters as he went. They slashed at him in vain, unable to land a strike on his lithe form.

"After him, you fools!" Liran roared to the other two. As they ran off he turned to look back at Tyler still lying on the ground. He sheathed his sword and reached down, grabbing Tyler by the shirt and lifting him off his feet. Tyler's brain was racing. The dream was getting too intense and he needed to wake up. He was in his sleeping bag back at the campground. Maybe if he just concentrated on it hard enough he'd be able to yell out in his sleep.

"As for you, I think I'll just leave you to rot in the streets. You're no use to me," Liran snarled, pulling Tyler in close. The hot breath stank. "Oh, and one more thing."

Tyler suddenly felt something plunge into his abdomen. Pain

filled every neuron in his body as his muscles tensed, the breath catching in his throat.

"That's for calling me a dragon," Liran hissed in his ear.

He threw Tyler back to the ground, the impact sending a new wave of mind-numbing pain through his system. Tyler's hand went straight to his stomach, clutching at the agony throbbing there. It came away covered in thick red blood. His own blood. Liran wiped his small blade clean and slid it back into the underside of his gauntlet. He spat in Tyler's direction and turned on his heel, jogging back into town in pursuit of Koto.

Tyler's vision began to tunnel as he stared down at the wound in his belly, blood oozing out over his clothing. He didn't understand what was happening or why it hurt so badly. None of it should be possible if it was just a dream. That's what it was, right? A strange burning sting pulsed through his stomach, spreading outward from the injury and into his guts. He could feel it crawling through his veins like ice, tracing up the center of his body towards his heart. Everything around him began to fade and only one horrifying thought filled in his mind.

Maybe, it wasn't a dream after all.

Tyler woke up with a start, shooting straight up from where he lay and immediately crying out in pain. He clutched his hands to his stomach, feeling the deep ache of torn flesh and organs below the surface. His skull was pounding and every inch of his body seemed to be in nearly unbearable agony. And all of that was followed by a swell of relief as he realized he was still alive. But for how long, he wasn't sure.

"Finally," a familiar voice said to his left. "I wasn't sure if that antidote would work or not."

It was Koto.

Tyler pushed himself away from him, wincing in pain as the bandages on his stomach began to turn red again, the wounds underneath bleeding through.

"Stop moving around!" Koto said, reaching out. "You're going to make it worse."

"You left me," was all Tyler could say. Koto wasn't to be trusted, not after he abandoned him with the lizard people. "You said you didn't give a shit about me."

"If I hadn't left, they would have killed us both. Believe me, Liran is *not* someone to be trifled with."

"Yeah, I found that out."

"I'm sorry he attacked you. I thought he'd just leave you and chase after me." Koto tilted his head slightly. "What did you say to piss him off so much?"

"I told him he looked like a dragon or a lizard."

"Yeah, that explains it," Koto smiled. "He doesn't poison just anyone. Thankfully I know his tricks. I always keep some antidote on me just in case I run into him."

"Fucking christ! He stabbed me *and* poisoned me? What is this fucking place?" Tyler clenched his jaw as a streak of pain shot up his torso. "Motherfucker this hurts!"

"You need to lay down before you make it any worse," Koto said, grabbing him by the arm and lowering him back to the bed.

He wasn't sure he trusted Koto, but for the time being, he was too hurt to do much else. For the first time, Tyler looked around at his surroundings. They were in a small room with a single dingy window on one wall. The bed sheets were clean but scratchy, and there was a small pile of blood-stained fabric on the floor with a pot of steaming water.

"Did… Did you bandage me up?" Tyler asked, turning his head on the pillow.

"There's nobody else in this nowhere town that would do it," Koto sighed. "They have a medicine woman but she took one look at you and told me not to bother. That you'd die even if she stitched you up."

Tyler felt his heart sink. "Am… Am I going to die?"

Koto lifted an eyebrow. "Why the concern? Worried this isn't a dream anymore?"

He closed his eyes, trying to fight back the tears that were threatening to spill forth. He didn't want to die.

"I don't know what you were high on in those woods, but something clearly addled your brain for a while," Koto said. "Whatever it was, it seems like you're doing better now."

"Doing better?" Tyler choked, hissing through his teeth as his stomach muscles tensed. "Fuck me... why is this happening? I just... I just wanted to be a good friend..." The tears were starting to stream down his cheeks despite every thought in his mind bent on keeping them at bay. He wished his mom was there with him. "What did I do to deserve this?"

"Hey," Koto cooed, leaning down close, brushing Tyler's hair away. It was an oddly intimate gesture. "It's okay. You're not going to die."

"Oh yeah? Are you going to sew me up then?" Tyler sniped, his voice a mix of anger and despair at his impending doom. "Even though it's not going to help?"

"No," Koto replied with a smile, pulling a small bottle filled with green liquid from his pouch. "I've got a healing potion."

Tyler's expression went from upset to irate in less than a second. His brows furrowed together as he gritted his teeth.

"A healing potion? Are you fucking kidding me?" he spat. "I'm sitting here dying and you think it's funny to fuck with me? Fuck you asshole!"

Koto looked genuinely surprised as he pulled back. "No... it's actually a healing potion."

"Right. So this isn't a dream, it's just a fucking video game. Sure."

"I promise, it's not a joke," Koto said softly, taking the stopper off the bottle. "I was saving this for a rainy day in case I ran into Liran, but you need it more than me." He paused for a moment. "And maybe... maybe it will help you think clearer as well. Then we can talk."

Tyler eyed the swirling green liquid with suspicion. He glanced down at the bandages across his torso, the red slowly spreading from his reopened wound. His brain was still pounding against his skull and his racing thoughts weren't making it any better. The day's events and the pain were enough to prove to him that he was no longer dreaming, but somehow, none of it felt real. It was almost like he'd been sucked into a crazy fantasy video game or a book on one of Danny's shelves.

Danny.

If he'd been transported into some crazy world, had Danny been taken as well? And Clay? He knew Clay could hold his own, but Danny was weak, thin, and his time was running out. If he came up against any sort of trouble like the monster Tyler had seen in the woods, he didn't stand a chance. Suddenly he realized how much trouble his best friend could be in. He had to find Danny and if that meant trusting Koto and some insane potion in a bottle, he'd do it. Besides, it wasn't like he had anything to lose, especially since he was going to die anyway.

"Give it to me," Tyler sighed, holding out a hand.

Koto handed it to him without a word. Tyler swirled the potion, watching the color shift and swirl, almost like it was full of starlight. Tipping it back he drained it in a single gulp, the strangely ice-cold liquid trickling down his throat.

For a moment nothing happened. Just as he was about to say something there was a sudden burst of heat in his stomach, like a fire blazing into life inside him. He clawed at his belly, the heat becoming too intense for him to bear. It crossed his mind for a split second that Koto might have tricked him into drinking acid or something. He choked on the words he wanted to say, coughing and sputtering as the heat grew.

Then, just as fast as it came, it faded away. Instead, it was replaced by a strange tingling sensation lower in his belly near the wound. He watched as the bandages shifted like something was squirming underneath them. Terrified, he cried out and tore them away, exposing the open wound into his torso. The sight of his own bloody intestines nearly made him faint, but what kept him there was watching them move of their own accord. In a horrifying display, he watched as they began to knit themselves back together, fixing the hole that Liran had punched in his guts. As they reformed, so did the muscle above them, the fibers curling across his entrails and weaving a patch over the hole. Sinew, fat, and skin also shifted, roiling like snakes as they slowly put themselves back in place. In a matter of moments, the wound was no more than a faint white scar. The tingling then moved to his leg where he heard a small pop, his knee joint shifting back into place.

As the tingling faded away tears began to roll down his cheeks again, renewed by the utter lack of ability to process what he'd just witnessed. He looked to Koto, his mouth half-open but unable to form the words.

"Don't worry, it's a bit intense for everyone the first time," he said, handing a clean cloth over to him. "I wasn't lying, you know."

Tyler nodded his head, still unable to speak. He was alive and suddenly free of pain. It didn't make any sense, but he was glad for it. Shuddering breaths were all he could take as he tried to stop himself from having a full-scale meltdown in front of a stranger.

"I... wasn't lying... either," Tyler managed to squeeze out between breaths. "I really thought... this was... a dream." He wiped the cloth across his face haphazardly. "I don't... understand... what's going... on."

Koto seemed surprised by his sudden change in demeanor. The ears drooped a bit as he turned his head to the side, the tail sweeping back and forth across the floor.

"Where are you from?" he asked, lacing his fingers together. "Do you know the name of it?"

"I'm... I'm from... Michigan."

NINE

Koto had been pacing the room for the last ten minutes listening to Tyler's story. It was obvious he was having a hard time digesting what had been said by the irritated twitching of his tail.

"So let me get this straight," he said, stopping in front of the bed where Tyler still sat. "You were out on a camping trip with your friends who stole a book that you tried to read. And Bramoria was mentioned inside the book?"

Tyler nodded.

"And this *Michigan* you're from isn't in Bramoria?"

"I'd never even heard of Bramoria until we opened that book."

"That doesn't make any sense," Koto sighed, slumping down into a chair.

"You're telling me."

"And these friends of yours, did they come with you?"

"I don't know," Tyler replied honestly, shrugging his shoulders. "Maybe I was the only one, maybe not. Clay would be fine here, he's always been good at taking care of himself. But Danny... Danny is really sick." He looked up at Koto. "I need to find him."

"Well," Koto sighed. "If he's dressed anything like you, he'll draw attention."

"We have to find him. Then I need to get us home." He leaned forward, resting his forehead against his knee, the smell of the wool duvet filling his nostrils. "My mom is going to be so worried about me. And what about Danny's parents? I'm sure they're going crazy trying to find him."

"I'm not sure I really understand or believe a lot of this," Koto said, taking a seat next to the bed. "But I *can* understand wanting to find your friend." He put a hand on Tyler's shoulder. "I'll help you find him."

"Why would you do that for me?"

Koto took a deep breath. "If you're not out in the world helping people, what's the point of being alive?" He glanced away, staring out the darkened window. "I spent too long turning a blind eye to the evil in this world. Now I'm trying to make up for that transgression."

Tyler lifted his head, staring at Koto who was still staring out the window with a faraway look in his eyes. What were the chances of waking up in the woods only to be found by an *actually* helpful person? He'd spent the past twelve years of his life in the public school system and had never found one. His mother seemed to be the only person who ever wanted to help him, even if it was almost always to appease her dreams she thrust upon him. Other than her and the guys, he really didn't have anyone to turn to in times of need. It struck him as odd that a total stranger was willing to help him when nothing he'd said made a lick of sense.

"Don't you think I'm crazy?"

"You seem too sincere to be insane, although the story you told is a strange one." Koto shook his head, pulling him from his thoughts. "But stranger things have happened in this world. Bramoria is constantly in turmoil in one way or another."

"If I had my phone I could show you pictures and *prove* I'm not lying." He reached down into his pocket and pulled out the cold rectangular stone. "But for some reason, all I have is *this*," he scoffed, throwing it down on the bed. "Useless."

Koto's eyes grew wide as he stared at the stone, his jaw hanging open.

"Where... Where did you get that?"

"I told you, my phone turned into a rock. Or at least that's what I'm assuming happened."

"That's not a rock." Koto lifted the stone gently and held it up to the candle's light, gazing through the transparent crystal. "This is a mage stone."

"A what?"

"A mage stone," Koto repeated, handing it back to Tyler. "They're incredibly rare. Only the strongest mages have them and almost all of them work for the king." He glanced back at the stone. "But yours isn't active. I wonder why?"

"Active? What does that mean?"

"Well, usually they glow, but yours just looks like a rock. Mind you, I've only seen one or two in my life."

"So… my phone turned into a magic rock?"

"I don't know what a phone is, but it may explain a little of what's going on." Koto tapped the stone with his sharp fingernail, the hollow glass-like sound filling the room. "Almost all the mages work for the king and do what he needs to keep the kingdom going. Usually, it's kept a secret, extremely dangerous, or both. They are some of the highest-ranking members in his army and shrouded in mystery."

"What does that have to do with me?"

"It's a long shot, but I think you might be one of the academy mages, possibly a student," Koto started.

"What?!"

"Hear me out," he said, holding up his hands. "Only the mages have these stones. It's possible that you were one of their ranks, but something went terribly wrong and wiped your memory. Maybe because you're a newbie." He paused. "Or, if you are a mage from another world, then it's possible that they called for you."

"Neither of those sound likely because I'm not a mage. I almost threw this away," he said, holding up the stone. "Magic isn't real, at least not in my world."

"Either way," Koto insisted, ignoring his comments. "If we can find another mage, maybe they can help you out. At the very least the stone will gain you an audience with them. They can do so many things that seem impossible. If what you say is true, maybe they can help you get home."

Tyler sighed, knowing he had nothing else to go on. "And where are they?"

"In the capital city of course," Koto replied, his ears falling with his voice. "The mages all live in the academy tower within the castle grounds." He looked up at Tyler. "However, I'm not welcome in the capital anymore and would rather avoid it. But there's also the Sage. He doesn't have a reputation of being the most likable character and he's damn near impossible to find if you don't know where to look, but I'm sure he'd be able to help too."

Tyler stared at Koto, having no idea what to think. Was he really about to traipse across the country looking for some mages to tell him who he was? Was it possible his entire life's worth of memories were completely made up? He didn't think so. Memories of his life, his friends, and his family seemed too real and too full of emotion to be fake. He didn't know anything about magic in Bramoria, but even without that knowledge, fabricating something that complex seemed impossible.

"And if it turns out I'm not from Bramoria, what can the mages actually do?" Tyler asked, turning the stone over absentmindedly.

"I'm not sure," Koto replied. "But they'd be able to find your friend pretty easily through scrying. And it might be possible to send you both back home. Some of them can travel across the world in the blink of an eye. The Sage does it all the time. I don't see why they wouldn't be able to help you do the same."

Tyler sighed, glancing back at the stone. He really didn't want to go on any sort of quest or adventure, not without Danny and *especially* not in some crazy made-up world that he'd been sucked into. All he wanted to do was go home. Driving across the state and going camping on a whim was one thing, getting stabbed by bounty hunters at a hyper-realistic ren fair was another. He missed his bedroom and the safety of his office chair, toiling away for hours building a fantasy world that he'd never have to possibly *die* in. That was all he wanted, not college, not a magic stone, and definitely not an adventure. Just him and his imagination where they could run free. But that wasn't important now. He thought of Danny and prayed he hadn't been sucked into Bramoria along with him. If something happened to his best friend, he'd never forgive himself.

"So where are we going?" Tyler asked, stuffing the stone in his pocket. "Are we seeing the mages or this Sage guy?"

"Well, the Sage doesn't ever stay in one place for long. He's a bit of a wanderer. But the mages are always at the academy. However–"

"Then we go there," Tyler interrupted. "I need to get home as fast as possible and I don't wanna chase some dude around the world who can't sit still." He slid his legs over the edge of the bed and pushed himself up. "And we have to find Danny if he's here. If not, the mages can help us track him down. They have to."

He took a few cautious steps, happy to feel no pain in his body. The potion had reversed all his injuries like they had never happened at all. But inside his brain, his thoughts were reeling from the emotional whiplash of the past few hours. So many life-changing things had happened and more than a few close brushes with death. Already it felt like too much to handle, but none of that mattered now. It was time to go home. He looked back at Koto, his jaw set with determination.

"So when are we leaving?"

"Look," Koto said, his ears laying against the top of his head. "I told you I can't really go back to the capital city. It's not safe there for me."

"So, what? You'd rather stay here and let those bounty hunters find you?"

"I didn't say that." He pushed himself up from the chair, raking his fingers through his hair. He glanced at Tyler, then out the window, pacing around the room. "Maybe I can guide you until we find someone else? At the very least Liran and his gang won't expect me to be heading north. They think I'm trying to flee the kingdom altogether."

"Are you?"

"Not right now it looks like."

Tyler headed for the door, placing his hand on the latch. "Are we ready then?"

"Slow down there, kid. We're gonna stay here for the night. I don't want to travel in the dark." He gave Tyler a once over. "And we need to get you some normal clothes that aren't covered in blood."

Tyler looked down at himself. He was wearing nothing but blood-stained shorts. His socks and shirt were both gone. A wave of self-consciousness washed over him as he crossed his arms over his chest in a vain attempt to cover himself up.

"Are the stores still op–" He stopped, suddenly realizing he had no money. "Nevermind."

Koto saw the look in his eyes. "I can purchase clothes for you."

"You really don't have to do that…"

He laughed. "Believe me, you're not gonna want to walk in the sun all day with nothing on that pale skin of yours. You look like you've never been outside in your life!"

He gestured for Tyler to come back into the room. "Stop there. Let me look at you."

Tyler felt himself blush against his will, suddenly conscious of Koto's discerning green eyes. "Wha… What?"

Koto made a slow circle around him, tapping his chin like he was thinking. Tyler began to feel like a piece of meat on display. He didn't know what Koto was looking for or if his intentions were more carnal.

"You don't have much of a build of any sort really," he finally said, taking a few more steps around him. "Your shoulders are wide, but you're so scrawny." His green eyes locked on Tyler. "Do people not eat you where you come from? How do you get anything done with so little strength?"

The blush faded and Tyler's voice immediately turned

sour. "I appreciate that. Thanks for making me feel good about myself."

"Kid, I'm not saying it to make you feel bad. But if you're gonna survive here in the outskirts, you're gonna need some serious training." He tapped his finger to his chin again. "Do you prefer a sword or a bow?"

"How the hell should I know?" Tyler quipped. "You just told me I'm useless anyway."

"Sword it is then. That'll be easier to teach a newbie. Bows require a level of strength and finesse that you don't look ready for."

Tyler was quickly feeling the graciousness he felt toward Koto subside. "Great. I'm so excited to be ridiculed for the next several days."

"Days?" Koto chuckled. "The capital is nearly a month away on foot. We're gonna be together for a while."

Tyler felt his chest tighten. A month. That was twice what he told his mother to expect and nearly a third of Danny's diagnosis. Taking a deep breath he tried to steady his nerves. He had to do this. If he wanted to see Danny or his mom again, he had to grit his teeth and bear whatever came his way.

"So when do we start?"

"Tomorrow morning," Koto replied. "But first dinner. I'm starving."

TEN

Tyler was dragging his feet, sweat pouring down his brow. The heat of the day was already intense and there wasn't even the smallest hint of a breeze. Birds were singing in the shade of the trees while he was left on the road, trudging along in the harsh sunlight. The air was filled with the smells of summer, but he was too busy trying not to pass out to enjoy it. For the hundredth time, he shifted his belt, trying to stop the leather from cutting into his hips. The sword at his side was heavier than he expected and completely useless to him. He wanted to collapse, or die, whichever was faster. At the very least it would save him from having to take another step.

"Pick up the pace," Koto called from a few feet ahead, a cocky smile on his face. "It's not even lunchtime yet! You want to make it to the capital before the winter solstice, yeah?"

Tyler scowled as Koto laughed at his own little joke. The cat was getting on his nerves. All morning he'd been making snide remarks about how slow, or skinny, or weak Tyler was. While they'd been picking out clothing at a local shop, Koto and the owner had a real laugh over how they should give him a discount because it took so little fabric to cover him. It was enough to set his teeth on edge for the entire morning. He had to keep reminding himself to unclench his jaw, especially if he wanted to have any teeth left by the end of their journey. He doubted a world that only had clothes made of linen and wool had a wonderful dental system. If Bramoria was anything like the shows he'd seen, he'd be lucky if he kept his teeth for more than ten years.

The thought caught him by surprise. Ten years. Was it possible that he'd be trapped in Bramoria for that long? Could he even *survive* that long? From the way Koto talked, it was as if danger lurked around every corner. Monsters, bandits, and bounty hunters seemed to be a normal everyday occurrence for the people of that world. Tyler had gotten a glance of the notice board in the tavern that morning and the monster Koto had slain definitely wasn't the only one there, although it had been the highest paying. There were other notices about goblins, rogue elementals, and even some tiny lemur-looking creatures called Fossars with bulbous eyes and sharp teeth. Tyler didn't want anything to do with any of them and hoped their trip would be an easy, monster-free one.

At long last, once Tyler could barely lift his own feet, they stopped for lunch, ducking into the cover of the trees that lined the main road to get out of the sun. Although it had only been May back in the real world, the climate in Bramoria seemed to be much warmer and the sun was particularly harsh.

Tyler held his hand up to shield his eyes, glancing into the sky. "Is the sun always that big?" he asked, squinting against the light. It was much larger than the one back on earth but seemed a darker shade like it wasn't as hot. Or at least, that's the only way he could logic it out why they weren't both on fire at the moment.

Koto looked at him with one eyebrow raised. "The sun is the sun. It has always been the same."

"It's bigger than the one back home," Tyler replied, turning away from it. He watched the sunspots on his retinas slowly fade as he took a bite of dried meat. "You know, I always thought all those fantasy book authors were being lazy when they talked about people eating jerky all the time." He took another bite. "Turns out they were right."

"What else would you eat?" Koto asked, taking a long drink from his waterskin. "Bread and cheese only stay good for so long. Although I usually prefer to hunt for my meat."

"You kill your own food?" Tyler asked, a disgusted look on his face.

"You don't?"

"No! We buy it."

Koto sighed. "You must come from a very wealthy family. That explains why you're so scrawny. With a house full of servants, there's no need to do things yourself."

"We don't have servants," Tyler quipped. "Everyone in my world buys their food from a store." He paused for a moment. "I guess there are some people out there who still like to hunt, but most just go to the local grocery store."

"And the hunters supply the meat to these stores?"

"Well, no... the stores buy them from suppliers who buy them from farmers I think. They do the same with vegetables, but those are grown by different farmers. Now that I think about it, I think most of the food at the store comes from a different country."

Koto stared at Tyler for a long moment, his eyes unblinking. "What a strange world you live in. It seems overly complicated for something as simple as food." He reached over and grabbed a plant from the underbrush covered in thorns. "Why go through all that when what you need is right here?" He reached out and pulled back the leaves, revealing clusters of dark red berries. "Food is everywhere. Only thirty feet behind you is a bird that when roasted makes for a scrumptious meal." He took a handful of berries and let the bush go. "The world is so simple, but people like to complicate it unnecessarily to make themselves rich."

Tyler could see something else behind his eyes, a sense of knowing that accompanied his statement. There was more to him than met the eye.

"So why can't you go back to the capital?" Tyler asked, changing the subject. "Is it because of your bounty?"

"You could say that."

"Can I... Can I ask what you're wanted for?"

Koto shot him a dirty look. "I didn't do anything *wrong* if that's what you're implying. I simply did what needed to be done."

"No, no!" Tyler said, waving his hands. "I'm just curious. Those guys talked about your father and the bounty from the crown. I was just curious why they'd go through so much trouble."

Koto popped another berry in his mouth, chewing slowly as he stared at the ground. "My father and I... we don't see eye to eye on a lot of things." He spat a few seeds into the woods. "There are things he did that I don't think are right and I wasn't willing to let that go. So I... left."

"And he didn't like that?"

"There were a lot of people upset that I left and most of them were within the castle." His gaze grew distant for a moment as if remembering something. "My father raised me to be the person he wanted, to take his place. But he never stopped to ask me what I wanted or what I thought was right. And when he convinced other people to follow his wrongdoings, I could no longer not take action. He was only ever concerned with his own dreams."

Tyler nodded. "I know that feeling."

Koto's ears perked up as his gaze lifted. "Oh?"

"My mom is that way. She has this grand idea of who and what she wants me to be." He paused. "But that's not what I want. And I can't tell her how I feel either, or at least it doesn't feel like I can."

"Seems like parents are the same no matter where you're from."

"Yeah, I guess so." Tyler kicked some of the leaves around with his new leather boots. "I understand what she wants and why, but I'm just not ready for it. But I don't want to disappoint her. She raised me after my dad walked out on us."

"I'm sorry to hear that."

"Nah, it's okay. He was a jerk anyway and honestly, I barely remember him." He looked back up at Koto. "Do... Do you think I'm a bad son for not doing what she wants?"

Koto shook his head. "No. In fact, I think that makes you brave. Standing up to your parents is the hardest thing any child can do."

Tyler felt his heart sink. If only he had the courage to actually tell her what he wanted. For years she'd been pushing him to join different groups, get better grades, and go to college. The only thing he'd successfully said no to was joining the football team. But now that he was wandering through Bramoria with his legs so sore he wanted to die, he was kicking himself for not being more active like she'd pushed him to be.

Koto was just braver than him. He'd walked away from his father and his entire life to pursue his own interests. Even if he didn't mean to, it made Tyler feel pathetic. All he did was run, just like he'd stopped going to see Danny when his illness got worse. It was easier to sit on his computer making up imaginary worlds than face the one outside his door.

"Well," Koto said, breaking the silence as he clapped his hands together. "I think it's time we get going. The road is long and if we can keep up this pace, we might get to the next village in a couple of days."

"A couple of *days*?" Tyler balked. "Why is everything so far apart here?"

Koto just smiled. "The world is a big place. You'll get used to it."

"Yeah, but will my legs ever recover is the question."

At that moment Koto held up a hand, his ears swiveling back toward the road. Tyler stopped talking and stood completely still. Immediately his brain conjured up images of a monster in the woods and his heart began to race. He knew Koto was capable, but he didn't really like testing his luck so often because eventually, he knew it would run out. Tyler turned slowly toward the direction Koto's ears were facing. There was nothing but the road. However, after a long moment, he could finally make out the distinct sound of wheels as a wagon came into view. Breathing a sigh of relief he looked back to Koto who was still on high alert.

"Should we talk to them?" Tyler whispered. "Maybe get a ride?"

Koto held his finger to his lips, shaking his head. "No. We have to stay out of sight."

"But I'm *exhausted*," Tyler whined. He glanced back at the cart, seeing nothing but an old man and his two horses. The cart itself was piled with crates, but no other people were in sight. "You can kill a monster but you are afraid of an old man?"

Koto started to speak but Tyler waved him off, turning toward the road and kicking through the leaves. For once he managed to catch Koto off guard and was out of reach before he could do anything to stop him. He walked right out of the woods and up to the road, waving with a friendly expression at the man as he drew close.

"Hello!" Tyler called out.

The old man immediately pulled his horses to a halt, stopping some thirty feet from Tyler. Even from a distance, Tyler could see the fear in his eyes, although he didn't understand why. He put on a friendly smile and took a few steps forward.

"Are you heading to the next village?" Tyler asked. "My friend and I are traveling and wondered if maybe we could ride along with you." He saw no change in expression on the old man's face. "Uh... we have money if you need payment for the ride."

"Stop where you are, thief!" the old man cried, pulling a crossbow from next to his seat and aiming it at Tyler. "Not another step."

Tyler held up his hands for the man to see. "I'm not a thief. I just want a ride." Then under his breath. "What the fuck..."

"Prove it!" the man yelled back. "How do I know the woods aren't full of your friends that'll rush me as soon as I put down my weapon? I know your tricks!"

"I only have one friend with me," Tyler replied. He turned

back over his shoulder. "Koto! Come on out!"

The old man narrowed his eyes, scanning the treeline along the road for any hint of movement. Eventually, Tyler heard the rustle of leaves as Koto exited the woods, his hands held up as well, the bow strung over his shoulders. He walked up beside Tyler, his hood pulled up, shooting him a furious look before turning back to the man.

"I apologize for my friend," Koto called. "But his intentions are pure, I can guarantee you that. He's also worthless as a fighter, so he poses very little danger to you." He put a charming smile on. "However, if you're worried about bandits, let's make a deal. If you give us a ride, we'll make sure you reach the next town without an issue. I'm a skilled warrior and would be more than happy to defend you from the dangers of the road."

"And why should I believe you?"

"Believe whatever you want. Just know that if I'd wanted to take your goods and leave you dead, I would have done so already."

"We'll see about that," the old man smiled.

There was a click and a twang as the crossbow string snapped forward, sending a bolt speeding directly toward Tyler. He didn't even get a chance to cry out as he threw his arms across his chest to block it, clenching his eyes shut in preparation for the pain. But none came. Slowly he opened his eyes one at a time. The old man was leaning forward in his seat, staring open-mouthed at the pair of them. Only inches in front of Tyler's face was Koto's outstretched arm, a dark shafted bolt held firmly in his hand.

He'd caught it.

"Really friend, that was unnecessary," Koto replied, flipping the bolt over and using it to pick dirt from under his nails. "Do we need to prove ourselves more or can we offer our services in exchange for a ride to the next village?"

The old man was nearly too stunned to speak. It took him a moment to find his words. "How... How did you do that?"

Koto pulled his hood back, revealing the long furry ears.

"Veordya are known for their quick reflexes." He waited for the man to respond. "Well? Are you gonna give us a ride or not?"

"You can join me," he finally replied. "Having keen ears and eyes on the road is a blessing I won't be passing up. Especially with all the trouble I've had."

"Glad to hear it."

Koto reeled back, the bolt still in hand, and threw it back toward the man. It flashed through the air and there was a dull thunk. The old man cried out as if struck, his body scrunched into a ball in his seat. However, Tyler noticed the bolt vibrating next to him, stuck in the wood boards of the seat. The old man slowly relaxed, unclenching himself and spotting the bolt. He looked back to Koto with fear in his eyes.

"That," Koto replied with a wicked smile, "was for trying to shoot my friend."

ELEVEN

The firelight danced across the wagon wheels and the nearby trees. A bird was roasting on a spit over the fire. It was Tyler's job to keep it turning as it cooked to make sure it didn't burn. He'd been doing it for nearly a half-hour and it felt like his arm was going to fall off. Koto had been the one to hunt it down as thanks to the old man for giving them a ride. Rendel was his name and he'd been a traveling merchant for most of his life until he'd set up shop in a small town to the west. However, it seemed it had been attacked in the middle of the night and burned to the ground, taking almost everything he owned with it. At the late age of seventy-five and with no other choice, he'd begun hauling goods again to make a living. He'd encountered bandits, beasts, and all manner of problems on the road, which slowed his progress. Still, he seemed happy enough to be out on the open road again, despite the danger. Tyler thought of the older people back home who took jobs as greeters at big box stores. Honestly, he wasn't sure which job was worse.

"But there is some good news," Rendel continued, poking at the fire with a small stick and looking at Koto. "At long last, the crown is caring for its people."

"What do you mean?" Koto replied, his eyebrows lifting. "That's not the royalty I remember."

"I agree. Spent my whole life without seeing so much as a single copper from the royals. They did everything they could to not be involved with the people. But something has changed."

He lowered his voice, looking around to make sure no one was passing by in the dark. "There are rumors that the prince has placed his own father under arrest and that the king now sits in his own prison."

Koto chuckled in disbelief. "How is that even possible?"

"The prince and his Paladins of Light overpowered him and locked him up with the permission of the queen." Rendel paused for a moment. "I hear he's to be tried for treason against the people of Bramoria."

"And the king's advisors just let this happen? The academy was okay with it?"

"I don't know," Rendel replied, shaking his head. "It's just what I heard. But I'll tell you what I saw with my own eyes. The king's men marched all the way to my small village with wagons after the attack. They were loaded with food, goods, and coins for the people who had just lost everything in the fire. In fact, it was the only reason I was able to afford to go into business again." He leaned back with a big smile, a few of his teeth missing. "Now what do you say to that?!"

"I say I can't believe it," Koto replied, shrugging his shoulders. "If the royal family is working for the people after decades of neglect, it's news to me. I used to live in the capital city and they didn't even help those just outside the castle walls. I find it nearly impossible to believe that they came all the way to your small village, but then again, here you are." Koto gestured to the wagon. "And with a cartload of goods to sell. I can't deny the evidence in front of me, however much I remember about the prince and his father."

"I was just as surprised as you are when they showed up. But I swear on the light of the sun, that's the truth."

"Did you ever find out who attacked your village?" Tyler cut in, turning so he could switch arms on the spit.

"The soldiers weren't able to find any evidence of who did it," Rendel said, poking his stick back into the fire. "Whoever they were, they didn't leave any tracks behind. Even the mage that came with them couldn't figure it out."

"They brought a mage?" Koto asked, casting an eye in Tyler's direction.

"I thought it was strange, but they said they were investigating similar attacks around the kingdom. It seems we weren't the only ones to be targeted." Rendel jabbed Tyler in the leg with the hot stick. "Keep that spit moving, boy!"

Tyler had been listening too intently and forgot to keep cranking. Glaring at the old man he began to turn it again, hoping it would be proclaimed done soon. The smell of the fat dripping on the fire was enough to drive him crazy with hunger.

"Do you know which mage it was?" Koto asked, drawing Rendel's attention away from Tyler.

"I didn't catch their name, but I saw them. Kind of a tall gal," he said, stretching his arms upward. "Blonde hair, skinny, and a little too flat in the chest if you ask me." He held up a finger as if remembering something. "Actually, she was the reason the soldiers got there so fast, I heard them talking about it. It seems the mages have been keeping an eye on the kingdom from their tower. When they see something go wrong they apparently order up a relief convoy to march out to the site." He shrugged his shoulders. "Too bad they can't figure out where the bandits are going to attack next along the road."

"The Divinarae," Koto breathed.

Both Tyler and Rendel looked at him in confusion.

"It's an ancient pool deep under the academy tower," he explained. "The mages use it to see Bramoria or divine the future. The last I heard it had been outlawed and sealed away by the king. He thought they would use it against him."

"You know an awful lot about the capital, young man," Rendel nodded. "You must have been a noble of some sort."

Koto's ear twitched. "No. Just a servant in a big house. But a man needs more than rumors and table scraps to survive." He looked at Rendel with a big smile, showing no hint of his lies. "A man has to do what he feels in his bones, whether it be adventuring, becoming a mercenary, or transporting goods." He clapped Rendel on the shoulder. "Isn't that right?"

"Aye, I'll agree with ya on that," Rendel replied, his toothless smile highlighted by the firelight. He glanced over at the bird on the spit. "Do you think it's ready?"

Koto poked at it with a clawed finger. "Looks done to me."

Tyler sighed, letting his nearly dead arm drop to the ground. "Finally. Holy shit..."

Around noon the next day, Tyler and Koto found themselves standing next to Rendel's cart on the edge of the village. They'd made excellent time and thankfully had met no problems on the road. Koto lifted a hand to Rendel as he snapped the reins and drove toward the other end of town to sell off his wares. Tyler waited until he was well out of earshot to say what he'd been dying to say since the day before.

"Aren't you glad I did that?" he asked, turning to Koto with a cocky grin on his face. "We got here in less time *and* without having to exhaust ourselves."

Koto turned away, heading into town himself with his hood up. Tyler didn't understand what his problem was. After all, he'd done them both a favor. Just because Koto was too scared to talk to people on the road didn't mean Tyler should have to suffer for it. He sighed to himself and jogged after Koto to catch up. They'd talk about it another day.

"Hey," Tyler said, putting his hand on Koto's shoulder. "Where are you going?"

Koto turned on him in an instant, grabbing him by the collar and slamming him up against a wall.

"What's your problem?" Tyler hissed, fighting to pull away. But Koto kept a tight grip on him.

"Do you realize what you've done by involving that old man?" Koto asked through gritted teeth, ignoring the people gawking at them. "If Liran and his men find out that he helped us in any way, he'll be killed on sight." Koto glared at him with his slitted green eyes. "You have doomed that man to death by letting him see our faces."

Tyler opened his mouth to argue but stopped. He couldn't think of anything to say.

"You are reckless and unthinking," Koto snapped, letting the collar of his shirt go. "You're not just a danger to yourself, but to others and that is something I will not stand by and allow you to do. Do you understand?"

This was a side to him that Tyler had never seen before. His lips were curled back in a snarl, exposing his elongated canines. It was surprising how ferocious he could look.

"I… I didn't think of that," Tyler sputtered.

"Yes. I know."

"I'm sorry."

"Your apologies won't save that man if he runs into Liran." Koto took a step back, pinching the bridge of his nose. "Look, if you're going to travel with me, there is one rule that you *must* abide by. I don't care what you do, but it must be for the good of others, not just yourself. Got it?" He took a breath. "There's no reason to be alive in this world *except* to help others. That's what I live by and while you're with me, you'll live by it too or you won't be alive at all. Understand?"

"Yeah," Tyler nodded, his heart pounding in his chest. He would have agreed to anything to keep Koto around. Without him, he didn't stand a chance. "Okay, so you like to help people. I can get behind that."

"Good. Then from now on, you'll follow my lead if you want to get to the capital alive."

"Alright, alright," Tyler replied, rubbing the back of his head where it had struck the stone. "You're really worked up about this '*doing good*' thing, I got it."

Koto gave him a long hard look. "Now, we're going to find the tavern and get rooms for the night. You're not to speak to anyone unless I say so."

"Yes sir…" Tyler sighed. He already wasn't enjoying this new side to Koto or being ordered around.

"Good. Now follow me and keep quiet."

Koto turned away and stalked down the street. For a moment Tyler stood there, still surprised by the sudden outburst of his guide. Up until that point he thought of Koto as the kind of good guy who only slew monsters. But the threat to his life shattered that illusion. Suddenly Koto wasn't just a hero in a video game like Tyler had originally thought. He was a person willing to do anything to accomplish his goals, even if it meant killing people who got in his way. This time there was no save point to go back to and no way to turn off the game if something went wrong or he pissed Koto off. After all the years of fantasizing and imagining being inside his own game, Tyler found himself there. And it was nothing like he'd expected.

TWELVE

T he tavern was hardly more than a bar with two small rooms for rent, one of which was already taken. Everything from the floor to the tables stank of stale beer and piss, burning the inside of his nose. It was easily one of the grossest places Tyler had ever been in and it was their only choice if they wanted to sleep under a roof for the night. Against his wishes, he'd been sent to the room to wait, Koto no longer trusting him to interact with the locals. The room was tiny and the beds were lumpy. A single table sat between the pair of them with a washbasin and a pitcher placed within it. The water was murky and the bowl dirty, both of which made Tyler want to avoid using them. But after the past two days without a shower, he could no longer deny the fact that he was starting to smell.

He glanced at the door. Koto would probably be gone for a little while and this might be his only chance at some privacy. Quickly he got up from the bed and started to strip, tossing his clothes over the end rail. Naked and already feeling self-conscious, Tyler opened the small table drawer and found a stack of linen cloths. Filling the bowl he dipped the cloth into the cold water and began to scrub himself. He started with the smelliest areas first, rinsing the cloth between uses. He'd gone through nearly three of them when he heard the door behind him begin to open.

Tyler attempted to tell them to leave, but all that came out was a garbled squeak as he grabbed the pillow from the bed and stuffed it over his groin, trying to hide his nudity. Koto glanced up, didn't bat an eye, and walked in with a tray of food, closing the door behind him.

"C-Can you p-please get out!" Tyler cried, still holding the pillow over himself.

Koto sat the tray down at the end of his bed and looked up with his brows furrowed in confusion. "Is something wrong?"

"Y-Yeah! I'm naked!"

"And?"

"Dude! Give me some privacy!"

Koto looked to the pillow then back up to Tyler with a knowing nod. "Ah. I see." He stepped back to the door and put his hand on the latch, glancing back at Tyler. "Don't take too long, I'd like to eat my food before it gets completely cold."

Tyler immediately turned red once he realized what Koto meant. "I'm... I'm just washing!"

"Right," Koto replied with a disbelieving tone. "Have fun."

With that he slipped out the door, leaving Tyler standing alone in the room more embarrassed than he'd ever been in his entire life. After a moment he threw the pillow aside and scrubbed himself furiously as fast as he could. He was horrified to think of Koto sitting outside the room waiting for him to do *anything* besides wash up. It was less than two minutes before he had all his clothes back on and was opening the door to call Koto back in.

"That was fast," Koto smirked, slipping inside the room and shutting the door behind him.

"I told you," Tyler replied, his face beet red. "I was *just* washing up. Maybe if you'd knocked before you barged into the room this wouldn't have happened."

"Don't worry," Koto said, taking a seat on the edge of his bed. "It's not a big deal."

"Easy for you to say." Tyler leaned down and snatched a piece of the crusty bread from the tray, biting into it as he plopped down on his bed. The scent of the fresh loaf took over his senses as the slightly sour flavor spread over his tongue.

"This… This is really good."

"You say that as if you're surprised."

"I am. I've never had bread like this before."

Koto opened his mouth as if he were about to ask a question, but he just shook his head and started picking through his own food. After a moment he sighed, pulling the bread away from his mouth before he could take a bite. "Listen, I wanted to apologize for earlier. I shouldn't have been so hard on you."

Tyler stopped mid-chew and looked up.

"With every passing moment, I realize how little you know about this world. And sometimes I can be a little… *intense*." He paused for a moment. "There's a lot of things in my life I want to make up for. Things that I've done. I just want you to know that I'm not trying to dominate you or anything. But if you're going to be in Bramoria, even if it's not your home like you say, you might as well leave it better than you found it, yeah?"

Tyler nodded. "I think I understand." He tore a small piece of his bread and popped it into his mouth. "I honestly didn't think that old guy would get in any trouble for knowing us. I'm sorry."

"It's alright. No harm done. I've already convinced him to leave town."

"Really? How did you do that?"

"Yes, he'll be going in the morning." Koto gave him a sly look. "And I told him the truth. He seemed quite happy to leave once he knew."

"Well," Tyler said, swallowing the last bite of his bread. "I'm glad he's going to be alright."

"Me too," Koto nodded. "I don't want anyone else hurt because of me."

Tyler looked up at the sad expression on Koto's face. His ears had dropped slightly and his tail came to a stop, but it only lasted a moment. He seemed to snap out of it quickly, scooping up a bowl of stew from the tray. Together they ate their meal in silence, enjoying the taste of a meal prepared by others.

The night drifted by slowly with easy conversation and

eventually, both of them laid down to sleep, the heat of the fire taking effect on them both. Koto seemed to find comfort quickly, but Tyler was having a hard time getting used to the lumpy bed and the scratchy blankets. His body was still sore from sleeping on the ground the night before, something he was not accustomed to in any way, especially without any padding. He missed his queen-sized bed at home. The mattress was old, but it was comfortable with a perfect indent in the middle the shape of his body. He missed soft pillows and cotton quilts, all the things he'd taken for granted until now.

Tyler's thoughts drifted back to home again like they always did before he fell asleep. It had been a few days since his last text to his mom and he wondered what she could be thinking. Eventually, she would start to think something was wrong, but even if she sent the police out after him, they'd never find anything but his car, if they even found that. As far as she knew, he was already at college. However, if Clay and Danny hadn't been pulled along with him, maybe they would be able to explain it to her. Tyler scoffed out loud in the dark. As if that would fix anything. Even if they knew he'd been pulled into the book, it wouldn't matter. He could barely believe where he was and he was *living* through it. How could he ever expect his mother to accept such a ridiculous story?

Then again, what if the guys had been pulled in along with him? He knew it would be no big loss for Clay, especially since he never wanted to go home again anyway. But for Danny, it could mean the last of his days in a strange world with no one around that he knew. Tyler felt his chest tighten at the thought of Danny alone, wandering through the wilderness. Or possibly already dead. He hoped, more than anything, that Danny had been left behind in the real world. At least he wouldn't have to worry about being eaten there. Guilt crept into his thoughts once more like it always did when it came to Danny. It was his fault Danny left home, his fault he was out in the world, real or fantastical, and his fault he hadn't been right there by his side for the past few months. If he'd been braver or a better friend, maybe he would have been able to convince Danny to stay on his treatments. Or maybe Danny wouldn't have relapsed if he'd kept him happy with his company. No matter which way he spun it, the entire situation seemed to be his fault.

A strange noise pulled Tyler from his downward spiral. He opened his eyes in the dark, the ceiling and walls highlighted by the dim glow of embers in the fireplace. It sounded like a dog and an unhappy one at that. He wondered if the poor creature was being beaten or fighting with a wild animal. It went on for a few minutes, a constant yelping and screeching in the night. At first, he wasn't worried about it. After all, Bramoria could be full of strange sounds that he'd never heard before and it was none of his business. Getting involved always led to trouble, so he tried to ignore it, stuffing his head under the pillow to drown out the sound. It wasn't until he heard Koto spring up out of bed that he knew something was amiss.

"Get up!" Koto cried, running to the window.

"Why?" Tyler whined, having finally just fallen asleep. "It's just a dog or something. Who cares?"

"That's not a dog." Koto jogged back to his bed and began to pull on his boots. "Those are Fossars and they've lit some of the houses on fire." The serious tone of his voice filled Tyler's chest with anxiety. "If you want a roof over your head come morning, you need to get up and help!"

"I can't fight..." Tyler said, swinging his legs over the side of the bed. "What do you want me to do?"

"Help people put the fires out!" Koto yelled, pushing himself up and grabbing his bow. "Use some of your common sense!"

With that, he flung the door open and rushed down the hall. Tyler was still sitting on his bed, listening to the sounds coming from outside. The more he strained his ears, the less the noises sounded like a dog and more like the monkeys he'd seen at the zoo. Peppered in were the screams of the townspeople, which made his skin crawl. He'd never fought anything in his life, much less a Fossar, whatever the hell that was. He glanced down at the sword leaning against his bed. It was about as foreign to him as the sports equipment in the school gym.

Pulling on his boots, Tyler got up from the bed. For a long moment, he stared at the sword, wondering if he should take it with him. The last thing he wanted to do was get in a fight and if he had the sword he'd look like a threat to the attackers. Instead, he decided to leave it behind along with his bag. He'd come back for them once they put the fires out. Besides, he was sure the villagers could handle themselves and the ruckus didn't sound that big to begin with. Everything would be fine.

The bar seemed mostly abandoned, but as Tyler stepped out the front door a mouthful of smoke and ash caused his lungs to seize up immediately. Coughing and sputtering he leaned against the outside wall. The smoke made his eyes water and he couldn't see much until the breeze picked up, shifting it away from him. At last, he was able to get himself under control and turned his gaze back over the town. The entire village looked like it was ringed in fire with flames reaching high above the houses, illuminating the hazy darkness with their orange glow. Embers and ash floated through the air and Tyler pulled his shirt over his mouth to avoid breathing any more of it in. The shrill screeches were louder, but now he could hear the yells of the villagers piercing through as they tried to say their homes and themselves.

Around the corner, an older man came running as if the hounds of hell were nipping at his heels. He skidded in the mud, trying to keep his balance. With one last slip, he went down, crashing to the ground. Before he could get back on his feet a ghostly white figure whipped around the building and landed hard on top of his back. He cried out in pain as long claws were raked across his back. The man looked up at Tyler, his eyes full of fear, a silent plea for help painted across his features. But before Tyler could react he watched as the creature bit down on the back of the man's neck, a loud crunch echoing across the clearing. The man slumped into the mud immediately, his body completely lifeless.

A wave of revulsion rolled through Tyler's body as he realized he'd just watched someone die for the first time in his life. His stomach churned, the bread and stew threatening to make a second appearance. Before he could process the thought a pair of bulbous glowing red eyes locked onto him. The creature on the man's back stepped off him, pulling itself up to its full height of nearly five feet. As it walked into the firelight Tyler got a better look at it. Most of its body was white and gray, giving it an ethereal quality. Its arms and legs were too long, too thin, and tipped in sharp claws that were dripping with blood. The eyes were masked by black fur, giving the face a haunted and sunken look while elongated canines, like a gorilla's, pushed out from under its lips. Behind it, a slender tail covered in black fur swung back and forth in intricate patterns. To Tyler, it looked almost like a monkey, but a hundred times more terrifying and far too big to be allowed. It had to be one of the Fossars Koto had spoken of.

He suddenly wished he had his sword. Taking a single step backward he put his hand on the handle to the tavern door. Before he could take another the Fossar sprang forward, galloping toward him on all fours. Without a second to spare, Tyler stepped aside to avoid the attack. Unable to get any traction in the mud, the Fossar slipped and crashed into the building, slamming into the stones at a bone-cracking speed. Tyler didn't waste time to see if it was hurt or not, instead, he darted out into the street, making his way toward the fires, trying to get as far away from the terrifying creature as possible.

Screeches and screams continued to fill the night as his feet pounded against the dirt and mud, trying to put as much distance between himself and the murderous ghostly creatures as he could. In the streets he saw other bodies lying face down in the mud, some of them killed with a single bite and others shredded until their entrails and blood were mixed into the muddy streets. He had to force down the bile rising in his throat as he ran. All the horror movies in the world could never have prepared him for the stench of blood and death that rode on the smokey breeze.

The ash and embers grew thicker as he approached the fires, forcing him to pull his shirt over his mouth again. He slid to a stop near a burning house, holding an arm up to block the intense heat radiating off of it. Glancing around he looked for any sign of Koto or the Fossars, but the dark shapes silhouetted against the firelight made it almost impossible to tell them apart. People ran back and forth with buckets, failing to keep the fires under control while others were swept off their feet by the monsters attacking the village. Everything was completely out of control and Tyler did the only thing he could, curse Koto for forcing him to leave his room. If they'd just stayed inside both of them would still be safe.

"Ty!" a familiar voice called from behind him. He spun around to see the lithe shape of Koto highlighted by the blaze jogging in his direction. For the first time, his hood was down exposing his tall ears. "Ty! What are you doing? Where is your sword?"

"You fucking *told me* to go help!" Tyler yelled back at him, his fear and anger getting the better of him. "And I don't know how to use the damn sword, remember? What the hell is going on?!"

"You need a weapon." Koto reached back to his belt and pulled out a dagger, handing it hilt first to Tyler. "Get back to the tavern! This is a lot worse than I thought!"

"Yeah, I can fucking see that!" Tyler cried, pointing to a dead body less than twenty feet away. "You wanna think about that next time before you send me out into a bloodbath like this?!"

"Ty, I–"

Koto stopped mid-sentence and pulled his bow up, an arrow on the string flashing through the air over Tyler's shoulder before he could so much as blink. Behind him, a dull thud followed by a horrendous screech split the air and he spun on his heel. He watched as one of the Fossar's clawed furiously at the arrow now buried in its neck. Blood spurted from the wound as the creature slowly sank to the ground, the red glowing eyes losing their light until it went completely still. Tyler's senses were overwhelmed and he felt like he might unravel at any moment.

"I'm taking you back," Koto said with a commanding tone, grabbing him by the arm. "Follow me."

With a harsh yank, Tyler was nearly pulled off his feet. He stumbled for a moment then began to match the intense pace at which Koto set off for the tavern. Together they ran, dodging between buildings, sliding around corners, and avoiding any sign of life. More than once Tyler caught a peek of another villager being chased down by the Fossars, some of them barely escaping behind closed doors. The more he saw, the more he wanted to rip his hand from Koto's grasp and fly out into the wilderness, never to be seen again. It took longer to reach the tavern than expected with all the detours Koto was taking to avoid a fight. However, as they rounded the last corner they came face to face with a small group of people backed up against the wall across the street from the tavern door.

Koto slid to a stop, letting go of Tyler's hand and pulling his bow up once more. Tyler grabbed him by the shoulder and turned him around.

"What are you doing?" he hissed, eyeing the unguarded tavern door. "We can get in without being seen. Just leave them."

Koto pushed him away. "I'm not a coward," he snapped, nocking an arrow on the string. "Get out of my way!"

With that he forced his way out into the open, ignoring Tyler's pleas. The first arrow whizzed through the air, catching one of the Fossars in the back of the neck. It never even got a chance to cry out as the arrow pierced all the way through, tearing a hole through its windpipe. The body crumpled to the ground amongst its friends who all looked at it in confusion. Slowly they began to turn their attention toward Koto who was already loading more arrows.

"Run!" he cried to the villagers, releasing an arrow and dropping another beast. "Take shelter in the tavern!"

A woman cried out as another arrow buried itself in the chest of the Fossar closest to her. The dozen ghostly creatures were hopping up and down, screeching in Koto's direction. They turned as a group and began to cross the street, each keeping a close eye on where his next arrow was aimed. Tyler watched from a few feet away as the villagers pressed themselves against the wall, inching their way toward the tavern. He wanted to dart from his hiding place and join them, but the beasts had already cut him off. Their glowing red eyes were all focused on Koto as he tried to take the rest of them down. But now that their attention was fixed on him, they saw the attacks coming. Only every third arrow or so found its mark and it wasn't always a killing blow. The beasts were dodging back and forth, laughing in their own monkey-like way as the arrows buried themselves in the mud.

In a matter of moments, the villagers had slipped inside the tavern and shut the door behind them. Tyler peeked around the corner to see the six remaining Fossars closed in on Koto who had only three arrows left in his quiver. He was outnumbered and in a moment his bow would be rendered useless.

"Ty!" Koto called over his shoulder. "I'm gonna need your help!"

Tyler was frozen with fear from his spot behind the wall. The ghostly faces, the thin long limbs, and the glowing red eyes pierced through him. All he could see was the man who'd been murdered in front of his very eyes and the shredded corpses he'd passed on the way through town. He didn't want to be next. His thoughts were in his room back home and the bed with the heavy quilt on it. He wished he was there.

"Ty!" Koto shouted, letting another arrow go. It hit its mark and he quickly nocked another. "Get over here!"

He just wanted to go home, to be anywhere but in that street where the road was made muddy with blood instead of water.

Koto cried out as one of the Fossars leapt forward and he

shot it in mid-air, the arrow piercing its chest. It landed in a heap next to him as another rushed at him. In a flash he tore the arrow from his kill and jammed it into the other, snapping the shaft off in the creature's belly. The wound was fatal, but there were still three more and he only had one arrow left. Slowly they all began to creep closer, keeping far apart from one another to force Koto to make a choice. He'd have to turn his back on two to attack the other.

Tyler still gripped the dagger in his shaking hand. He knew how fast the beasts could take a man down and Koto was surrounded and outnumbered. Although he wanted nothing more than to run away, something was keeping him in place, a sense of honor that he wasn't familiar with. Taking a deep breath he stood up straight, tightening his grip on the dagger. He had to help Koto if he ever wanted to get to the capital or back home. Without him, he was lost in a strange world with no way out.

The twang of the bowstring and a screech told him he'd waited too long to act. Tyler's head snapped up as one of the Fossars went down, an arrow sticking out of its chest. Meanwhile, the other two had rushed Koto, both of them leaping onto his shoulders, biting and clawing at any spare piece of flesh they could find. Digging his heels into the mud Tyler raced into the street with the dagger held high. The creatures didn't see him coming as he collided with Koto, driving the dagger into the back of the beast with its teeth sunk into the man's shoulder. Tyler was surprised at how easily the knife slipped between its ribs. It turned as if to fight, but Tyler tore the creature away, throwing it to the dirt as the light left its eyes.

Koto was crying out in pain as Tyler turned back, the last Fossar had its teeth buried in his forearm and was clawing at his eyes with its spindly limbs. He came around with the knife, but the creature saw it coming. In a flash it let go of Koto and leapt through the air, wrapping its body around his torso and burying the claws into his chest. Tyler screamed in pain and dropped the blade, clutching the Fossar by the neck to stop it from biting his shoulder or face. Both fell to the ground in a tangle of limbs, mud, and fury. They rolled back and forth, fighting for an advantage that would assure their victory. Tyler squeezed and squeezed at its windpipe, trying to make the creature pass out, but it only seemed to infuriate it more. Claws raked across his body and he felt the long tail wind around his neck. With incredible strength, it began to constrict and he immediately felt the pressure in his skull as the blood was cut off from his brain. In a matter of seconds, his vision began to tunnel and he could feel his strength leaving him as he was no longer able to draw breath. The orange firelight was fading and all he could think of was home.

Suddenly the creature above him stopped screeching, its eyes growing wide. It stared down at Tyler until the light left its eyes, the tail around his neck loosening. Immediately he hefted the beast off of him and rolled to his side, coughing and sputtering in the mud. Every inch of his body was on fire with the multitude of deep cuts bleeding under his shredded clothing. His vision widened once more and he looked up. Koto was standing over him with the dagger in his off-hand, blood running down the opposite arm. One of his ears was nearly shredded and he looked like he was on the verge of passing out. Embers floated through the air around them, their forms cast in an orange glow.

Koto stared at him for a long moment. "Ty... help."

With that, his knees buckled and he fell to the ground, coming to rest in the blood-soaked mud next to Tyler.

THIRTEEN

It had been two days since the attack on the village and Koto was still lying in his bed at the tavern, slipping in and out of consciousness. He looked like he was made of bandages rather than a person, but at least he was still alive. Tyler had enlisted the help of the villagers to bring him inside after the last of the Fossars were killed. He'd spent nearly all of Koto's money paying the local medicine woman to sew him back together. She'd done the best she could, but parts of him would be heavily scarred and his ear would never look the same. Still, he was alive and that was what mattered. He'd awoken a couple of times just long enough to drink water or babble something incoherent, but Tyler was still waiting for his lucidity to return.

Tyler, on the other hand, was covered in his own series of wounds, but nothing so bad that it required stitching, which he was thankful for. Even so, he was exhausted. For the past two days, he'd been terrified out of his mind to sleep. Every time he closed his eyes he saw the ghostly faces and the glowing red eyes in his head, chasing him with their blood-stained teeth and tearing other faceless people apart in front of him. He'd awaken multiple times a night, his heart pounding in his chest and his vision playing tricks on him in the dark. More than once the simple sound of a dog barking or a raised voice would send him into a panic, making him unable to get back to sleep until the dawn came at last. His sword stayed untouched next to his bed and the dagger lay on the small end table, still covered in dry blood. He wanted nothing to do with fighting ever again. The images of villagers torn apart in the streets, their entrails laying in steaming piles next to them, were impossible to get out of his head. Up until that night he'd never seen death before, but now that he had it was all he could think about.

The all-consuming thoughts were only disrupted when Koto stirred or the medicine woman came by to check on him. But it wasn't enough. He thought of going out into the town and trying to help the villagers but quickly brushed it away. The aftermath of the attack was not something he wanted to see or interact with. He already heard the grief-stricken wails beyond his window, he didn't want to experience it up close. Besides, he was scrawny and weak, just like Koto had said. What possible use could he be to people who lived hard lives every single day? Instead, he kept mostly to the room or the tavern itself. He'd taken a liking to ale, a harsh bitter drink that apparently didn't require proof of age to order. The past couple of days had been nothing but food, ale, and fighting intrusive thoughts until he eventually passed out and was haunted by his dreams once more.

When Tyler returned to his room that night after dinner, one ale too many in his churning stomach, he found Koto sitting up in bed with his injured arm draped over his bare torso.

"You're finally awake," Tyler slurred slightly, leaning against the doorframe. "I was starting to think you'd never come to." He stifled a belch, bile stinging the back of his throat. "Are you hungry?"

Koto was silent for a long moment. "What... What took you so long?" he asked quietly, his green eyes resting on Tyler's.

"What do you mean?"

"In the street... why didn't you help me when I called for you?"

Tyler sighed, shifting his weight further against the doorframe. He didn't want this to be their first conversation. It could wait. "You need to eat. It's been a couple of days. I'll go get you something."

"Ty," Koto called after him, but Tyler ignored him and the nickname, heading back down the hallway to the main bar.

He put in an order with the barkeep and sat down on a stool, crossing his arms over the bar and resting his head on top of them. Koto had no right to ask him such a question, to *blame* him for not coming to his rescue. Tyler had been more than honest with him about his capabilities. He couldn't fight and he didn't want to get sucked into crazy shit every time something went wrong. It wasn't fair for Koto to question him or to ask him in the first place to go save people he didn't know in a world he wasn't from. If they'd just stayed in the room and left the villagers to themselves they'd both be better off. Koto wouldn't be injured and Tyler wouldn't have his every moment haunted by the memories of what he'd witnessed that night. His life would be forever changed because of those horrors and it was all Koto's fault. If there was anyone who should be asking questions and placing blame, it was Tyler.

A tray was put down in front of him and Tyler pushed himself back up from the bar. He looked up to see the owner of the tavern staring down at him. He was a friendly sort of person, the kind of bartender someone would feel compelled to confess their troubles to. His smile was warm, his visage unintimidating, and he had a chubby bearded face that made him look wiser than he probably was.

"Is that friend of yours awake?" the barkeep asked, leaning against the bar from the inside.

"Yep," Tyler sighed, grabbing the sides of the tray.

The owner put a hand on the tray, holding it in place. "Then give him this," he said, producing a small leather bag with a drawstring. "It's not much, but the village wanted to thank him for his help and nearly losing an arm in the process." He glanced over the bar. "None of this would be left if he hadn't stepped in. Those Fossars are deadly at the best of times. We can usually fend them off, but when the entire troop attacked that night, we didn't stand a chance." He turned his gaze back to Tyler, his eyes growing watery. "You're friend is the only reason our little village still exists. So thank you."

"Uh... sure," Tyler replied, having no idea what to say. The sheer amount of gratitude emanating from the barkeep made him nauseous. Then again, it might have been the ale. "I'll let him know." He paused awkwardly, glancing back up the hall. "I'm gonna go now. Thanks."

The barkeep nodded in his direction and went back to the other handful of customers in the tavern. Tyler picked up the tray and headed back down the hall towards his room. For a brief moment, he wondered if he should tell Koto at all about what the owner had said. He knew it would only inflate his need to be a *good person* that much more and it was already getting in the way of Tyler reaching his goal of getting home as fast as possible. The more Koto tried to help people, the longer it took for them to get to the capital. And the more he thought about it, the more infuriated he became. Koto had offered to *help* him, but so far all he was doing was making things harder.

For a long moment, Tyler stood outside the door, wondering if he should hide the pouch of coins and fighting with himself about sharing the praise from the villagers. Maybe he could use it to get himself to the capital without Koto's help. It seemed shady and underhanded, but Tyler was desperate and thus far Koto had only put him in more danger. He needed to get to the mages so he could figure out where Danny was and get them both home. He knew nothing about magic, but he didn't suppose it would be cheap or free. Besides, Koto would probably do something stupid with the money anyway, like donate it to someone in need and force them both to sleep on the cold ground again. Tyler was sick of it and Koto didn't need the money anyway.

Setting the tray down Tyler picked up the small pouch and stuffed it into the back of his belt, careful to place it so that it wouldn't make any noise. Taking a deep breath he pushed the door open and carried the tray inside, kicking it shut again behind him.

"You're gonna need your strength," Tyler said, taking the

tray over and sitting it on Koto's lap. He avoided the man's gaze, too guilty and angry to look him in the eye. "The owner needs this room for other people who are more in need," he lied, making it up on the spot. "We need to leave soon and get back on the road toward the capital."

"Oh," was all Koto said, staring down at his food.

Tyler glanced up to notice his ears drooping to the sides of his head, one of them mangled permanently and covered in stitches. He went over to his own bed and flopped down, the coin pouch digging into his lower back painfully under the belt. For a long while, there were no words spoken between them as Tyler stared up at the ceiling, trying to force the guilt from his system. Koto ate slowly with one hand, unable to use the other due to its severe injuries.

"Ty? Can y–"

"Why do you call me that?" Tyler interrupted before he could get the question out. He was still seething that Koto had put him in so much danger. "I don't need a pet name from you. It's not like we're friends or anything."

Koto paused for nearly a full minute. "I... I apologize." He lifted his bowl awkwardly and nearly spilled the stew on himself, his off-hand lacking in coordination. "I'm sure you're eager to get home. We can leave tomorrow."

"Early."

Koto nodded, his voice lacking its usual enthusiasm. "As you wish."

The next morning they were both up before sunrise. Tyler had found it easy to get out of bed and get ready for the day even at such an early hour. He even helped Koto gather up his things and get dressed so that they could leave faster. Anything so that he could avoid the barkeep from revealing his secret. Thankfully the bar was empty before dawn and the tavern owner had yet to stir from his quarters. With quiet steps, they left the keys to their room on one of the tables and snuck out the front door.

Koto kept mostly to himself. He'd been quiet since the night before when Tyler had been harsh with him, but that was all the better in his mind. Over the past few days, he'd been getting tired of Koto treating him like he was stupid, threatening him, and even getting them into trouble. As far as he was concerned, Koto keeping to himself for a while was a bonus. The less he talked, the less trouble they would get in on their way to the capital.

Winding through the half-burnt village, Tyler led Koto toward the northern end of town where the main road continued on into the wilderness. At the edge of the village, Koto stopped, looking out over the landscape in front of them as the first hints of reds and pinks filtered into the sky.

"The next town is a few days away. I'll take you there and no further," Koto said suddenly, his voice gravelly from sleep. "It's a bigger town and a trading hub for the kingdom. You'll be able to find a mercenary or caravan to take you the rest of the way from there."

Tyler glared at the back of his head for a long moment, irritated that Koto had the nerve to have a problem with *him*. After all, he was the one that saved him from the Fossars in the end.

"Fine," he replied, not bothering to cover up the venom in his voice. "I can make my own way after that."

He watched as Koto visibly sighed and readjusted his shoulders. "I guess we better get a move on then," he said, his voice lacking all warmth and enthusiasm.

Tyler gritted his teeth. His mother had a habit of doing the same thing whenever she was upset with him and it made his skin crawl. The constant disappointment and guilt-tripping was the only reason he'd made sure to get good grades in school. And by trying to please her he'd paid the price of getting a full ride to a college he wanted nothing to do with to prep for a life only to make her happy. It seemed like every time he'd tried to please someone, no matter what world it was in, it backfired on him.

Keeping his head down Tyler started down the road, leaving Koto in his wake. He was too angry to speak as he stomped away. Nothing ever went the way he wanted it to. Life seemed to be an endless series of unfair events that made sure to fuck him over as often as possible.

FOURTEEN

Koto held up his off-hand, motioning for Tyler to stop. It was the fourth time that day and he was getting tired of it.

"What is it now?" Tyler said without lowering his voice. "You've been doing this for two days straight. Can we just keep moving?"

"Someone is coming," Koto replied, his voice barely a whisper.

"No, they aren't. Just like they haven't been the past seven hundred times you've done this."

Koto was quiet for a moment, his good ear turned toward the road. After a long pause, he headed toward the trees on the left side of the road. "Quick, follow me!"

Tyler sighed. He was getting sick of this charade. It almost seemed like Koto was wasting his time on purpose. His mood hadn't improved any the past couple of days and it was beginning to feel like they'd never reach the next town, especially when they were stopping and hiding from invisible passersby every twenty minutes.

Reluctantly, Tyler stomped toward the woods, his arms crossed over his chest. He chose a spot a few trees away from Koto and sunk down to the ground, finding a comfortable position amongst the roots. Koto glanced his way and shook his head before turning back to the road. Tyler caught it out of the corner of his eye and looked away. He was tired of the silent judgments Koto was always making about him. It had crossed his mind more than once to leave him behind over the past two days, but the fear of being alone in a strange place kept him there. Whether he liked it or not, Koto was his only chance at staying alive in Bramoria, a land that seemed to grow more inhospitable by the day.

For a long moment, they both sat in silence, listening to the sounds of the summer woods around them. Everything seemed completely normal and it irritated Tyler even more. But just as he pushed himself up and opened his mouth to berate Koto again, he felt cold metal press against his neck.

"Not a fuckin' word boy. You got that?" a gruff voice breathed in his ear, the harsh breath nearly making his eyes water.

Koto's eyes widened as his gaze fell on Tyler. Without hesitation, he drew the dagger from his belt and began to rush forward.

"Ah ah ah!" the man holding Tyler called. "Not so fast if you want your friend here to live."

Koto slowed but didn't stop moving forward. "He doesn't have anything you want." He reached back to his belt and pulled out his coin purse with a few coins left for killing the monster almost a week ago. "Let him go and you can have it."

"Would ya look at that?" the man muttered in Tyler's ear. "Looks like your pal's got your back after all." He looked back up at Koto. "I've been keepin' an eye on ya for a couple days now and to be honest, I wouldn't have known you two were friends at all!" He laughed to himself, the knife coming away from Tyler's neck before giving him a shove to the ground. "But now that *my* friends are here, we'll just be takin' everything ya have."

Tyler pushed himself up from the dirt and leaves, bolting over to where Koto stood and hiding behind him. In front of him was the man who'd held him hostage. His hair was dark and greasy, looking as if it hadn't been washed for some time. His skin was richly tanned and coated in a thin layer of dark hair as well. The face was smudged in places with dirt, but his beard was neatly kept with two braids ending in white beads hanging from his chin. He looked almost friendly if not for the curved dagger he held in his hand that had just been up against Tyler's throat.

The rustling of leaves and plants began to fill the spaces between the trees, echoing through the forest. Both Koto and Tyler glanced around noticing the dozen or so men that were slowly surrounding them. Each of them was equally scrappy looking with some kind of weapon in their hands. They all wore simple clothing covered in patches and stains just like their leader, giving them an almost pauper-ish appearance. Tyler listened to his heart pounding in his ears as they drew closer. He had no idea what to do. They were outnumbered and outmatched by far, especially with Koto injured.

"You need to run," Koto whispered to him out of the corner of his mouth. "As fast as you can. Don't look back."

"But..." Tyler began, surprised by his words. "What about you?"

"I'll be fine. Don't worry." Koto gave him a soft smile. "You need to get home, so go."

Tyler felt guilt suddenly well up inside him. "But–"

"Go!"

Koto gave him a shove, nearly tripping Tyler in the process. But he found his footing and kept going like he'd been instructed. He spotted a gap between their pursuers and dug his heels in, running as fast as he could.

"Tiragan!" the leader shouted. "Bring him back! Alive or dead, I don't care!"

Suddenly the pounding of Tyler's feet was joined by another. He pushed himself harder, breaking through the outer ring of men and heading deeper into the forest. Leaping over roots and barreling through bushes, the branches and thorns tore at the exposed flesh of his arms, small rivulets of blood welling up in their wake. But he ignored it. Koto had sacrificed himself to save Tyler and he wasn't going to let it go to waste. Thoughts raced through his mind laced with the sudden guilt over how he'd treated Koto, how he'd lied to him. But it was too late. There was nothing he could do about it now except get away as fast as he could.

However, the other man was already gaining on him.

Without looking back, Tyler took a sharp turn right, ran for a few yards, then went left, trying to lose his pursuer amongst the trees. He weaved through the forest, hoping that something would eventually throw the other person off or cause them to finally give up. Instead, the footfalls grew closer and closer until Tyler was convinced they were nearly on top of him. He panicked, dodging around another tree. This time the footsteps seemed to die away for a brief moment. A smile came to his lips as he thought they'd given up, leaving him victorious. But as he came around another tree he felt a sudden blow against his side and all the breath was forced from his lungs.

Tyler was thrown to the ground, every inch of his body crying out from the sudden impact. Leaves and dirt flew into his eyes and mouth as he cried out. Roots and fallen branches dug into his back as he struggled to get away, blinded and coughing. In the thrashing, he couldn't make out his attacker's face, but it didn't matter, he struck at anything he could find. He let out a fierce roar as he kicked and punched, doing anything he could to break free.

"Stop fighting!" a man's voice yelled, grabbing one of his wrists.

"Get the fuck off me!" Tyler cried back, trying to force the other man off him. "Let me go!"

"Tyler, stop!" the voice shouted.

He froze in place. How did the man know his name? Gasping for air he used his free hand to wipe away the dirt and debris that had gotten in his eyes. Leaning over him was a familiar face that he could barely believe.

"Danny?"

"Hey buddy," Danny replied, a warm smile spreading over his features.

"What... what the fuck are you doing here?"

Tyler couldn't believe what he was seeing. It was Danny,

but not the one he remembered. This Danny had bright eyes and vibrant skin, although the red spots still remained. His clothes were different, his figure was more filled out, and he seemed to absolutely be glowing with life.

"So... I guess I'm not dead," Danny laughed, letting go of Tyler's wrist.

"What the hell does that mean?"

Danny smiled. "At first I thought this was some kind of dream, then I thought I'd died and gone to the coolest afterlife that's ever existed. But now that you're here, I'm not so sure."

"I don't think I'm dead," Tyler muttered, looking over himself. "Not that this fucked up world hasn't been trying really hard to make that happen."

"Yep, you sound like you." Danny pushed himself to his feet and held out a hand. "I suppose this is probably real then. Or maybe it's all fabricated." He smiled wider, taking Tyler's hand and pulling him to his feet. "I don't really care either way!"

Tyler brushed the leaves from his clothing. "Are you okay? What's going on? Why are you with those people? Where's Clay?"

"Woah there," Danny chuckled. "One question at a time." Tyler couldn't believe how good he looked. "I'm fine. I know it sounds crazy, but it seems like we're in some sort of weird fantasy world, like the ones in my books. This is definitely the coolest thing that's ever happened to me if I'm being honest."

"What the hell is cool about this place?"

"For the past few weeks, I've been learning how to hunt, fight, go o–"

"*Few weeks?!*" Tyler interrupted. "What do you mean, a few weeks?"

"That's how long I've been here." He seemed confused by the question. "How long have you been here?"

"Like four or five days at most!" Tyler's mind was reeling. Everything he thought he knew was starting to come apart. "I woke up by myself in the middle of the woods with nothing but my sleeping bag. I didn't know where you or Clay went!"

"That's weird." He just smiled. Danny grabbed Tyler by the arm and started leading him back through the woods. "I didn't even think to go looking for either of you. When I woke up I was already in the keep with those other guys. They told me I'd been sick and were glad to see I was feeling better again. After a few days of food and rest, I was feeling more myself than ever." He looked at Tyler, an embarrassed look on his face. "I didn't ask anything about this world. I just started living in it."

"Are you okay?"

"Okay? I feel amazing! This is everything I ever dreamed of." Danny patted the thick-bladed sword hanging at his side. "I've never felt more alive."

"But... what about... aren't you sick?"

For the first time, Danny paused, turning over his hand to look at the red spots on his skin. "I don't know." A smile came back to his face. "But I also don't care. This place is so incredible and I'm not gonna waste a moment of my time here worrying about what tomorrow brings."

"But what about go–"

"Tiragan!" one of the men shouted from ahead. Tyler didn't realize they'd gotten there so fast. "What's going on?"

"False alarm," Danny called back with a wave. "This is my friend!"

"What about the other one?"

Danny turned to Tyler. "Is he with you?"

Tyler paused for a moment, his guilt doubling as he realized he'd actually have to talk to Koto again and apologize for being a dick. "Yeah," he sighed. "He's with me."

"Also a friend," Danny returned to the man. "Let him keep his goods for now."

"Are you... are you a bandit?" Tyler asked in a hushed tone.

"We do what we need to survive." He was all smiles. "It's not the most ethical thing in the world, but we never hurt anyone or leave them with nothing."

Tyler didn't know what to say as they rounded a corner

and saw the others standing in a circle around Koto who had his blade still drawn. He looked up at the pair of them in confusion, Danny with his arm around Tyler's shoulders.

"Listen up Shadow Squad," Danny called. Tyler immediately lifted an eyebrow at the name. It sounded ridiculous. "These are my friends and our guests. It seems they've been traveling and as you can see," he gestured at Koto and his bandages, "they've run into a bit of trouble. With the boss's permission," he nodded to the large bearded man who threatened Tyler first, "I'd like to bring them back with us to the hideout and give them a chance to recover from the road."

The others all turned to their leader, looking for his opinion on the matter. He lifted a hand and ran his fingers over the two braids of his beard, playing with the beads for a moment.

"Well, anyone who is a friend of Tiragan is a friend of ours."

The others shouted in agreement.

"Return anything you took lads and let's get these two back to the keep for a good meal and warm beds."

Koto stood in the center of the group, a dumbfounded look on his face as his coin purse was handed back to him and multiple people clapped him on the shoulder as if they'd been friends for years. He threw a glance Tyler's way before allowing himself to be led off back toward the road by one of the bandits. Tyler, on the other hand, was still staring at Danny who wore the biggest grin he'd ever seen.

"Tiragan?" Tyler asked. "Who the hell is that?"

"I've got so much to tell you," Danny laughed. "There'll be plenty of time on the walk. Come on."

Gesturing for him to follow, Danny set off with the others, jogging up to the leader of the group to speak with him for a moment. Tyler stood for a long moment glued to the spot. He couldn't believe what he'd seen and heard. His entire world had changed in a matter of moments. Danny was in Bramoria and not only that, he'd joined a gang of thieves and looked amazing besides like he was somehow miraculously recovering from his illness. In the past four years, Tyler had never seen him with so much light in his eyes. But even if this strange world was doing him some good, his time was still running out. Tyler couldn't allow himself to hope, not when the symptoms were still showing. Eventually, they'd need to go home and he shuddered at the thought of Danny passing before he got to see his parents one last time. They'd always been the best people Tyler knew. They deserved that. That and Bramoria was teeming with danger. It would only be a matter of time before Danny came up against something he couldn't handle. He was fragile after all, but Tyler knew he'd never allow anything to happen to him. Not now that he'd found him. The sooner they got to the academy, the sooner they could go home.

FIFTEEN

T he hike to the bandit's keep took nearly the rest of the day, the bright sun caressing the horizon as they drew close. Deep pinks and purples filled the sky as the light caught the underside of the fluffy clouds, giving the world a magnificent glow that was unlike any Tyler had seen before. Or maybe he'd just never really paid attention. After all, this was the most he'd been outside in years.

Contrary to expectation, he and Danny had spoken very little during the trek as he was kept busy by the other members of the gang. It seemed he'd made himself useful in Tyler's absence and become a respected member of their group, even in his weakened state. The others relied on him for advice, to watch their backs, and treated him like a welcome friend, as if they'd known each other for years. The further they walked, the more jealous Tyler became. For the past few years, he'd been Danny's only friend, the one who'd come visit him no matter what. Except for the last few months, he'd been the one always there and he was surprised how easily he'd been replaced. He wanted to step between Danny and the bandits, knowing they were a bad influence on him. It was obvious since he'd already taken to thievery as a means of enjoyment. But that didn't matter. In a few days they'd be out of there and on their way to the capital, he was sure of that.

"You're gonna want to see this," Danny said suddenly, jogging over and grabbing Tyler by the arm.

The path was on a slight incline and Danny dragged him to the top of the hill. At the peak, they both stopped and stared in awe. Golden sunlight spilled across the landscape, covering the trees and grass in a sheen of metallic gold that was too vibrant to be real. At the bottom of the hill was a low stone building with turrets on either end and people milling about. It almost looked like a small castle, although it was covered in vines and not in the greatest of shape. Danny lifted an arm, pointing to the westernmost tower.

"Watch," he whispered. "This is my favorite part."

Tyler squinted, noticing something glimmering in the sunlight. As the sun dipped lower the light struck the shimmer and suddenly a burst of rainbow-colored light exploded across the landscape, coating everything in a dazzling display. Tyler couldn't help but gasp as he watched the colors sparkle and dance over the keep.

"What is it?" Tyler asked.

"It's a crystal," Danny replied, smiling as he looked on. "Nothing more. But if you turn it this way and look into it, it will show you your dreams."

Tyler turned down Danny with an eyebrow raised. "Did you just quote *Labyrinth* at me?"

He laughed. "I've been holding onto that one for weeks. Finally, someone's here who understands it." He punched Tyler in the shoulder lightly. "But it really is a crystal."

"What does it do?"

Danny shrugged. "Nothing. It's just there to be beautiful. Like the prism glass people hang in their windows. The guys see it as a point of pride, a small piece of wonder in their harsh lives." He paused, his expression growing distant. "I think it's wonderful."

"I'm worried about how much you like this place," Tyler sighed, turning back to watch the display.

"Don't you?"

"What? Hello no. This place is awful!"

"That's sad," Danny said matter of factly.

"Why's that?"

"To stand before so much beauty and not see it. I feel bad for you."

Tyler felt his guts twist in a flash of anger. "Is that another stupid movie quote?"

"You've changed, Tyler," Danny said simply with a small sigh. "What happened to the guy who convinced me to run away from home and go on an adventure with him? The one who used to sit up late at night making fantasy worlds in his games? We used to run around the yard pretending to fight dragons and rescue princesses all the time."

Tyler scoffed at the sentimentality, although the words stung. "That guy grew up. He almost got killed the moment he got here and that's been repeating on almost a daily basis since." Tyler didn't understand why Danny couldn't see the truth of Bramoria. He had to show Danny why he was wrong, even if it was harsh. "We need to get back home. Do you think your parents deserve to never know what happened to you?" He paused for a moment, wanting a reaction and not getting one. Danny just stared off into the distance watching the rainbow of colors dance over the landscape. "They've spent their lives caring for you and... and you don't have that much time left. They should be able to see you again. To say go–."

Tyler had to stop himself. He couldn't say the last word no matter how much he tried. It caught in his throat like a softball. He wasn't ready to say goodbye to Danny either and even thinking about it made him want to scream. Why did everything have to be so unfair all the time? Wasn't it bad enough he'd never get to live the life he wanted?

"They've had me for eighteen years," Danny said. "It's time I had some life to myself." He paused for a moment, turning to Tyler with his sparkling blue eyes full of sunlight. "It's true they took care of me and they know I appreciate it, but I've spent too long cooped up in that room, living my life between the pages of books. It's time I got to truly experience it for once." He gestured out to the world around him. "And this place... this place is a dream come true. If I could live here forever, I would. But since I can't, I'll make the most of it."

Tyler watched as Danny's eyes grew glossy. He'd never known him to cry in front of others about his predicament. For a long moment, he stood there, silence filling the space between them as the sun sank lower on the horizon. At last, he lifted an arm and wiped his eyes on his sleeve.

"Do you really want to go home?"

"Yes," Tyler answered without hesitation. He was terrified the truth would slip out if he waited too long. "I *need* to go back home."

Danny nodded. "Alright. I'll make sure you get there then. And before you argue with me," he said, holding up a hand to cut off Tyler's rebuttal. "Give me this adventure. You and I both know it's going to be my last and I want to die happy. Can you do that for me?"

"I..." Tyler began. "How the hell can I say no to that?"

"You can't," Danny grinned. "That's why I said it that way."

Tyler felt a smile spread over his face despite himself. "I still think you should go back with me."

"Let's just play it by ear." Danny clapped him on the shoulder and began to lead him down the hill as the last vestiges of sunlight slipped behind the horizon. "You need to introduce me to your friend with the fancy ears. He must be a nice guy to have been taking care of you all this time!"

Tyler felt a stab of guilt in his guts. He'd been treating Koto like shit for days and he'd offered to sacrifice himself at the first hint of danger. There was an apology owed, but Tyler wasn't sure how he'd ever be able to go through with it.

"What do you mean? I can take care of myself," Tyler replied, trying to shift the conversation away from Koto. He'd deal with that later.

"Oh please. The way you were flailing back there tells me you still have absolutely no idea how to fight."

"And you do?"

"I told you," Danny chuckled, gesturing toward the group and the keep. "They've been training me for weeks." He patted Tyler on the back and headed off toward the front doors with the others. "Meet you in the kitchens!" he called over his shoulder and jogged away.

Tyler was about to go after him when Koto came into his peripheral vision. They glanced at one another and continued toward the keep without speaking. The coins in the back of Tyler's belt dug into his lower back as if they knew what was eating away at him. A constant reminder of the deception he'd taken part in. Before he could gather up the courage to say anything, one of the bandits came up between them.

"I'll take ya down to yer rooms," he said in a thick drawl, gesturing for them to follow. "You'll have to room together, but there's plenty of beds to go 'round. It's the least we can do for friends of Tiragan."

"That won't be a problem," Koto replied, returning a friendly smile. "I appreciate the hospitality." He glanced down at his arm, pulling at the soiled bandages. "I'll need to get washed up. Is there a place I can do that?"

"We can make a hot bath happen and get fresh wrappings for yer wounds. We turned over a small caravan of soldiers last week and ya wouldn't believe the number of supplies they had on them. I've never seen a wagon so stuffed!"

Koto's ears twitched. "Alright," he replied with trepidation. He took a deep breath. "Is... Is that something that happens often? The soldiers I mean."

The bandit nodded. "More and more lately. Ever since the prince took over the kingdom with his mother the soldiers have been wandering about delivering supplies to those who've suffered from attacks."

"The last village we were in was nearly burnt to the ground by Fossars," Koto replied, rubbing his wounded arm absentmindedly. "Has that happened in other places?"

"I haven't heard of Fossars causing any issues beyond the normal stuff." He lowered his voice and raised his hands to form mock claws. "The rumor is that there are dragons on the loose."

Tyler stopped in his tracks, raising an eyebrow. "You've got to be kidding. Dragons?"

"I know, it sounded crazy to us too. But then again, the mages are investigatin' the attack sites, which gets ya wonderin'."

"We heard about the mages and the supplies, but not about what was causing the problem." Koto seemed as surprised by the news as Tyler. "But dragons seem a bit far-fetched. Nobody has seen one for thousands of years. They're barely even a legend anymore, much less attacking villages."

"Nobody is sure. But whatever is doing it is keepin' to the outskirts of the kingdom and comin' in the middle of the night. The towns are set ablaze and nearly destroyed in minutes, then it's gone like nothin' was ever there." As they reached the door to the keep he pulled it open for them. "Nobody knows the truth, but I'll tell ya one thing, the damage is real and the new king is takin' it seriously."

"Is he really sending aid?"Koto asked, stopping in the doorway. "That doesn't sound like the prince I kn–... heard things about."

"He is and I'll prove it to ya."

The bandit led them into the keep. Inside the main walls was a barren courtyard with barrels of supplies stacked against the outer walls. A giant fire ring stood in the center with smoldering embers from a recent fire. Stumps were stationed around it in a circle as if it were a common meeting place for the members of the Shadow Squad if that was even their real name. In one corner there were several horses tied up as if they'd just been brought in from a patrol with their riders chatting nearby. Tyler followed silently, keeping his gaze in any direction but Koto's. He saw a sentry posted at the top of every turret marking the four corners of the keep. At the very top of the tallest tower was a ballista with a single man keeping watch over the valley. Tyler wondered what kind of things they had to fight away with that much power. All the time he and Koto had been walking he'd been concerned about monsters in the woods. He'd never thought to look to the sky for danger. But now with the talk of dragons, he was wondering if there was any place that was safe in Bramoria.

At the far end of the courtyard, they were led through a set of heavy wooden doors and into a large square chamber with vaulted stone ceilings. There were several of the gang sitting at small tables or getting drinks from the bar at the far end near a door that looked like it led to the kitchens. Danny was nowhere in sight, but Tyler thought he could hear his voice over the din. He took a step in that direction and felt a hand on his shoulder.

"Let's get ya cleaned up before we eat, yeah?" the bandit said, smiling widely enough to showcase a missing molar. "No offense, but yer filthy."

Tyler glanced down at himself. His clothing was covered in dirt and leaves from his attempted escape into the woods. However, the man in front of him was easily just as dirty.

"Fine," he sighed.

"Don't worry," the bandit smiled. "There'll be plenty to eat when yer done."

That wasn't what Tyler was concerned about, but he didn't have the energy to argue. Both he and Koto followed the man to the opposite end of the chamber and through a stone arch that led to a set of stairs spiraling downward. Even though they were only a few feet underground, the air turned significantly colder and Tyler could see moisture building up in the corners of the stonework. He thought it might feel warm during the winter, having the ground as insulation, but with the summer in full swing, it felt like stepping into a freezer. When they finally reached the room where he and Koto would be staying, he was happy to see a fireplace on the far wall already blazing.

"Here's yer room. Jus' relax for a minute while I have some hot water brought down so ya both can wash up."

"Thank you," Koto responded politely.

Tyler turned to thank the man as well but the door closed

before he could get a chance. Silence filled the room as they both stood there awkwardly, not looking at one another. Koto eventually made his way over to the bed and sat down, cradling his injured arm.

"Does... Does it hurt much?" Tyler managed to force himself to ask.

"Not too badly," Koto replied, not lifting his gaze from the bandages.

Crickets.

"Look," Tyler said, grabbing the back of his neck and leaning to one side. It was time to say something while they were alone. He might not get another chance. "I... I've been a real jerk to you."

Koto looked up.

"I'm not usually like that... it's just this place has got me on edge." He shifted nervously, reaching a hand to the back of his belt. "There's something else too." He produced the coin pouch and walked it over to Koto, tossing it onto the bed. "That was from the villagers at the last town. It came with their thanks."

Koto glanced at the bag then back at Tyler. "Why did you conceal it?"

"Because I was mad... because I'm *still* mad." He locked eyes with Koto, trying to force down the anger that had been bubbling inside him for days. "You forced me to leave that room when you knew I had no way to defend myself. Up until the other night I'd never even seen a dead person much less tried to kill anything. I... I could have died." He could feel tears of frustration forming in the corners of his eyes against his will. "And if you'd died I would have been all alone again in this crazy fucking place again." He took a few steps back and slumped down to his bed, holding his head in his hands. "I hate this world... I just want to go home."

A long silence stretched between them. After a minute or two, there was a creaking from the other bed and steps on the stone floor as Koto crossed the room. The bed next to Tyler bowed slightly as he sat down.

"I'm sorry," Koto replied with a sigh. "I shouldn't have asked you to do that. That was unfair of me."

"You didn't know those Fossars were there…"

"No, I didn't, but I knew something was wrong and I still told you to go. I made you feel like you didn't have a choice and that was wrong." Tyler felt a hand on his shoulder. "I'll try to be better about that. When I see people in need I can get a little thoughtless. I took a personal vow to do whatever needed to be done to help the people of Bramoria to repay my debt, but I need to remember that is my journey, not yours."

Tyler couldn't stop himself from asking. "Why do you want to help people so much? Is it just to be the opposite of your father or something else?"

Koto shifted nervously. "It's… more complicated than that, but for now let's suffice to say it's what drives me to live." He turned his gaze down at Tyler. "Surely you have something that drives you?"

"I guess," Tyler shrugged. "But I'll never get to do it, so it doesn't matter."

One of Koto's ears cocked to the side. "Why not?"

Tyler sighed. "My world isn't like yours. We can't just run away and do whatever we want. It doesn't work that way." He lifted his gaze, meeting Koto's for a moment before looking away. "Most people live their whole lives and never do anything they want. That's just the way it is."

Koto was quiet for a long moment, thinking to himself. "Maybe it's better you're here then," he finally said. "You can do whatever you like here, right? There's no one to stop you."

"I wish it was that easy," Tyler said, shaking his head. "But there are people back home who are depending on me."

There was a knock at the door, breaking the tension in the room.

"Don't worry," Koto said, patting him on the knee. "I'll make sure you get home. I made that promise to you and I intend to keep it. Maybe I can focus on helping you for now instead of everyone else." He pushed himself up from the bed and turned toward the door. "Come in!"

SIXTEEN

I t was nearing the end of the third day at the bandit keep and Tyler found himself atop the exterior wall. Leaning against the stone he stared into the western sky as the sun sank closer to the horizon. He'd been there every night since they arrived and he never got tired of watching the rays of light pierce the crystal at the peak of the tower.

"Up here again, huh?" a familiar voice said from behind him.

"Yeah. It's just really nice up here, ya know?" He turned to his right to see Danny lean against the wall beside him. "I never really got the chance to do this back home."

Danny laughed. "You would have if you ever left the computer in your room."

"Every time I leave my room my mom has a whole fucking list of chores for me to do and even more things she wants me to be better at," Tyler sighed. "At least if I'm up there she thinks I'm studying or some shit."

"I think you're lucky," Danny said after a moment. "My parents never let me do anything for myself, much less ask me to do chores."

Tyler gave him a sideways glance. "Believe me, you're not missing anything."

"Hmm," Danny hummed, his tone indicating he didn't quite believe Tyler. "But here we can do whatever we want and both of us can make up for lost time. This place is better than anything I've ever imagined." He paused for a moment. "I wish I could live here forever."

Tyler felt his heart skip a beat. He knew exactly what Danny meant. He wanted more life. More time to explore the world and see who it would turn him into.

"Even with the dragon thing?"

"Yeah, sure! Why not?" Danny slapped him on the back. "What's swords and magic without a little dragon fighting thrown in?"

"Magic," Tyler scoffed. "I believe that about as much as I believe in the dragons. What a bunch of bullshit."

"Is that so?" Danny asked, leaning forward and holding his hand out.

Tyler eyed it suspiciously. "Do you want me to hold your hand or something?"

"Just watch."

Tyler lifted an eyebrow as Danny closed his eyes, but didn't say anything. He just stared at Danny and his outstretched palm, wondering what in the world was going on. For a moment, nothing happened. It was just a hand and it wasn't doing anything. He didn't understand what it was supposed to prove.

"I get it, I'm gullible," Tyler sighed. Danny didn't react. "Really happy you enjoy messing with me like this. It's hilarious," he added sarcastically.

But Danny didn't reply, instead, he continued to concentrate with his eyes closed. As Tyler was about to open his mouth and make another comment he stopped. There was a shimmer in the air above Danny's palm, like heat coming off pavement on a hot summer day. For a moment it was invisible, but at last, the smallest pinprick of light began to form in the air. Tyler felt the heat swell as it suddenly burst, blue flames coalescing around Danny's hand.

"Oh my god!" Tyler yelled, taking a few steps back. "Water!" He leaned over the inside wall and shouted into the courtyard. "We need water up here, NOW!"

A few men scrambled off to get water, thoroughly

confused, but as Tyler turned back he could see Danny laughing, unconcerned with his limb that was currently on fire.

"Dude, relax. It's just a bunch of hocus pocus."

"Stop quoting movies at me!" Tyler yelled, not understanding what was happening. "What the fuck is that?!"

Danny gave his hand a twirl and snapped his fingers into a fist, dousing the flames entirely. "It's just like I said, a little bit of magic."

Tyler looked at the unblemished hand then back to Danny. The sudden heat had completely disappeared. "Where the hell did you learn that?"

"I picked up some tricks here and there," Danny laughed, pulling a glowing red rectangular stone from his pocket just like Tyler's. "And I woke up with this in my pocket. I thought it was my–"

"Your phone?"

"Yeah." Danny tilted his head to the side. "How did you know?"

Tyler pulled the stone from his pocket. It was the same shape, but not glowing. "I thought at first that my phone was taken by you and Clay as part of the joke, but then Koto called it a mage stone?"

"Yeah, that's what it is." Danny took a step forward, squinting his eyes as he looked over Tyler's stone. "I wonder if our phones transformed when we came over, however that happened. I wrote it off at first, but now that you're here with the same thing, I'm not so sure." He looked back up at Tyler and a thought flashed behind his eyes. "Do you... Do you think the mages in the capital city are from our world too since they have stones?"

Tyler paused. "I... I hadn't thought of that."

"I feel like the mystery of this place is starting to reveal itself." Danny handed the stone back to Tyler. "This reads like a quest and the main storyline one at that."

"This isn't a game, Danny," Tyler sniped. He watched Danny's smile falter. "I've already almost died twice. I don't want to do it again." He turned back to the sun that was now nearly below the horizon, the crystal above beginning to lose its luster. "We need to go home."

"I know you've got a lot to look forward to back there," Danny sighed. He leaned down on the railing, propping himself up on his elbows. "I'll make sure you get there."

"It's too dangerous. What if yo–"

"Tyler," Danny said firmly. "You already promised you'd let me do this. Even if this quest kills me, this is what I want."

Clenching his jaw shut, Tyler kept his eyes forward, unable to look at his friend for fear he'd start crying again. He didn't want Danny to come along and get hurt, but he realized leaving him behind with the bandits meant saying his final goodbyes now and that was something he couldn't do. Spending time with Danny was all that mattered, even if it meant learning to protect him. Although Danny was ready to give up on treatments and his future, Tyler wasn't. They were in a world with magic, after all, that had just become crystal clear. There had to be a way to save him, right?

"Alright," Tyler said at last, knowing he had no other choice. "We'll go together."

"Looks like you'll be able to make good on your promise."

"What promise?"

Danny put a hand on his shoulder. "You said you'd give me the best summer ever." His blue eyes came to rest on Tyler's. "And this is way better than I expected."

Forcing a smile Tyler watched as the last vestiges of sunlight disappeared from the sky. He wanted to kick himself for saying such a thing. Everything was his fault. If he'd never have convinced Danny to leave they'd both still be back in their small town dreading the end of summer, both of them headed for a future that they didn't want. But now they faced dangers unlike either of them had ever seen. It was up to Tyler to make sure Danny saw as much of it as possible, even if he had to bit his tongue the entire way.

"I've got yer water!" a man yelled as he ran down the

walkway carrying two buckets that were sloshing from side to side, spilling most of their contents.

"Ah!" Danny laughed. "Just put it down here my good man!"

He jogged up to them and placed the buckets on the ground. Taking a step back he looked at both of them expectantly. Tyler had made it sound like an emergency and the man seemed confused about what was going on.

"Thanks, John," Danny said, waving his hand. "You're dismissed."

"Oh... alright," he replied, cocking his head to the side. "I... okay bye."

With a shrug he turned away, making his way back toward the stairs to the courtyard. Tyler felt foolish for making such a scene, but then again, his friend had been suddenly on fire. If that didn't warrant panic, he didn't know what did. Danny watched the man start down the stairs before he looked back to Tyler.

"Help me with this," he said, lifting one of the buckets to the railing.

Tyler followed suit, hefting the other up beside it.

"On my mark, dump it over the side."

"What?"

"Just do it."

"Okay..."

"One... two... go!"

They both dumped their buckets at the same time. It wasn't until he heard the shouts from below that Tyler realized one of the patrols was directly underneath them. The man cursed up in his direction as he turned to chastise Danny, but he wasn't there. Glancing up he saw his friend already twenty feet away, sprinting down the walkway and leaving him to take all the blame.

◆ ◆ ◆

"Are you sure it was okay to leave them like that?" Tyler asked as they crested the hill the next morning, the keep still cloaked in the darkness behind them. "Shouldn't you have told them what you were doing? What we were taking?"

"Sometimes the hero has to go his own way," Danny muttered, patting his horse on the side of its face. There was one for each of them now, 'borrowed' as Danny put it from the courtyard. "Besides, I left them a note. They'll understand. People come and go from the squad all the time and they've got more than enough cash on hand."

Koto stepped up beside them, freshly bandaged and cloaked against the cold morning air. "It's probably for the best. If you're going to the capital city, you'll want some distance between you and the bandits if you want to get into the academy. They don't take kindly to people who steal from the king."

Danny didn't answer but stared back down at the keep as the sky began to lighten all around them. His body stood tall and proud with a sword lashed across his back, but in his eyes was a sadness that Tyler had seen many times before. He was looking at the keep for the last time and he knew it. It was his silent way of saying goodbye.

Tyler stepped up and wrapped his hand around Danny's. "We'll leave when you're ready."

Danny smiled at him, looked for a moment longer, then nodded his head. "Alright. Let's go."

Together the three of them mounted their horses and set off down the hill back toward the road. Tyler found it a bit awkward at first, but with a little guidance, riding became easier to bear. The sounds of birds slowly filled the air as the sun began to rise, lighting the sky with pinks and blues. Dew clung to the grass giving it an almost frosted look although the air was already growing pleasantly warm. On the southern horizon, Tyler could just make out the single blue moon of Bramoria sinking out of sight. With Danny at his side, he finally felt at home. Even though it came with more worry, he was glad to have someone familiar by his side in that strange world. He just hoped that he could protect Danny enough to keep his promise.

SEVENTEEN

The days passed by peacefully as they followed the road north. Their new steeds made the journey much easier, which Tyler was thankful for. He was tired of going everywhere on his own two feet. Besides, the riding left him with enough energy to start training at night so he could defend himself and Danny should they run into any more trouble. Koto agreed only after Tyler assured him that he wanted to learn for himself, which wasn't really the truth, but Koto seemed convinced nonetheless. Each night he and Danny would take turns sparring with Tyler using sticks, taking every opportunity to land a blow and teach their methods via pain and frustration. It wasn't long before Tyler found himself methodically searching for weak points in their techniques, trying to land a blow no matter the cost. It was reckless, but by the end of the second night, he was able to land a few on Danny. Koto, although injured and fighting with his off-hand, managed to avoid all his attempts.

"You're leaving yourself too open," Koto repeated, striking his stick across Tyler's ribs as he rushed by. "Your irritation is getting the better of you. Control yourself."

Tyler turned to face him, his skin hot and his arms shaking.

"Fighting isn't about being the strongest or striking first, it's about patience and calculation." Tyler rushed him again, but he flicked his stick to the lower left and parried the blow.

"Obvious. You give away your attacks with your body. Don't lean into it until you're ready to land the blow."

"Easy for you to say," Tyler panted, leaning on his stick for a moment. "All you've taught me is how to hold this thing and nothing else. I have no idea what I'm doing!"

"Have you not been listening? I've been teaching you this entire time." Koto lunged forward and rapped the stick on the top of Tyler's head. "Don't let your guard down!"

Danny laughed from the campfire as Tyler rubbed his throbbing skull, checking his hand for blood. He was getting tired of Koto constantly making him look like a fool, especially in front of Danny. It irritated him beyond all reason. He glared in Koto's direction, gritting his teeth and sprinting toward him once more. Swinging as hard as he could, he aimed for Koto's wounded arm, hoping to catch him on his bad side. For a split second, he thought it would connect, but Koto was too fast. His stick caught Tyler's, spun it out of his grip, and tripped him all in the blink of an eye.

Tyler crashed to the ground in a heap, getting a mouthful of dirt and grass. He felt something hard press against his shoulder and looked up to see Koto standing over him, both sticks now held in his hand.

"That's enough for tonight," he said and tossed them away. He held out his undamaged hand to help Tyler up.

But Tyler only glared at him.

"Come on," he said with a smile. "This is just training. Don't get upset, it's nothing personal. Everyone starts at the beginning."

Sighing Tyler took his hand and was helped to his feet. He spit out the grass, wiping the debris away from his face and clothes. "I'm never gonna get this."

"Yes, you will!" Danny called from the fire where he was roasting a few fish for their dinner. "It took me a week or two to start actually landing some hits. You're already moving faster than I did."

"I feel like an idiot." Tyler walked over and plopped down

next to the fire, cradling a bruised elbow.

"You're a computer nerd, dude. It's gonna take some time for your body to get used to *actually* moving."

"Says the guy who spent the past four years in bed."

"And somehow I still got more exercise than you apparently."

Koto tossed another log onto the fire and took a seat on the opposite side. "You two must be good friends," he chuckled. "You bicker like an old married couple."

Tyler felt his cheeks flush, but Danny just smiled.

"We've been friends since kindergarten," Danny said, poking at one of the fish with his finger. "It's been almost thirteen years since we met."

"I can't believe it's been that long." Tyler leaned onto his undamaged elbow in the grass. "It's strange how it feels like forever and a moment at the same time."

"Life feels that way," Danny nodded. "When you're waiting for something, life is slow. But when you don't want it to end, the clock seems to tick faster and faster."

Tyler looked up, seeing the morose expression on his best friend's face. He wished he could help or find a way to give Danny more time. There wasn't anyone in the world who deserved it more than him. A thought crossed his mind.

"Danny... How did you get your mage stone to work?"

"Oh, that's easy," he replied. "You just have to kill someone and bathe it in their blood while doing this neat little ritual I found."

Tyler's mouth fell open. "Wha–"

"Dude, I'm kidding," Danny laughed, punching him in the leg. "You're way too gullible."

"For fuck's sake," Tyler sighed. "Then how did you do it? What's this big secret?"

"Honestly, I don't know." Danny took the glowing red stone out of his pocket and turned it over a few times. "At first it looked just like yours, but then one day it didn't. I'm not really sure what happened."

"Mage stones are activated by their users," Koto interjected. "It takes an immense amount of skill, knowledge, and no small amount of talent to awaken a stone." He nodded in Danny's direction. "It seems you met those qualifications without training. That's something not even the most talented of mages in the academy has done."

Tyler pulled out his own stone and stared down at the lifeless crystal. So he just wasn't good enough. It really was that simple. Even after all his time in school and making sure he tested well to please his mother, it wasn't enough to allow him to do magic in Bramoria. He felt nothing but contempt for the stone in his hand. It was just one more thing in his life that he didn't have a choice about. He was happy Danny could do the things he dreamed of, but why couldn't he? While Clay and Danny lived in their fantasy worlds to escape reality, he had to toil away to please everyone else. And now that he had the chance to live the same fantasy, everything had gone wrong. A piece of him wanted to see the beauty in the world like Danny had told him, but all he felt was contempt for it. It didn't matter if he was in the real world or not, what he wanted never came to fruition. Instead, he was left to always play the background character, a casual observer who was neither special nor brave, just someone who helped the others achieve their goals and never his own. He'd read enough books to know that they were never the heroes of the story, just passing faces between the pages.

"Ty?" Koto asked, his head tilted to the side. "Are you alright?"

"Yeah," Tyler shook his head, trying to break himself from the downward spiral of thoughts he'd sunk into. "Sorry. I just got lost for a minute."

Koto looked as if he wanted to inquire further, but Danny interrupted him. "Fish is done!" he called, pulling a stick away from the fire and handing it to Tyler, then Koto. He pulled a small pouch out of his bag and set it on the ground beside him. "And a little salt if you want it."

Tyler pulled the pouch open and was surprised to see its contents were blood red.

"Oh, that's just the color of the salt here," Danny smiled, reading his expression. "It threw me off at first too. Just think of it as pink salt back home. It doesn't taste any different."

"It looks so gross..." Tyler said, thinking of all the blood he'd seen during the Fossar attack. "I think I'll pass."

"Suit yourself," Danny replied, sprinkling a healthy portion over his fish. He handed the pouch to Koto who took a small pinch for his own. "I'll be glad to find a tavern in the next town," he said, taking a bite and blowing the hot air out of his mouth to cool the steaming fish down. "The food here is delicious. I can't tell you the last time I had bread that didn't come from a bag."

"Bread in a bag?" Koto asked, looking up from his meal. "Like bread you carry home from the baker in a bag?"

Danny laughed. "No, it's sold in a bag." He put his fish down and began miming his story. "It's this perfectly rectangular loaf of bread and it's mostly air and sugar. It weighs almost nothing and it doesn't have any flavor either. They sell it in a plastic bag at the grocery store."

"Ah, this *store* again. Ty mentioned those." He nodded in his direction. "Although I've never heard of *plastic* before."

"Hmm," Danny hummed, rubbing his chin. "I guess it's like a cloth but it's waterproof, airtight, and you can see right through it."

"If you can see through it, how do you know it's there?"

Danny and Tyler looked at one another. "It's shiny I guess?" Tyler added. "It's pretty easy to see actually."

"This world you're from is full of mysterious trinkets. Are you sure these things aren't magic?"

"Wait till we tell you about guns," Danny grinned. "That would literally blow your mind."

Koto lifted an eyebrow and shook his head. "Sometimes I begin to wonder if you're actually from another world and then one of you opens your mouth."

"We haven't even begun to scratch the sur–"

Danny stopped, his head whipping around to the south as he looked back down the road, a look of concern on his face. One of Koto's ears twitched and swiveled in that direction as well. Tyler looked over his shoulder, but he didn't see or hear anything. He sat down his fish and reached for the hilt of the blade sitting next to him on the ground. For a long moment, they were all silent, nothing but the crackling of the fire and crickets filling the night. Above them, the stars twinkled noiselessly in the distance. Tyler watched as Danny's expression slowly relaxed, the firelight dancing across his features.

"Must have been nothing," he finally said, turning back to the fire. "I'm still getting used to the noises in this place."

Tyler let his grip on the sword relax. "You had me worried. Don't do that."

"Sorry," Danny grinned, rubbing the back of his head. "Must have been my imagination."

"No. Something's coming," Koto said softly, his voice barely above a whisper. "And it's moving fast."

The sound of thumping in the distance caught Tyler's attention and he turned back to the road. In the dark he couldn't make out much, the blue moon not casting much light as it was waning. His eyes followed the curvature of the path, then the tops of the trees that made up the horizon. The sky was filled with starlight, but in the distance, something strange caught his eye. It was a dark shape heading in their direction, only given form by the stars it blocked out.

"I see it," Tyler began.

But he was cut off as a tremendous roar filled the sky followed by a gout of flame. The fire, nearly white with its intense heat, lit up the underside of the low flying figure. A thick black body with clawed feet, long curving horns, and wide dark wings surrounded by roiling smoke was illuminated. Immediately Tyler knew what it was. He'd seen them in his dream.

Dragon.

All three of them hit the ground as the creature sped over top of them, the gust of wind from its wings kicking up embers and ash, blowing their small campsite to smithereens. Everything that wasn't tied down was blown apart, even the trees near them creaked under the strain of the wingbeats. Their horses startled, rearing back and snapping their tethers. Without hesitation they galloped into the forest, getting as far away from the dragon as they could.

Tyler cried out as a few hot embers landed on the exposed skin of his neck. He jumped to his feet, dancing around to get away from the burning sensation. As he patted the last of them out he looked up to the sky once more, the dark shape of the dragon already half a mile away. In the far distance, he could see the lanterns of the city they were headed for. Another gout of fire lit up the night and he realized the rumors the bandits had told him were true.

"He's going to attack the town," he said, pointing in its direction. He glanced back at the other two who were trying to kick dirt over the fire to put it out before it got out of control. Breathing a sigh of relief he started to sit back down. "I guess it's good we made camp here for the night."

Tyler saw Koto get to his feet and take a few steps toward the town before he stopped himself. His ears drooped slightly as he turned back to Tyler. "I want to help, but..." He glanced down at his injured arm.

"And we will," Danny said, pulling the bandolier straps across his body that held his sword. "A hero never turns down a fight!"

"It's a fucking dragon!" Tyler cried. "We don't stand a chance!"

Danny glanced back, a huge grin spreading across his face. "I like those odds," he muttered.

"This is a game, Danny!"

"Catch me if you can!"

Before Tyler could get another word out Danny dug his feet into the dirt and took off at a sprint for the town that was easily a mile or more away. Tyler turned to Koto. "What about the horses? Our stuff?"

He patted the two coin purses at his side still full of money. "We'll get new. Your friend is going to need our help if you want him to survive." His expression was almost apologetic as he shouldered his bow and started to jog after Danny.

"Fuck," Tyler sword to himself. "It's just one goddamn thing after another." He kicked a glowing log that had rolled over and burned a hole in his bedroll. "Monsters, bounty hunters, bandits, and dragons. I fucking hate this place."

With a growl of frustration and fury, Tyler grabbed his sword and threw his pack over his shoulders. Even if he didn't want to get involved, he had to protect Danny. Grinding the balls of his feet into the dirt, Tyler ran after the other two, hoping that he wasn't running headfirst to his doom.

EIGHTEEN

Nearly half the town was ablaze by the time they came to the gates which had been thrown wide open. People clutching children and belongings were rushing out of the city into the surrounding woods, trying to escape the wrath of the dragon swooping overhead. Guards shouted and ran in all directions, trying to guide people out of the city amidst the panic. Somehow Tyler had managed to catch up with Koto and Danny, but by the time they reached the gates, he was on the verge of collapse. He stopped to catch his breath, both hands on his knees as he doubled over from the stitch in his side. Already he could feel the waves of heat pulsing off the city as thatch roofs caught fire and burned up in a matter of moments.

Overhead another roar filled the sky as the dragon dove toward the eastern side, a massive line of white flame shooting from its open mouth. Screams filled the air and were cut off prematurely as the flames consumed the area, the townsfolk caught in the conflagration. Danny was already pulling his sword from the sheath, staring at the burning buildings with a smile on his face.

"This is where I'm meant to be," he said gallantly and took off through the gates.

"Wait!" Tyler cried, but it was too late. Danny was already around the corner and disappeared from sight. "Goddammit!" Tyler shouted, pulling his own sword from the sheath. He looked over at Koto who couldn't use his bow with only one arm. "We have to find him!"

Koto nodded, pulling a dagger from his belt. "Keep close to me," he said as they both crossed through the gates.

Inside the wreckage was complete and the heat was so intense that Tyler could barely breathe. The streets were filled with villagers yelling and crying as they desperately tried to escape the flames. A rumbling of wooden wheels made Tyler glance over his shoulder and he reached out to pull Koto aside as a horse galloped by pulling a wagon that was engulfed in fire. The animal sped away down the street, crashing into everything and everybody as it went. As it rounded a corner the wagon caught the edge of a building and suddenly stopped, throwing the horse to the ground. Immediately the building caught fire, the cries of a wounded animal mixed in with the cacophony. It was utter chaos as they turned away and tried to wind their way through the smoke-filled streets in search of Danny.

Koto looked up and pointed toward the dragon who was diving again toward the eastern side of the town. "He'll be going after the beast! That's where we need to be!"

"You've got to be kidding me!" Tyler yelled back as they ran. "Is he fucking stupid?"

"He's reckless, I'll give you that!"

Together they rounded a corner, finding themselves on a long wide street that led straight to the heart of the town. Ahead they watched as the white fire rained down across the market square once more, vaporizing the carts full of goods that were parked there. In the distance, they could just make out an armed figure silhouetted against the flames. With a simple nod, they doubled their speed, trying to get to Danny before he was burned alive by the terror in the sky.

"Danny!" Tyler yelled as they got closer. "Danny, come back! Get the fuck away from there!"

But the figure didn't respond. Instead, Tyler watched as a ball of blue flame erupted into existence, crawling over Danny's outstretched arm. He lifted his hand to the sky, pointing at the dragon flying overhead.

"Danny, don't!"

But it was too late. With a flash, the ball of flame condensed and created a beam of bright blue light that raced through the night like a shooting star. True to his aim, it struck the underside of the dragon and exploded into turquoise fire wrapping itself around the monster's body. The beast cried out and turned its glowing yellow eyes on Danny. With a sudden shifting of its body, the dragon changed course and pressed its wings to its sides, diving toward the ground where Danny stood. At the last moment, it flared the massive wings out and landed with a tremor that Tyler felt vibrate up through his feet, the wind blowing some of the more damaged houses to the ground. Both he and Koto skid to a stop at Danny's side, the three of them staring down a massive dark beast wreathed in roiling black smoke, only the yellow of its eyes piercing through to fix on each of them in turn.

"You've met your match, beast," Danny said, holding out his hand once more that burst into flame. He pointed a fire-wreathed finger at the monster. "You'll hurt these people no more!"

The fire condensed once more and shot out from his hand, heading straight for the creature's face. But this time it was ready. Taking a deep breath it opened its toothy maw and let out a jet of flame. The two collided between them, the explosion blowing all of them off their feet and throwing them back several yards. Tyler felt the sword leave his grip as he tumbled, the others crashing into him as he rolled over the hard ground. When he finally stopped moving he lifted his head, wiping away the sweat, ash, and grime from his eyes. The dragon looked surprised by the explosion, but mostly undamaged. Meanwhile, the three of them looked quite a bit worse for wear.

"That was unexpected," Danny smiled, pushing himself up from the ground. The fear and pain almost seemed to invigorate him. "I guess we'll have to do this the old-fashioned way."

With a cry he lifted his sword and charged at the dragon,

facing it head-on.

"Danny, stop!" Tyler shouted, but it was too late again. "Fuck!" he cried out, forcing himself up from the ground as fast as he could.

He glanced to the side and saw Koto lying still on the ground, but he didn't have time to worry about him. Without a weapon and without a plan, Tyler ran after Danny who was almost face to face with the dragon already. He kept his eyes fixed forward, not allowing anything to pull his attention away from his friend. Danny made it to the creature within seconds, reeling back his sword to strike, a battle cry filling the air. Tyler watched as the blade passed right through the dragon as if it was made of nothing but smoke. Danny froze in place, staring down at his sword, confused by what had happened. But before he could take another strike the dragon snapped a claw forward and swept Danny's feet out from under him.

"Danny!" Tyler yelled, skidding to a stop.

With a second claw, he shoved him to the side, lifting him up and tossing him into a nearby stone wall. Tyler cringed hearing the cracking noise as Danny struck the wall and crumpled to the ground in a heap. Already he could see the glint of blood in the firelight.

Then the dragon turned its sights on Tyler and reared its head back once more as it took a deep breath.

"Oh fuck..." he muttered.

He didn't have time to do anything else but throw up his arms, knowing it would do no good. A jet of white flames rushed toward him and he knew he was as good as dead. For a brief moment, time seemed to slow, the heat of the fire slowly growing more and more intense as he watched it race toward him. Just before it struck Tyler saw a dark hooded figure suddenly materialize in front of him, a hand outstretched toward the dragon. The fire collided with the figure's palm and split around them both, deflected by some unknown force. As the flames subsided the figure stepped forward holding a gnarled staff topped with a large dark blue crystal in his off-hand.

"This," he said in a deep masculine voice, "is not how the story goes."

He tapped his staff on the ground twice, sparks shooting from the wood as it struck. Suddenly the smoke around the dragon shifted violently as if caught up in a windstorm. It swirled around the creature, picking up dust, ash, and embers as it grew in strength. The dragon roared and slashed out uselessly as it was lifted from the ground and turned over and over. The fire on the nearby houses roared in Tyler's ears, suddenly fed by the rush of air. The figure lifted his staff once more and struck it to the ground. All at once the swirling smoke and the dragon froze in mid-air and began to condense into a sphere, pulling everything in that wasn't staked down. It shrunk until it was the size of a beach ball, fire and crackling blue energy swirling around it. For a moment everything went silent, only the faint whirring of the sphere audible in the market square. Suddenly it was blown apart, releasing a concussive wave of air that knocked Tyler to the ground and put out many of the fires at once, casting everything into near-total darkness.

The figure in front of Tyler turned around, his staff the only source of light in the sudden dark. He couldn't make out the face under the hood, but he saw the slight nod before the crystal flashed and the figure disappeared entirely. In his place was left a small floating bottle of glowing green liquid. For a moment it hovered in the air before it lurched forward and pressed against Tyler's chest. He reached up to catch it as the magic that held it there faded. He stared at the bottle in recognition. It was a healing potion, just like the one Koto had used on him.

Without taking time to process everything he'd seen, Tyler got back to his feet and ran across the decimated market square in search of Danny. It took a few minutes to find him since the blast had collapsed a few of the houses. But at last, he discovered his friend partially buried under some smoldering rubble. He was covered in soot and too much of his own blood. Without hesitation Tyler grabbed him by the arm and dragged him out of the debris, feeling the socket in his shoulder give slightly. Finally free of the still-burning ruins, Tyler knelt down next to Danny. He wasn't breathing and it looked as if several of his bones had been broken when he hit the stone wall.

"You're g-gonna be alright D-Danny," Tyler stuttered, his hands shaking as he tried to unstopper the bottle. His heart was racing a mile a minute. "It's g-gonna be f-fine. J-Just hold on."

Tipping Danny's head back and pulling his mouth open, Tyler slowly dripped the potion onto his tongue, afraid to drown him if he did it all at once. There was a long moment where he held his breath wondering if Danny would swallow on his own to make the potion take effect or if he was already dead.

"Come on, Danny," he said, cradling his friend in his arms, tears forming at the corners of his eyes in frustration. "I need you to drink this. I didn't come all this way just to have you die on me."

There was a slight shifting as Danny's eyes fluttered and he finally swallowed, taking the first bit of the potion at last before he sucked in a ragged breath. A quiet moment stretched out before Tyler saw the first hints of his wounds closing up and a slight creaking sound as his bones began to shift. Suddenly Danny's eyes flew open and he cried out in pain, tears instantly streaming down his cheeks. The potion was taking effect.

"It's alright," Tyler said, doing everything he could to not lose it himself. "It's alright. Just drink this and it'll go away." He tried to push the potion into Danny's mouth, but he was beside himself. "Work with me, Danny! You have to drink this!"

Finally, he managed to force the rest of the bottle's contents into his mouth and clamped his hand over Danny's lips to stop him from spitting it out. His eyes grew wide and he looked up at Tyler.

"Drink it!"

Danny swallowed and Tyler let him go. Immediately he began to writhe as if in pain, his skin bubbling and shifting as it knitted itself back together. Below the surface, Tyler heard the snaps of several bones popping back into place. A large crack in

Danny's right thigh caused him to scream out in pain before he collapsed back into Tyler's arms, completely unconscious.

Tyler just held him, tears streaming down his face. The rest of Danny's wounds pulled themselves together and the intensity of the healing process started to fade. He was still breathing, but completely unconscious. Tyler just sat there coughing in the smoke and ash that filled the air, doing everything he could to not let his emotions overtake him.

For a long moment, he just sat there, keeping tabs on Danny's breaths to make sure he wasn't making up the miraculous recovery in his mind. As the minutes passed he started to calm down and his thoughts began to race. Where had the cloaked figure come from? How did he destroy the dragon? And most importantly, why did he help them in the first place? He'd said something about a story, but Tyler didn't understand what he'd meant. Something about the figure had seemed familiar, but he brushed it away. There were more important things to worry about like how to get out of the burning town and take Danny somewhere safe to rest.

"Is he okay?" Koto asked, startling Tyler badly.

"Yeah... Yeah, I think so," he replied, his hands still shaking. "Are you?"

"More bruises, but I'll live," he nodded, walking around to the opposite side of Tyler and kneeling down. "Where did the dragon go?"

"You didn't see the mage that killed it?"

"No. When I woke up it was already gone."

"Danny was attacked by the dragon and nearly killed, but that mage showed up and destroyed it. Then he gave me a healing potion to save Danny." Tyler paused for a moment. "Do you know who it was?"

Koto looked over the pair of them, his expression blank. "I have no idea..."

NINETEEN

I t had been more than a day since the attack as Tyler and Koto sat in the warm sun near the road with Danny lying close by under the shade of a tree. The tavern had been partially burnt and many of the locals were without homes, so it was the best they could do for the moment. None of them were particularly hurt from the ordeal and Danny had reaped the benefits of the healing potion, curing all his wounds. Even with all the healing it provided, Danny was still unconscious. Tyler was starting to get worried by his lack of movement. He was still breathing and seemed to be doing fine, he just wouldn't open his eyes.

"It's going to take some time," Koto said for the tenth time that morning. "Those potions work in a snap, but it takes the mind a while to realize it's no longer hurt."

"I hate sitting here," Tyler whined, looking down the road at the burned village to the south of them. "We need to get to the capital." He glanced at Danny. "And I still need to yell at him. A lot."

They'd left the village behind them, not wanting to arouse the suspicion of the villagers, especially since a few of them had seen Danny's display of idiocy and possibly his magic. But it was still too close for comfort in Tyler's mind. He wanted to get away as fast as possible and leave that dreadful night behind him. He'd almost lost Danny and now more than ever he realized how much he wasn't ready for that to happen. Bramoria was teeming with danger and with every passing day, it seemed to draw closer. With dragons on the loose, no place was safe. He was starting to wonder if they'd ever make it to the capital.

Koto sighed. "If he's not up in the next few hours we'll find a way to wake him. For now, just let him rest."

Tyler lay down in the grass with a huff, splaying his arms out and letting the breeze dance over him. He wished he could appreciate the calm and quiet left in the wake of the dragon, but his mind was full of too many thoughts. Instead, he tried to find something, anything to distract his attention. He turned to the right, noticing a ladybug crawling across a blade of grass. It slowly crept over the surface, stopping for a long moment as if taking in the sun as well. With a quick movement, it sprang forward, grabbing a tiny green bug in its jaws, and proceeded to methodically tear it apart, consuming each tiny piece. To Tyler, it was incredibly unsettling for something so small. But he stared anyway. After a minute or two, the ladybug finished the last bite and began to clean its mandibles with its front legs as if nothing was amiss. Flaring its carapace it unfolded its wings and took off into the air, leaving the scene of the crime far behind. As Tyler's vision refocused he saw a wagon flanked by people heading their way.

"What's that?" he asked, sitting up on his elbows.

Koto glanced to the north and his ears went flat against his head. "The king's soldiers," he murmured in panic. Immediately he pulled the cloak hood over his head and tucked his tail away. "It's too late to hide. Whatever you do, don't tell them who I am. Okay?"

"Sure..." Tyler replied. "I doubt they're after you anyway." He looked back at the wagon and noticed there were several more behind it, each piled high with goods. On either side the wagons were flanked with armored soldiers, their chest plates catching the sunlight. At the very front was a tall figure sitting atop a horse. "Maybe they can help us."

"If Liran and his bounty hunters are looking for me, you can be sure the king's men know my name as well." He shifted to sit next to Danny, trying to use the shadow to his advantage. "Just leave me out of it."

"Alright. Whatever you say."

The soldiers continued to approach and Tyler moved a few feet away from the road to let them pass. He stood and watched as the leader became more and more clear. They were a well-dressed man, his chin held high and the broad shoulders giving him a strong look. His clothing was well made and shimmered in the sun along with a metallic circlet placed on his head. To either side of him walked a soldier, both of them unique in their garb. The one to the right was dressed lightly and comfortably with a sword hanging from each hip. He wore a cheerful smile and seemed to be enjoying the day. The other however was dressed in dark billowing fabric and held a dark metallic staff at his side topped with a white stone. He was not smiling. In fact, he looked downright exasperated.

"I don't understand why you insist on coming out here yourself," the man in the cloak croaked. "There's no reason for you to be out here. Your place is back in the city. There's things that need your attention there."

"The people have been living under the rule of a false king for too long. I'm not gonna be one of those useless tyrants. You should know that by now Gordy," the man on the horse replied.

"My name is Gordath. I've told you time and again not to call me by that terrible name."

"I think it suits you," the smiling man on the right observed, laughing to himself. "It helps lighten up your permanently terrible mood."

"Just because you already have a stupid name Nikolas, doesn't mean I want one too."

"You two are so great to have around."

The man on the horse shook his head, smiling the entire time. He looked up to see Tyler standing off the side of the road and raised a hand. Instinctively Tyler waved back, but stopped partway through and turned his head to the side. The man on the horse looked extremely familiar. He took a few steps forward to get a better look.

"Stop right there, peasant!" the man in robes shouted, brandishing his staff. "No one goes near the king without an invitation!"

"Gordy, calm the fuck down," the king sighed.

The voice sounded familiar too.

"Clay?" Tyler asked suddenly. "Is that you?"

The king gazed at him for a long moment, his eyes going from head to toe and back again. He placed the reins over the saddlehorn and pulled one leg over, dropping to the ground with ease. The dark metal pauldron on his shoulder rattled slightly against his chest plate, both of them shimmering in the sunlight. His entire left arm was armored all the way down to his fingers which were tipped with dark metallic claws.

"Your highness, I really must insist–"

"Can it, Gordy," the king said, holding a hand up to silence him

He walked right up to Tyler and stood there for a long moment. Then, without warning, he punched him in the arm.

"Tyler!" he laughed, pulling him in for a hug. "Dude, what the fuck are you doing here?"

"Is that really you, Clay?"

"It's King Clay now," he said, holding his chin up high. "Although everyone around here insists on calling me by a hundred different titles."

Tyler stared at him for a long moment. "Why is everyone else getting a cool story and I just woke up in the woods with nothing?"

Clay's expression shifted to one of surprise. "What do you mean everyone else?"

Tyler pointed behind him to Koto and Danny sitting under the tree. "Danny's here too."

"What?!"

Before Tyler could say anything, Clay rushed across the clearing to the tree and knelt down next to Danny. He gazed for a moment at Koto who kept his face concealed but turned his attention back to the unconscious figure of his friend.

"What happened to him?"

Tyler caught up with him, leaning against the tree. "The village was attacked by a dragon last night. This idiot," he pointed to Danny, "decided he wanted to be a hero and rushed in with just a sword and a magic rock. Good thing some rando mage showed up and saved us."

Clay froze and turned back toward him. "A mage was here?"

"Yeah," Tyler nodded. "He killed the dragon all by himself and just disappeared. In fact, he's the only reason Danny is alive. If he hadn't left that healing potion behind, Danny would be…"

"What did he look like?" His face had twisted into somewhat of a scowl as he reached forward and grabbed Tyler by the collar. "Tell me everything you know about him."

"I-I don't know!" Tyler stammered, pulling at the metal gauntlet that held him tightly. "His hood was up! He had a blue rock on his staff and that's all I saw!"

"Gordanth! Nikolas! Get over here," Clay called over his shoulder, finally letting Tyler go. He stood up and walked back toward the other two that were already rushing his way. "Take the others ahead and have the supplies handed out amongst the villagers. It seems the mages were right again. We're being watched."

He leaned forward and whispered something only they could hear. Tyler watched from his spot near Danny, rubbing his chest where the gauntlet had scratched him. He didn't understand what was going on.

"I'll stay with you my lord," Gordanth began, but Clay cut him off.

"I can take care of myself. I'll meet up with you momentarily."

"But your highness—"

"That's an order, Gordy."

The mage loudly sighed as he turned away, heading back to the wagons. Nikolas stood for a moment longer in front of Clay as they spoke amongst themselves. A minute later he nodded and headed back to the wagons as well, hoping atop Clay's mount and leading the soldiers toward the village. Clay watched them pass by before he went back to where Tyler and Danny were sitting.

"Sorry about that," Clay said with a small smile. "There's a lot going on." He looked over to Koto who was still sitting against the tree with his hood up, trying not to be noticed. "Who's your other friend here?"

"Oh him? Uh..." He glanced back to Koto, searching for some hint as to what he should say. "That's... um... Jerry."

"Jerry?"

"Yep. Good ole' Jerry," Tyler nodded. "He's been helping me since I got here. We were headed to the capital to meet the mages when we found Danny."

Clay cast a suspicious glance at Koto who still hadn't looked up. "To meet the mages? Why?"

"So I can go home."

Clay stared unblinking into Tyler's eyes. "You... *want* to go home? Why?"

"You don't?"

"Why the hell would I want to go back there?" Clay laughed, gesturing to the world around him. "This place is way better. I'm a king if you haven't noticed. Sure as hell beats being a poor nobody back home."

"But what about..." Tyler stopped. He couldn't think of anything.

Clay's tone shifted. "No, please. Tell me what was so great about my life back home." He waited a moment longer, crossing his arms over his chest. Tyler turned away from his gaze. "That's what I thought." He turned his attention back to Danny. "How long has he been like this?"

"Since the attack. He woke up while I was giving him the healing potion so he felt all his bones snap back into place. It didn't look comfortable."

"What happened to him?"

"The dragon treated him like a cat toy."

"Christ..." Clay breathed. "Poor Danny." His eyes flicked up to Tyler. "How... How has he been?"

"Surprisingly well until the dragon. It's like he's not sick at all, except for the spots. It doesn't make any sense, but then again, neither has anything else since I got here." He leaned forward brushing a stray hair out of Danny's face. "He said he's been here for weeks, but I've only been here for a few days."

"I've been here almost a year," Clay said without missing a beat.

Tyler's jaw dropped. "W-What? How is that possible?"

"I don't know," he said, shaking his head. "I thought I was all alone here."

"Do you know how you got here?"

Clay nodded, but he held a finger up to stop Tyler from asking any more questions, giving a sideways glance at Koto. "We'll talk more after the town is taken care of. I have to see to my people. I'll come back for you and Danny after sundown. Then we can catch up."

"But Clay–"

"After sundown," Clay repeated with authority.

Tyler knew there was no use in arguing. "Alright..."

Clay smiled and stood up, turning back toward the road. "Hey Tyler," he said with a small smile. "It's good to see you."

"You too."

The jangling of his armor faded as he headed toward the city gates, catching up with the tail end of his caravan. Tyler sat on his heels next to an unconscious Danny wondering what in the world was going on.

TWENTY

T yler shook his head. "You've got to be joking," he said, sitting at a table draped in expensive fabrics and more food than he'd seen in over a week. "The book?"

"You didn't put it together?" Clay laughed, tossing an apple to Danny who had finally woken in the late afternoon. "This is the kingdom of Bramoria, the same as the welcome message in the book. I thought it was obvious."

"Oh yeah, sure," Tyler replied, rolling his eyes. "I should have just accepted that we'd been sucked into a book you stole. That makes perfect sense. Happens all the time."

"Gosh… that was so long ago. I'd nearly forgotten."

"It was literally a couple of days ago."

"For you," Clay smiled. "I've been here for so long… I was already starting to forget about the world we came from."

"How could you forget?"

"Being king doesn't leave you a lot of time for reflection."

"Didn't you just become king?" Danny asked, taking another bite of the shiny red apple.

"Yes," Clay nodded, taking a few grapes for himself. "But I've been working on having my father imprisoned for almost a year now. It took a lot of doing to pull it off. I had to make a lot of friends first."

"Your father?" Tyler leaned forward in his seat. "He's here too?"

"No! Of course not," Clay laughed, waving him off. "But

somehow I ended up with a piece of shit dad in both worlds." He paused for a moment, spitting a few seeds from his mouth into a bowl. "But this time I had the power to do something about it." His eyes glazed over for a moment, but then he shook his head, looking up at the pair of them. "But enough of that. What have you two been up to?"

"I woke up in a bandit hideout," Danny smiled, puffing himself up a bit. "And I've been stealing supplies from your soldiers."

Clay's eyes narrowed. "We were wondering who was doing that. Are they nearby?"

"Oh yeah," Danny laughed, taking another bite. "They're a couple days south of this town. But they're good people. They nursed me back to health and trained me to take care of myself. I was living with them until we tried to rob Tyler."

"That's a relief at least," Clay replied, leaning back on his down pillows. "We'll have to send them a personal thanks from the king when we get back to the capital for caring for you so well."

"Yeah, I've just been trying not to die," Tyler cut in, getting slightly annoyed that the other two seemed to be enjoying their time in Bramoria so much. "Almost failed at that three times now. Really love it."

"How did you manage to get into so much trouble so fast?" Clay asked, a big smile on his face.

"First I woke up in the woods all alone with nothing but my sleeping bag and was immediately attacked by a monster." He lifted a finger. "Then I was stabbed by a bounty hunter who was after someone else." He lifted another. "And then I was nearly burned to dust by a dragon that *someone*," he threw a pointed look at Danny, "decided to run up on half-cocked."

"Oh, we're fine," Danny laughed, finding the whole thing amusing. "Besides, the hero never dies, everyone knows that."

Clay lifted an eyebrow. "Oh. So *you're* the hero?"

"Obviously. Poor sick kid goes to a new world, learns to fight with swords and magic, then gets called on a grand adventure to help someone in need." He tossed the apple core onto the table. "Classic farm boy story."

"The only reason you're still alive is because of that mage and his potion," Tyler interrupted.

"Yeah, because I'm the chosen one." Danny dusted off one of his shoulders. "That's why he saved me. If it was anyone else, they'd be dead."

"Sure, whatever," Tyler said, waving off the insanity spilling from his lips. He turned his attention back to Clay. "But I still don't understand how we got here."

"I told you. The book was magic." He leaned forward, placing his elbows on the table. "You two fell asleep and I was still looking at the book until it started to suddenly glow. I watched as the world around me disappeared, leaving me in total darkness. I was scared at first, but then everything started to take form again. It could have been hours or only a moment, but the next thing I knew I was sitting up in my bed-chamber in the castle with the book still held in my hands." He looked between the two of them. "And the weirdest part was, the pages began to fill themselves with what was happening."

"What do you mean?" Tyler asked, his brows furrowed.

"It's almost like the book began to write itself." He shrugged. "It was neat at first, but then it kinda got boring." He sighed and leaned back on the pillows. "I don't really want to read about every time I take a piss or get a boner, ya know? I'm already living it."

"Oh my god…" Tyler sighed, resting his head in his hands. He took a moment to compose himself. "So we're living inside a book?"

"I think it's more like we're writing one without knowing it."

"Okay… So how do we get the fuck out?" Do we need to burn it or something?"

"I don't think it's going to be that easy." Clay leaned forward and laced his fingers together, resting his chin on his knuckles. "In the past year, I've tried a lot of things. At first, I thought maybe I could turn back time by tearing the pages out, but no matter how many I pulled, I found another underneath it with the same writing, and the book looking as if nothing had happened." He shook his head. "Every time I messed up I did anything I could think of to try to undo the writing on the page, but nothing would change it." He glanced up at Tyler. "I don't think destroying it is possible. Besides, I don't think it would do any good anyway. Whatever magic brought us here has already happened. The book isn't controlling it anymore."

"So how do we leave then?"

"Maybe we have to finish the adventure," Danny piped in, shrugging his shoulders. "Kind of like Jumanji or something. First person to beat the game wins."

"I hope this is more like the Robin Williams version. At least then it will be enjoyable," Clay laughed.

"Is this really a big fucking game to you two?" Tyler snapped, slamming his hands on the table. "We're trapped in this crazy fucking place and you two want to *play the game*?!"

Clay's face suddenly hardened as he glared at Tyler. "Do you have a better idea, Tyler?"

He silently glared back.

"You seem to like to get upset about this, but you don't have anything constructive to add to the conversation. I know you're frustrated, but you need to calm down and just enjoy it or shut up. This place is a hundred times better than home and you know it. If you weren't so upset about your fucking scholarship and preppy school you'd be having fun right along with us."

Tyler felt the artery in his neck throbbing and pushed himself up from the table.

"Tyler, what's wro–" Danny started, but he lifted a hand to cut him off.

Without a word, he stalked out of the tent and into the night air. The soldier's camp was just outside of the city on the western side. Tyler crossed through it to the far end where it gave way to rolling hills in the distance. He stopped at the edge of the hill, staring out at the dark horizon, thousands of stars twinkling above and a pale blue crescent moon hanging low in the sky.

They just didn't understand. Clay didn't have anything or anyone he cared about back home. Danny on the other hand had everything but it would be gone whether he liked it or not. But Tyler had a parent that was depending on him and that he didn't want to disappoint. He'd spent years making all of her dreams for him come true and even if he didn't *want to* leave home, he at least wanted to explain it to her. To just run off and disappear from the face of the earth was too cruel, especially after his father had done the same thing and that was the last person he wanted to be like. She deserved better than that. Even if Clay and Danny didn't care to ever go home, he didn't have a choice. It was the right thing to do and he wasn't going to stop trying.

"What are you doing out here, Ty?"

Tyler glanced over his shoulder to see Koto walking up to stand beside him. His hood was up and his tail was still tucked into his belt. He'd disappeared the moment the king's men came back to fetch Danny earlier in the day.

"Where have you been?" Tyler asked in a rather gruff voice. Koto looked at him for a long moment before he took a deep breath. "Sorry. This reunion isn't going as well as I thought it would."

"What's wrong?"

"They just... they don't understand," Tyler started, letting the tension out of his shoulders. "Clay doesn't have a good life or family back home, so he just wants to stay here. And he's a king, it's not like I can blame him. Danny on the other hand has everything handed to him on a silver platter at home and a loving family, but..." Tyler couldn't force himself to say anymore.

"He's sick. You mentioned that." Koto turned his gaze toward the stars. "And it's not the kind of sickness you recover from, is it?"

Tyler shook his head.

"I see."

"They have no reason to go back. And because of that, they just keep telling me I'm stupid for wanting to go." Tyler crossed his arms, shifting his weight to one hip. "They think they know my life, but they don't. Everybody always makes assumptions, but they don't actually ask if they're true or not."

Koto was silent for a long moment. "Have you told them the truth?"

"They wouldn't listen to me anyway, so what's the point?"

"Hmm," he hummed. "They don't sound like very good friends if you can't tell them how you really feel."

Tyler's head snapped toward Koto. "They are my *best friends* in the whole world! How could you say that?"

"Friendship is based on mutual communication and trust. If you can't share the truth of yourself with someone, that doesn't make them much of a friend. Likewise, they should be willing to listen to you, not just pass judgments." He glanced over Tyler. "It seems like you have people who enjoy your support, but don't like to return the favor."

Tyler felt a churning in the pit of his stomach. "That's not true. You don't even know them or how we were back home."

"You're right, I don't. But I can see how you feel now and my gut tells me something is off."

"And what makes you such an expert?" Tyler growled, crossing his arms tighter over his chest, trying to hold the anger back. "You're just like them, a runaway who never wants to go home again. Not to mention you ran off today and left me all alone with them."

"I told you, my father was a terrible man and I'm doing my best to add some good back to this world, and to make up for my past sins." He gestured back to the camp. "Any one of these men could recognize me and send me back home in chains without fulfilling that mission." His voice lowered. "Is your need for attention more important than my safety?"

Tyler ground his teeth together. He wanted so badly to scream at Koto, to tell him he didn't understand a damn thing. But the words he said highlighted how selfish Tyler was at that moment. How he was taking out his frustration on Koto who didn't deserve any of it, the person who'd come over to check in on him. That more than anything made the blood pound in his ears. Koto was right and he hated it.

As he opened his mouth to find some sort of retort he was cut off by a screeching that pierced the night air. Both of them turned toward the noise, craning their necks up toward the sky. There, another dark figure sped toward them, the long neck and wide wings wreathed in smoke catching the faint moonlight. A long jet of reddish flame erupted from its mouth, filling the night with a sudden flash of light. Tyler felt his arms fall to his sides and his jaw hanging open.

"Oh, you've got to be FUCKING kidding me!"

TWENTY-ONE

Shouts erupted from the city as soon as the first roar's echoes died away. The soldier's camp came alive in an instant, each of them rushing about trying to pull on bits of armor and belts with their swords hanging off them. They pointed to the sky with looks of horror on their faces, the dragon drawing closer by the second. Those in charge shouted orders that were mostly lost among the cacophony of sound. Both Tyler and Koto looked out over the camp, wondering how any of them stood a chance against such a creature with just their swords. That hadn't worked well for Danny and he'd even had magic on his side. As far as Tyler could see, the entire place would be nothing but a smoldering pile of ash by morning.

He thought of his friends left back in the camp the moment his eyes fell on the king's tent and the door flap was thrown aside. Both Clay and Danny walked out, flanked by Gordanth and Nikolas who had come to protect their leader. Clay stopped for a moment, speaking to Danny, then the three moved out toward the road, leaving him next to the tent. Tyler watched in fascination as Gordanth ignited his staff, the gem giving off the brilliance of sunlight in the dark. The three of them walked out into the road in plain sight and the dragon immediately turned its head and took notice. It had found its prey.

Roaring filled the sky once more as the dragon shifted its trajectory and nosedived straight for the trio, the black roiling smoke surrounding it trailing behind. Nikolas drew both his swords, readying himself to fight. Gordanth began to chant and move his fingers through the air in a complicated motion, a faint glow coalescing around him like thousands of fireflies clinging to his cloak. The magic built into a massive orb of greenish energy until it looked as if he could hold it no longer. Clay stood perfectly still, eyes fixed on the dragon as the magic exploded from Gordanth's grip. It hurtled toward the creature who attempted to dodge too late and took the full brunt of it in the face. Crackling electricity arced around its body, each of the limbs going stiff as if it were paralyzed. Unable to flare out its wings to slow the descent, the behemoth crashed into the ground, the vibrations strong enough to be felt for miles.

A cloud of dust and dirt filled the night air. From inside, the light of Gordanth's staff could still be seen but nothing else. A tense moment passed where Tyler wasn't sure who'd survived the crash. Eventually, the small breeze pulled it away, revealing Clay still standing there. His guards stood to either side, all of them unmoving and unphased by the beast now only a handful of feet in front of them. Black smoke still rolled off the dragon's body like waves of heat. Nikolas lifted his swords, ready to rush the creature, but Clay held up his armored hand to stop him. Immediately the man backed down, bringing the swords to his sides and bowing his head. Clay took a few steps forward and reached out his armored hand, resting it on the snout of the dragon that was slowly starting to come back to life, only momentarily dazed by the crash. Glowing flames began to lick at the sides of its muzzle, the golden eyes constricting as it opened its jaws filled with razor-sharp teeth, its growls rumbling over the open area.

Clay stood his ground. In fact, he didn't even remove his hand from the creature. He just stood there, staring the beast down as the flames in its mouth grew brighter and brighter. Tyler was still frozen in place along with everyone else, watching the unbelievable spectacle that was happening in front of their very eyes. Why wasn't Clay moving? For a moment Tyler thought the worst, wondering if he was purposefully trying to kill himself. He'd always been a bit of a daredevil and never cared for his own mortality. But he'd been so adamant about loving Bramoria. Why would he suddenly give it up for some stupid stunt?

Then the dragon began to shake, slowly at first but grew quickly into violent tremors, the eyes rolling back in its head. Even the dark fumes around it seemed to vibrate, twisting and churning in strange directions as if they were part of the creature's body itself. The flames died away as it reared back, trying to get away from Clay. But something stopped it, like an invisible force that tethered it to Clay's armored hand. Tyler watched in horror as the dragon began to be crushed from all sides. First, the jaw snapped inward, then a rib. One after another the bones in its limbs and neck cracked and shattered as the creature was pulled inward, collapsing in on itself. Blood, smoke, and fire tried to escape but was pulled back by whatever had a hold of it. In a matter of moments there was nothing left but a swirling black ball in the center of the road, much like the one Tyler had seen the night before created by the mage.

Clay stared at it for a long moment, his arm outstretched. At last, he flicked his fingers upward and the sphere shot into the sky. As he turned away it exploded in a brilliant flash of purplish light. The concussive wave could be seen in the air as everyone clapped their hands to their ears, nearly going deaf from the blast. Tyler's own rang as he stared. He had no idea how to process what he'd just seen. Apparently, Danny wasn't the only one that could do magic. He felt a hand on his shoulder, startling him from his stupor.

"Are you alright?" Koto asked. His voice seemed hazy and far away.

"Yeah," Tyler replied, sticking his fingers in his ears. "I can't really hear much."

"Come on. Let's check on your friends."

Tyler nodded and followed. He looked up to see Clay speaking heatedly between his two defenders, but was unable to make out what they were saying. Clay raised a hand and gestured for both Danny and him to join them. By the time they both made it to the small circle the ringing in his ears had faded enough to allow him to speak without shouting.

"What the hell was that?" Tyler asked in an accusing tone, gesturing to Clay. "What did you do?"

"I got rid of it." He looked Tyler up and down. "You're welcome."

"Yeah, but how?"

Clay sighed. "We can talk about that later. Right now we have more important things to worry about." He glanced at Danny. "Are you alright?"

"Yeah. No damage here," Danny smiled. "Too bad you didn't leave any for me."

"There was nothing to leave," Clay replied seriously. "That *wasn't* a dragon."

Everyone's expression shifted to one of confusion, but nobody said anything to contradict him.

"Whatever that was, it was summoned by someone very powerful and they obviously want me dead." He turned to Tyler. "The mage who saved you had a dark blue crystal you said?"

"Yeah. But how do you know–"

"That's the Sage. He's been after the royal family for a while. His minions are everywhere. He'll stop at nothing to take us out."

Koto perked up next to Tyler but kept his mouth shut.

"It seems he not only wanted my father gone but me as well. And he's obviously willing to kill innocent people in order to draw me out." Clay's face fell as he looked back at the village. "I feel foolish for taking the bait. These people were hurt because of me."

"Why's he after you?" Danny asked, putting a hand on Clay's arm. "What happened?"

Clay sighed. "My father in this world is just as bad as my dad back home. But apparently, this one had a bit more of a bloodlust." He glanced up at Gordanth and Nikolas. "I'm told he sought out the Sage at one time for help. During his stay, he learned many things, but what he realized most was that the Sage was more powerful than him by far, probably more powerful than anyone in Bramoria." His voice lowered as he cast his eyes down. "The night he left he murdered the Sage's apprentice and badly injured his pet. He also stole a few magical items as well and some of them he gave away as cursed gifts to amuse himself." Clay looked down at his armored arm, rolling the metallic fingers through the air. "He was not a good man."

"So why not just tell the Sage you're not like him? Won't he listen?" Danny gestured to the camp. "Look at all the good you're trying to do for the people."

"It would seem he's beyond my reach at this point. His wrath knows no bounds, especially if he's willing to sacrifice the innocents he used to protect." Clay looked back to Gordanth and Nikolas. "He has to be stopped."

Tyler stared at Clay as he spoke. He'd never heard his friend sound so serious. It was true he'd been in Bramoria for a year already, but his manner of speaking and the way he carried himself implied a weight on his shoulders that hadn't been there before. The rowdy teenage boy Tyler knew was now a king and bore the responsibility of that role. It was his duty to protect the people of Bramoria. Even if they were just inside a magic book of some sort, the screams coming from the nearby town made him realize a strange truth. The mangled and burned bodies, ruined homes, and destruction that surrounded them was too real to be denied. Whoever the Sage was, it was clear he was the villain of the story.

"So what do we do?" Tyler asked, breaking the silence.

Gordanth lifted a hand to cut off Clay's response. "The *king* is going to go back to the capital city where the academy can protect him until we learn the Sage's location." He gave a nod to Nikolas who ran off toward Clay's tent. "The castle is already warded from the Sage's magic. We can call a council meeting once we're there and consult the Divinarae."

"We should be staying here and helping the people," Clay rebutted, turning his sights on the mage. "We can't just abandon them!"

"The soldiers will stay here with their captains and take care of everything. They already have their orders."

"What do you mean they already have their orders? What's going on?"

Nikolas sprinted back from the tent and came to a halt next to the king, a sheathed sword in his hand. "Here you are, your highness."

"I don't need thi–"

But before he could say anything else Gordanth tapped his staff to the ground, a large circle of geometric patterns spiraling out from it in an instant. Runes swirled through the warm evening air, giving off a faint yellowish glow of their own.

"I'm not asking permission this time," Gordanth said, staring Clay in the eye. "Enough of this foolishness."

With a second tap, the circle burst into bright golden light and Tyler felt his body jolted upward, the air torn from his lungs.

For a brief moment he thought he'd died, but as his eyes adjusted he found himself standing in a star-filled landscape with no horizon or floor. His feet felt like they were on solid ground, but as he looked down he realized there was nothing to see but the stars and galaxies swirling beneath him. Bright colorful light spilled over his body, cast by the nearby nebulas and stars. It was unlike anything he'd ever seen before. He stared, fascinated by this new place he found himself in. It was a long moment before he realized he wasn't alone. Out of his periphery, he saw a dark figure approaching.

"Clay?" he called out, his voice hollow and echoing in the void. "Clay, what is this?"

The figure did not answer. But as it grew nearer Tyler saw the dark hood pulled high and a gnarled staff in its left hand. At the very top was a glowing blue crystal.

"What do you want?" he said, pulling his fists up as he took a step back. "Don't get any closer!"

From under the hood, a deep voice answered. "This is *your* story, Tyler Wilson. Don't waste it."

"What the fuck is that supposed to mean?" he hissed through his teeth. "I don't want your fucking story, I want to go home!"

"Stories happen whether people want them to or not. That is life." He paused for a moment. "Your friends are already telling their own stories." He tilted his head to the side. "But you resist. Thus far your story is one of avoiding choices and confrontation."

"Why are you trying to kill my friends?" Tyler yelled. "Leave Clay alone! I don't know why you saved Danny, but I know who you are and I'll tell them everything!"

The figure laughed, the bassy voice echoing strangely in the expanse. "How could you possibly know me when you don't even know yourself." He took another step forward. "But if you wish to learn more about the truth of this world, read the book." He lifted his staff and the crystal began to glow. "Bramoria holds more secrets than you could ever know. Something it has in common with you and your friends especially."

"How do you know about the book?" Tyler paused, his thoughts racing. "It was you…" he said, pointing a finger at the cloaked man, anger pulsing in his stomach. "You're the one that trapped us here aren't you?! I'll fucking kill you for this!"

He rushed forward, hands outstretched ready to strangle the hooded man alive. Before he could reach him the staff shifted and the starscape around him disappeared in a flash of white. Less than a second later Tyler found himself standing in a stone room surrounded by his friends and Clay's guards.

"Where is he!?" Tyler screeched, turning on the spot. "I'll fucking kill him!"

"What are you talking about?" Danny asked, grabbing him by the shoulder. "What's wrong?"

The other four just stared at him with looks of confusion at his outburst.

"The Sage! He was just here, talking to me," Tyler seethed. "He was spouting off some crazy shit about stories and secrets and the book. He's the reason we're trapped here!"

"We're out of his reach now," Gordanth said, lowering his staff to the floor. "The castle is warded from his influence."

"But he was just here!"

Clay stepped up and put both his hands on Tyler's shoulders. "He's just trying to get in your head." His brows furrowed together. "My dad used to manipulate me all the time to take me off my guard or confuse me. Don't let him in. It just gives him power."

"But he told me t–"

"Tyler," Clay said seriously. "Just let it go. Anything he said to you is a lie. Let it go." He gave Tyler a small smile, reaching a hand out to pull Danny in. "You're both safe here with me. I promise."

Tyler furrowed his brows but nodded to the pair of them. He glanced over to see Koto standing a couple of feet away, his hood fallen down around his shoulders exposing his tall cat-like ears. He had a look of abject horror on his face as he stared at the stone walls. Clay followed Tyler's gaze, his lips parting in surprise before his expression turned to one of hatred.

"Kotolor Garrunda," he breathed, reaching for his sword.

Both Gordanth and Nikolas took a step forward, arming themselves as well. Clay's blade flashed out, the tip resting against Koto's clavicle.

"Clay! What are you doing?" Tyler gasped, reaching for the sword.

Clay knocked his hand away. "You've got a lot of nerve getting so close to me again Kotolor." His voice was full of venom. "You murdered your father and tried to take care of me too the same night. Come back to finish the job, have you?" He pressed the blade closer, drawing a tiny rivulet of blood. "Did the Sage send you back to kill me? How is your master by the way?"

"What?" Tyler asked, turning his gaze to Koto. "Is... is that true?"

Koto didn't respond, he just cast his eyes to the floor.

"Paladins!" Clay yelled across the room. Immediately the doors flew open and several men in full plate armor piled in, each holding a long spear toward Koto. "Take this man to the dungeons to await execution! Make sure he's stripped of all his belongings!"

Tyler watched as his friend, or who he thought was his friend, was nearly tackled by the paladins. He cried out as his arms were twisted behind his back and he was forced out of the room flanked by several guards. It seemed the Sage had infiltrated the castle's defenses after all, but thankfully was unsuccessful.

TWENTY-TWO

The room Clay had set him up with was incredible. Every available surface was draped in silks and finery, things he would never have been able to afford even in the real world. But Tyler was feeling too sorry for himself to enjoy it. There were no words to describe what he felt after finding out Koto was a criminal and working with the Sage. Over the past week, he'd been annoyed with the man, but he'd started to enjoy his company and trust him as a friend. To find out he'd killed his own father and attempted to take Clay's life was a rude shock. At first, he couldn't believe it, but the more he thought about it, the more he realized Koto had been avoiding speaking of his father and trying to get him away from Clay the moment they ran into one another. He'd even tried to convince him that his best friends no longer wanted anything to do with him and were treating him poorly. He was angry with Koto for deceiving him but moreover, he was angry with himself for being so stupid and gullible. It seemed to be a running theme during his stay in Bramoria.

Tyler flopped down on the soft bed, throwing his arms over his head as he sank into the down mattress. He'd been stupid for trusting a complete stranger anyway. Koto was a dangerous criminal and that's all there was to it. He was locked in the dungeons and no longer a threat to anyone else thanks to Clay. Now that he was in the capital and safe with his best friends, it was time to start figuring out how to go home. Clay had already arranged a meeting with the mages the day after next to see if it was something they could do for Tyler as a favor from the king himself. It seemed like an impossible amount of time to wait, but as the smell of his own body wafted over him, he realized he was happy for the delay. It would give him a chance to get cleaned up and get some decent clothing before he had to meet the most powerful people in all of Bramoria.

A knock at the door interrupted his thoughts. Regrettably pulling himself away from the softest bed he'd felt in over a week, he crossed the room and opened the door. On the other side stood a beautiful young woman with pale skin and bright green eyes. Her blonde hair was long and shiny, pulled into a loose braid across her back. She wore a thin gown with a belt across her waist, the fabric highlighting the curves of her body and leaving little to the imagination. He noticed a rough scar around each of her wrists.

Tyler swallowed hard, immediately placing his eyes on hers and forcing himself not to look down again. "Uh... Can I help you?"

"Our great king has sent me to collect you for your bath," she smiled with a small curtsey. "Please follow me, Sir Tyler."

"It's just Tyler."

"Of course."

"Do... Do I need anything?"

A brief flash of confusion crossed her face, but she quickly recovered. "The king has arranged for your bath, a change of more suitable attire, and an evening's company to your liking. We will take care of everything."

"Company?" He shifted nervously. "What d-does that mean?"

"The king has requested that all your needs be seen to." She paused for a moment, her eyes falling to his waist.

He understood her meaning. "I... uh... that's okay. Just a bath."

"Is there something not to your liking?" she asked as if it were nothing more than a business transaction. "The castle has many courtesans on staff and I'm sure we can find someone more suited to your personal tastes."

"No no!" he said, not wanting to offend her. "I don't think you're ugly or anything... I just... it's... I..." He continued to open and close his mouth like a fish out of water, desperate to find a way out of the uncomfortable conversation.

"It's your first time," she stated matter of factly.

He nodded, not sure why he was admitting it to her. "But you can't tell Clay. I'll never hear the end of it."

"Of course," she nodded. "The other servants and I are here to please you. I'm sure we can find something that is to your liking and comfort. We live to serve."

Everything about the situation felt strange. "Okay. I guess I'd like to take a bath then."

She held out a hand, gesturing him down the hall. "Right this way, Sir Tyler."

The bath was a long walk to the west wing of the castle and down three flights of stairs to the ground level. After a maze of hallways and doors, Tyler finally found himself in a large room with a massive copper tub full of steaming water. The air was full of fragrance that he breathed in deeply through his nose. It took a moment to identify it as honeysuckle. For some reason, there were also several people in the room of varying genders and states of undress. All their eyes turned to him as he stepped through the door and immediately felt his face flush bright red.

"We'll help you remove your clothing and wash, Sir Tyler," the young woman said, reaching up to grab the dirty collar of his shirt.

"No no!" he squeaked, shrinking away from her touch. "I can do it by myself. I don't need any help."

"Of course," she said, bowing her head.

Tyler grabbed the hem of his shirt and started to lift it, but then stopped. All eyes in the room were still on him. "Um..."

A man, no more than a year older than him, walked over and put a hand on his hip. He wore nothing but thin linen harem pants pulled so low that they were barely holding on. His skin was richly tanned with a warm glow and he wore several small silver hoops in his ears. There was a large bruise on his left shoulder and similar scars on his wrists.

"Let me help you with that," he said in a soft voice, leaning close to Tyler, his dark brown eyes gleaming.

He smelled richly of cedar. Before Tyler could respond his shirt was lifted over his head and tossed to the floor. The man gave him a crooked smile and grabbed his hand, leading him over to the bath. Tyler knew his face was beet red as they crossed the room. He was so embarrassed he couldn't even speak. The thought of half a dozen people watching him bathe was terrifying. Stopping at the tub the man turned around and reached for his belt, pulling it free in one swift motion.

"Alright, okay!" Tyler said, on the edge of passing out from holding his breath. "I can do this myself. Please let me take a bath alone."

The man's face fell. "My apologies sir," he said, bowing his head and taking a step back. "We were on orders from the king. But if you wish to be left alone, that can be done."

"I... don't... I just..." Tyler didn't know what to say, but his embarrassment was quickly replaced by guilt as everyone in the room wore a worried expression. He noticed each one of them looked rather skinny and many of them sported scars around their necks or wrists. Something felt off. "Will... Will you get in trouble if I send you away?"

Eyes danced to one another, but nobody made a sound.

"Please," Tyler said a little softer, trying to appear as unthreatening as possible. "I'm new to this and I don't know the rules."

"It's not our place to say," the man responded, his head still bowed.

"I... give you *permission* I guess? Please tell me."

The man glanced at the blonde woman that led Tyler there. He swallowed hard and looked back up at Tyler. "The king gives orders and we *must* follow them. That is the life of a servant." The others in the room looked horrified at his words. "It is our duty to please."

Tyler understood. The eyes and the scars told him everything. They were slaves of the crown and if they didn't do what Clay told them to do, they'd be punished. But would Clay really do that? He'd only been in Bramoria a year. Could it be possible he was already okay with medieval slavery and would allow it in his own home? It seemed more likely that he just had his hands full with the dragons and his father's old laws were taking time to abolish. Still, something about it made Tyler's stomach turn.

"Can everyone please turn away while I get in the tub at least?" Tyler asked, keeping his voice gentle. He didn't want anyone to think he was upset. "I'm a little shy..."

Everyone turned around at his command, although the man in front of him gave him a tiny smirk before turning back. Something about him made Tyler's stomach flutter, but he pushed the feeling away. He felt that way every time any person flirted with him. But the last thing he wanted was to be feeling any sort of way when he smelled like an elephant's butthole.

Making sure everyone's eyes were turned away, he quickly stripped off and stepped into the tub, hissing through his teeth as the hot water enveloped his skin. Slowly he sank down into it, resting his arms on the metallic lip. Immediately he felt the scent of honeysuckle wash over him and his muscles relaxed. A bath seemed like such a common thing back home, but in Bramoria, it was the lap of luxury.

"Is the water to your liking," the blonde woman asked, kneeling down next to the tub.

"Yeah," Tyler sighed. "It feels great."

"Good," she nodded. "If there's anything we can do to assist you, please let us know."

"I... I'm kind of hungry." He quickly sat up, realizing he'd just created more work for them. "If that's not a problem! I don't want you to have to go out of your way or anything!"

"Easily arranged." She stood up with a smile and called

two of the others over to her. The three of them left the room at his request. He hoped it wouldn't get them in trouble.

"Do you need any help?" the man in the harem pants asked, resting his chin and hands on the edge of the tub.

"I've washed myself before," Tyler chuckled, trying to hide the embarrassment of being naked in front of other people. He tried to place his hands casually over his groin to hide himself. "I can do it."

"Yes, but have you ever had *someone else* wash you before?"

"N-No…"

"May I?" he said, picking up a cloth and dipping it into the water.

He moved around behind Tyler and began to run the steaming cloth over his neck and shoulders. It was weird at first, but as he slowly began to realize he was in control and could call it off at any moment, he started to relax. The others in the room milled about, stoking the fire to keep the tub water warm and finding other things to keep themselves busy since Tyler wasn't giving them any orders.

The neck washing slowly turned into a massage and Tyler nearly fell asleep. When the time came for further scrubbing below the waterline, he insisted on doing it himself. Food was eventually brought up and it was far more than Tyler expected. He asked the others to join him in eating it, not wanting it to go to waste, but all of them refused even though they looked underfed. At long last, the entire ordeal ended with him standing in front of a mirror with a new pair of breeches, dark knee-high leather boots, and a soft linen shirt that billowed around the sleeves.

"You look handsome," the man said, brushing away a few stray fuzzies on Tyler's shirt.

"I look like a pirate," Tyler snorted.

The man and the blonde woman looked suddenly worried.

"If there's something not to your liking," she said quickly, "we can have it exchanged."

"No no!" He stopped her from pulling at his shirt, holding his hands up. "It's fine. I really like it, I'm just not used to this sort of clothing."

Both her and the man visibly relaxed.

"Is there anything else we can provide for you?"

It was getting late and even though the courtesans were doing their best to not look it, they were tired.

"Only one thing," he said, looking between the pair of them. "What are your names?"

Both seemed surprised. The blonde woman spoke up first.

"My name is Ninsar."

"Mine is Faus," the man replied as well, a smile playing at his lips again.

Something about him made Tyler feel exposed like he was seeing right through him. "It's nice to meet you both." He held out a hand. The two gave him an odd expression before each shaking his hand in turn. "Uh... I might need someone to take me back to my room," he said, scratching the back of his head. "I don't remember how to get there."

"I can take you," Faus volunteered, lacing his arm around Tyler's. "Follow me."

The walk back to his room was quiet and longer than he remembered. Faus kept stroking the back of his hand as they walked through the endless hallways and doors. He wondered how the man wasn't freezing to death with no shirt and barely any pants. It seemed almost cruel that he should have to walk around in so little. Although, after a few stolen glances, Tyler decided that he would have done the same if he had a similar physique.

"Here we are," Faus said when they finally reached the door. He pulled it open and led Tyler inside, closing it behind him.

"Uh..."

Faus held a finger up to his lips. "Don't worry. I'm just going to help you get ready for bed."

"I... don't need help?"

Why it came out as a question, Tyler didn't know. Faus lifted an eyebrow and smiled.

"How about I make sure your fire is set for the night while you get yourself ready?"

Tyler couldn't think of a way to deny him. "O-Okay."

Faus made his way over to the fireplace and bent down to add a few more logs to bring it back to life. Tyler stood stock still for a long moment, not understanding why his cheeks were burning so badly. Somehow Fause was getting under his skin with his furtive glances. Finally, he snapped himself out of it and rushed to the bed. He pulled off his boots and clothes, tossing them haphazardly over the chest at the end of the four-poster. With nothing else to put on, he slipped under the cool covers completely nude. He didn't suppose there were any gym shorts in Bramoria, but he was going to make it a point to have some made if he had to stay more than a few nights.

Faus moved about the room dousing candles. Afterward, he came to the bed and began folding Tyler's new clothing neatly into a pile. He stepped to the head of the bed and sat down next to Tyler, leaning back so that he was resting on his torso on one elbow.

"Anything else you need?"

"I d-don't think s-so," Tyler stuttered, cursing how stupid he felt.

Faus gave him a hard look before reaching up and patting the side of his cheek. "As you wish."

He stood up from the bed and turned to walk away, but he stopped as Tyler's hand grabbed his own and he turned back.

"Wait," Tyler said, pulling him back. He forced down the butterflies as Faus took a seat again. Pushing himself up in bed he took a deep breath. "There are some things I want to ask you. I know you're not supposed to say them, that's pretty clear, but I need to know."

Faus went from playful to immediately uncomfortable.

"I promise I won't say anything to the king. You have my

word."

"I… will say… what I can."

"Thank you," Tyler nodded. "I don't know what you've heard about me, but I don't know much about this place. Bramoria I mean." He twisted the covers in his hands as he glanced down at the scars on Faus' wrists. "Are you a slave here?"

The man's lips remained sealed, a look of fear on his face as he kept his eyes fixed on Tyler. For a long moment, they just stared at one another. Then his head nodded ever so slightly.

"Okay. Thank you. And the king knows this?"

Again, an almost imperceptible nod.

"It wasn't just his father who enslaved you?"

Faus cocked his head to the side. "I… I was brought on just a few months ago by our current king. I've never even met his father."

"I thought he *just* became king?" Tyler didn't understand. "How long has he been doing that?" He looked at the bruise on Faus' shoulder. "Who did that to you?"

Faus looked toward the door. "I don't think this is appropriate. If you no longer require my services, I should retire for the evening."

"I'm sorry," Tyler sighed, knowing he'd already given in all the answers he needed with his reaction. Quickly he shifted the conversation. "He's my best friend. I'm just worried about him is all. I want to make sure he's okay."

For a long moment, Faus was silent. He stared into Tyler's eyes, searching them for something. Finally, he sighed. "The king has been in control of the throne for some time," he said at last. "His father relinquished his power when he fell deathly ill almost a year ago."

Tyler stared back, furrowing his brows. That wasn't the story he'd been told. Clay specifically said his father was a terrible man and had him imprisoned for treason against the citizens. More than a few things were starting to feel off and more kept piling on by the moment. He glanced back at Faus' bruise. Clay had done that, it was clear from Faus' reaction earlier. There was no reason for him to lie, especially about information that could get him possibly killed if he was caught sharing it. Tyler stared at him for a long moment, processing what he'd said. Still, he didn't want to believe it but there were too many questions now. And there was only one way to find out the truth, something that both Clay and the Sage agreed on.

"One last question Faus," he said, keeping eye contact. "Where does the king keep his book with the gem on the cover?"

TWENTY-THREE

The meeting with the academy mages went poorly. Tyler was more annoyed than ever as he walked out of the gilded room at the base of the tower. The mages were happy to boast about how powerful they were but when he asked them to send him home, all of them clamped their mouths shut in an instant. Clay had asked them to keep researching and although they agreed to do so, he knew there was no hope. Their reactions had told him everything he needed to know. After a few awkward moments, they'd gone back to discussing the issue of the dragons and the Sage, trying to figure out what to do about it and how to better protect their king. Danny on the other hand seemed completely nonplussed by the information. Tyler knew he wanted to stay in Bramoria, but he was still sick. The meeting was dismissed before he could bring up finding a cure for him.

"Danny," Clay called from inside the chamber. "Can you join us for a moment?"

Tyler looked up to his friend walking alongside him, but Danny was already gone, having turned back in and shut the door behind him. He was alone in the hallway, the other mages filing away toward their respective offices throughout the tower. He wondered if he should wait for his friends or take the rest of the day to himself. He'd already been in the castle two days waiting for the meeting but had found little time to explore. A part of him wanted to go to the dungeons and talk with Koto and gather some information, but he had a feeling Clay wouldn't approve of that. There was still the issue of finding the book, but it was kept in the king's chambers at all times, which of course remained under constant guard. Faus had given him the answer, but there was no way in without Clay's permission or without being discovered. Sure he'd promised to show the book to Tyler when he had a free moment, but so far he'd been busy every waking minute of the day since they'd arrived. Not only that, but he was constantly surrounded by guards, mages, and his advisors. There was no time for the three of them to be alone.

Choosing to head out into the castle grounds, Tyler wove his way through the tower halls until found the front door. He stepped out into the warm sunlight, stretching as his boots clicked against the cobblestone path. The castle was a safe place to rest for the time being, but he was troubled. More than a few things were out of place and most of them revolved around Clay and his stories. Tyler knew he was busy, but the more he found out, the more it seemed like he was stalling about showing him the book. He'd made it plain he wanted to catch up on Clay's life while he'd been in Bramoria, but that had garnered a quick dismissal for some new meeting. Tyler had known him long enough to know when he was avoiding talking about something. Although he'd had lots of time to practice in his new position, he still gave himself away. And that's what worried him. In the past Clay had always avoided talking about home when things were at their worst. What could possibly be going on that Clay didn't want him to know? Were things worse than they seemed? Did Faus have his story wrong? What about the slavery, the bruises, and Clay's father? Why was Clay lying to him?

Tyler stopped at the edge of a small pond where several orange and white fish were swimming in lazy circles around the lilies. He stared at his reflection for a long moment in the greenish water. Whatever Clay was hiding, he'd find it in the book and come up with a way to help him. For now, he just had to figure out a way to sneak in without getting caught. It was clear his friend was in trouble and Tyler needed to help him, even if it meant going behind his back to do it. But he knew he couldn't do it alone, not with his minimal knowledge of the castle and its workings. He glanced back at the white stone tower, wondering if Danny would help. Shaking his head he turned back to his own reflection. Danny was unreliable at best nowadays. For some reason living in Bramoria had gone to his head and he'd become reckless and foolish. Rushing into things that nearly killed him and barely coming out on the other side with a false sense of immortality was a red flag that Tyler couldn't ignore. He wished he knew what to do about that but there were already so many questions flying through his head that there was no room for another.

"Once I get Clay some help, we can help Danny together," Tyler muttered to himself, crouching down next to the water. He skimmed his fingers over the surface causing tiny ripples to wander around the lily pads. "This summer is *not* going how I thought it would."

The orange and white fish swam over to where his fingers brushed the water, their round mouths breaking the surface as they searched for food he didn't have. His plan had been to run off with Danny and Clay. To remove them from the difficulties of their lives. Clay needed a break from his father and Danny had spent too much time trapped within the walls of his home. He hadn't anticipated that they would steal a magical book and get transported to a fantasy world where both of his friends would suddenly turn into completely different people. Most of the time it seemed like Tyler was the only one who had any sense left. He definitely was the only one that still thought of home. The other two only found ways to ignore him when he spoke of it, which irritated him to no end. For some reason, they didn't see it as a problem, but Tyler was convinced Bramoria was changing them and not in a good way. He had to do something to make them see the truth.

"Faus..." he whispered under his breath, the solution popping into his mind.

That was it. Faus had made it clear he'd been in Clay's

private chambers before and he was a trusted member of the serving staff. If he knew where the book was, he could get it for Tyler. It would be a big risk, but once Tyler figured out what was going on, he was sure he could convince Clay not only to forgive Faus but to free him and the other slaves. All he needed was answers, after that everything would be easy.

"I don't know how you convinced me to do this," Faus whispered, leaning his back against the stone wall around the corner from Clay's chambers. "This is going to get me killed."

"I promise it won't," Tyler said, waving him off. "I know Clay, he's a good guy, but this whole *king* thing has got him really stressed out. If I can just figure out what's going on, we can get this all cleared up."

"And how do you know that?"

"The book will tell me the truth about everything, Clay said so himself." Tyler put a hand on Faus' shoulder. "Look, I know this is a big risk for you, but I'm going to make sure you and your fellow slaves are taken care of, okay? There's a lot at stake here for me too, so don't think I'm doing this on a whim."

Faus breathed out a slow sigh. "I really hope you're right." He glanced at his shoulder that was still bruised, although lightened up considerably. "I know what he's like when he's angry."

"I've dealt with Clay plenty of times while he's angry, believe me, I can handle it."

Faus raised his eyebrows before he glanced around the corner once more and took a deep breath. "I can't believe I'm doing this." He reached back and grabbed Tyler by the collar, pulling him in close. "You better be right about this. If any harm comes to me or the other slaves, just remember I know every passage in this castle, secret or otherwise."

Tyler gulped, knowing the man wasn't lying. "I understand."

The show of fear brought a smile to Faus' face as he patted him on the cheek. "Alright. Meet me in your room. I'll have your book."

"Okay."

Faus gave him one last glance before he straightened himself up and walked around the corner. Tyler listened for a moment as he walked down the hall and stopped in front of the guards. They exchanged a few words that he couldn't make out before he heard the door to the king's chambers open. Faus was in.

Tyler turned on his heel and headed in the opposite direction, winding through the hallways back to his room. He made sure to count the turns in his head. Left, right, another right, left again, then straight through to the end of the hall. It was a miracle anyone could find anything in the giant stone maze of the castle, but he breathed a sigh of relief as he saw the door to his room once more. Slipping inside he pushed the door closed behind him and leaned his forehead against the wood. All he had to do was wait for Faus to return and then he'd finally have his answers.

Turning around he saw the rich tapestries on the walls and a large mahogany desk against one corner. His heart nearly stopped as he realized it wasn't his room at all. There was a shifting from the four-poster bed draped in thin damask curtains. A figure stood up, silhouetted against the fabric, and stepped out into the candlelight. For a moment he didn't recognize her in the elegant gown, a silver tiara balanced on her head, but his jaw dropped as those details faded away.

"Mom?" he whispered, still not believing his own eyes. He blinked a few times and squinted, just to be sure. "Mom, what are you doing here?" Rushing over to her side he took her hands. "What's going on? Why didn't anyone tell me you were here?"

She stared at him with a blank look on her face. "Who... Who are you? I don't believe we've met."

His heart skipped a beat. "What do you mean? It's me, Tyler!"

She tilted her head to the side. "I don't know you, I apologize." Quickly she replaced her confusion with a smile. "You must be one of my son's friends."

"I am *your* son..."

"Oh no," she laughed, waving a hand as if to bat away his little joke. "My son is the king of Bramoria. Surely you've met him if you're staying here in his castle?"

"Y-Yeah," he managed to get out. "He brought me here himself." He couldn't believe what he was seeing. How was his mom in Bramoria and why didn't she know who he was? Why didn't Clay tell him about her? He would have said something if he knew, wouldn't he? But then again, how could it even be possible he didn't know she was there?

"W-When is the last time you saw your... s-son?" Tyler asked, tensing as he awaited her answer. His heart was pounding in his chest, the anxiety threatening to overtake him.

"Why just this morning," she smiled. "We have breakfast together every day."

He didn't know what to think. "Do I look familiar to you at all?" he asked, searching for some hint that she still recognized him.

"No, I'm afraid not. Have we met before?"

"You don't remember anything about my full ride to college? About graduation? About... Dad?"

She gave him a perplexed look, shaking her head. "I apologize. I'm not sure what you're talking about."

Tyler didn't know what to do. He wanted to reach out and shake her. To scream and yell until she remembered who he was. It was cruel enough that he was trapped in this make-believe world, but for his mother to be there and have no idea who he was... that was too much. How could Clay keep that a secret from him? What was going on? It felt like everything he knew was crumbling around him. As he gazed up into her apologetic eyes he let out a sigh. Hopefully, the book would tell him and then he'd set it straight. But for now, there was nothing he could do without causing a ruckus.

"I... I apologize," he finally said. "I was looking for my room and it seems I chose the wrong door."

She smiled again. "It happens all the time. This castle is rather like a labyrinth."

"I'll leave you alone. Sorry to have disturbed you."

Realizing she was one of the royal family, he gave her a slight bow and left the room, unable to lift his eyes to her again without bursting into tears. With the door shut softly behind him, he traced his steps back until he found his mistake. He'd gone right instead of left on his last turn. Eventually, he found his actual room and shut the door behind him.

His mind was racing. Nothing felt real after the shock of seeing his mother. Crossing the room he fell onto the bed face first, completely overwhelmed with no idea what to do. He stayed that way until a soft knock at his door roused him. Faus let himself in, a large bundle of cloth in his hands. He brought it over to the bed and sat it down, pulling the fabric away to reveal the same book with the honey-colored gem that Clay had stolen from the vanishing bookstore. Without a word, Tyler pulled it toward himself and flipped it open, ready to get some answers as to what was going on.

TWENTY-FOUR

Tyler started at page one and didn't stop until he'd read every single page in the book. Twice he sent Faus out for food and water, feeling safer with his company while he learned what had been happening in Bramoria over the past year. Several times he stopped to ask questions, but Faus had almost no knowledge of anything beyond the castle walls. Fortunately, the book explained most of it, and what it told Tyler was unlike anything he'd ever imagined. There was a lot more wrong in Bramoria and with Clay than he'd anticipated. As he read the last few pages he found that the book mostly focused on Clay and thankfully didn't mention the book theft from his room or who'd done it. At the very least that would keep Faus safe from any punishment until Tyler could figure out what to do.

The courtesan had been pacing around the room for the last hour, the day growing late. When Tyler finally snapped the book shut he rushed over to the bed, sitting down at the edge. His demeanor was that of a nervous cat.

"Alright, we need to get this back," he said, a look of worry on his face. "The king will know it's missing immediately. It's one of his most prized possessions."

Tyler didn't want to let the book go, but he knew Faus was right. Facing Clay head-on after having stolen his property was probably not the best way to handle the situation. After what he'd read, he now realized how truly powerful Clay had become in the past year. Not only was he a gifted fighter, but also an extremely gifted mage. It seemed all three of them had been given mage stones when they crossed over into Bramoria, but Clay had taken great pains to master his.

"You're right," Tyler nodded with a sigh. "I need to talk to Danny about this first. If it's the two of us, I think we might stand a chance at talking some sense into him." He wasn't sure if he believed the words coming out of his mouth, but he had to try. "Besides, I don't want you getting into trouble."

"I appreciate that." He pulled the book from Tyler's hands and wrapped it in a sheet. They'd already worked out how to sneak it back in, pretending to be changing the bedclothes out for the night. "Come on, let's get this over with."

"Alright," Tyler said, pushing himself up from the bed.

Together they left Tyler's room and headed down the maze of corridors. The path was starting to become familiar to Tyler as he began to memorize the different tapestries and ornamentations hanging on the walls. He found himself partially leading the way toward Clay's room as they drew closer. At the last corner, they stopped, peeking around the edge to see the two guards standing watch over the door as usual. Once again Faus turned back to Tyler.

"The king isn't back yet," he sighed in relief. "He always keeps four guards when he's in his room. I'll get this put away. You should head back to your room."

"Are you sure?" Tyler asked, still worried about having kept the book for so long.

Faus leaned forward and planted a small kiss on his cheek, making Tyler blush in surprise. "Promise. I'll meet you back there."

Unable to think of anything else to say, he just nodded. Faus straightened himself up and walked around the corner with the bundle of fabric in his arms. This time Tyler didn't linger, he immediately turned back toward his own room, confident Faus could handle the task. He'd gone no more than a few steps when he turned a corner and ran face-first into someone, the clattering of armor filling the hall as they both tumbled to the ground. Before he had a chance to recover he felt a rough hand on the back of his neck yanking him to his feet.

"Watch where the fuck you're going, servant!" a husky baritone cried, throwing him aside like he was nothing more than a bag of potatoes.

Tyler slammed into the wall and shook his head. He lifted his gaze and saw a small group of armored guards standing in the hallway, the one that'd thrown him helping his compatriot up from the ground. Between them a figure pushed its way through, shouting at the others.

"You watch yourself, captain!" Clay yelled at the man as he managed to force his way to the front. "That is my best friend and my personal guest here in the castle!"

The captain looked at Tyler and all the blood drained from his face. "S-Sorry sir!" he managed to get out. "I d-didn't realize..."

"No, you just assumed," Clay interjected. "As usual." He gave the captain one last stern look before he turned to face Tyler, holding out his unarmored hand to steady him. "Are you alright?"

"Yeah," Tyler replied, rubbing the side of his head where it had hit the other soldier when they collided. "Just surprised me, is all." He glanced up to the captain, worried how Clay might react. He'd read a few things in the book that made him worry for the captain's safety. "No harm done."

"Are you sure?"

"You know me, Clay," Tyler forced himself to laugh. "I'm always hurting myself. I've had worse than this."

Clay gave him a small nod. "Yes, I do." He shot a quick glare at the captain before turning back. "What are you doing in this part of the castle?"

Tyler felt his heart nearly stop. He hadn't planned to run into anyone and didn't have a story prepared. "I... uh... was looking for you. I didn't know when your meetings ended, so I came to see if you wanted to hang out."

Clay's brows furrowed together. "You wanted to *hang out*?"

"Yeah," Tyler shrugged, trying to look nonchalant. "Is that weird or something? We used to do it all the time back home."

"I suppose not." He relaxed a bit and smiled. "I keep forgetting you haven't been here that long. To you, we just left home last week, but for me, it's been a lot longer. I'm not used to the old way of doing things."

"I guess you're a pretty busy guy now, running the whole kingdom and all." Tyler looked around, desperately wanting to get away from Clay. He didn't feel safe around him anymore after reading the book and without Danny, he wasn't ready to confront him about what it contained. "I'll go back to my room. I'm sure you're exhausted."

Tyler started to walk away when he felt a metallic hand grip his shoulder to stop him.

"No, I can hang out for a bit," Clay said, turning him back around. "It'll take me a while to wind down anyway and you're right, I should take some time for myself."

"I don't want to impose…"

"Nah, don't worry about it, dude."

Clay returning to his more casual speech patterns gave Tyler a moment to relax. Maybe he wasn't as bad as the book had made him out to be. After all, books were subjective things anyway. Tyler wanted to give his friend the benefit of the doubt and at least a chance to explain himself. He couldn't have gone that bad, not in just a year.

"Come on," Clay smiled, leading Tyler back the way he'd come. He turned over his shoulder. "Captain! Have food and drink brought up to my room right away!"

"Yes sir!" the captain replied and immediately sprinted away, his armor clanking down the hallway.

"That man is such an oaf," Clay chuckled. "I really need to find someone to replace him."

"Oh?" Tyler tried to slow his pace to give Faus more time.

He wasn't sure if he'd gotten back out of Clay's room yet. "Why's that?"

"He's just a moron, like all the rest of the soldiers here," he replied, obviously not caring who overheard him. "Everyone wants to impress me, so they do stupid shit to get my attention thinking they are doing what I want." He pulled Tyler forward, forcing him to speed up. "But nobody here knows what I want."

"You know what I want," Tyler began, trying to get Clay to stop. "A nice walk through the gardens in the moonlight. Doesn't that sound amazing?"

"What kind of gay shit is that?" Clay laughed, clapping him on the shoulder painfully with the metallic hand. "You've been here a week and you're a fairy now?"

Tyler felt his cheeks blush red with a mix of embarrassment and anger. Clay had never been the kind of person to talk to him like that, especially when it came to his sexuality. Sure he teased, but he'd never been derogatory before.

"Oh come on," Clay laughed again, seeing the look on his face. "You know I'm just messing with you."

Tyler forced a smile. "I know."

"If you really want to walk through the gardens, we can. But I need to change first."

Before Tyler could say anything to stop him, Clay stepped up to his door and pushed it open. Both of them stepped inside and the first thing Tyler's eyes landed on was Faus standing in the middle of the room next to an ornate wooden stand. He had his fingers wrapped around the corners of the book as if he were just putting it back into place. His eyes grew wide and immediately he stepped aside and kneeled on the ground.

"Your highness," he muttered, his head bowed. "I apologize, I was trying to clean your room before you got back. I'll get out of your way immediately."

Clay's eyes were fixed on the man in front of him. Tyler opened his mouth to speak but Clay's hand shot out in front of him, silencing him immediately.

"It is not your duty to clean my room. Why are you here

without my permission, Faus?" Clay's voice was suddenly dark and serious. It made Tyler's skin crawl as he realized he sounded just like his father. "Who sent you here?"

"I... I came because one of the servants is sick," Faus lied, keeping his head down.

"Hmm," Clay hummed.

His eyes glanced at the book once more, hovering on it for a moment longer than Tyler liked. His face didn't give anything away as he stepped forward, walking around the pedestal and running his fingers over the surface of the tome. Tyler watched in horror as he lifted the latch on the side and put it back in place, locking it shut. He'd forgotten to replace it when he finished reading.

"So... you came to do a little reading, did you Faus?" he asked, stepping around to stand in front of him.

"No sir."

"Don't lie to me!" Clay yelled, his metallic fist colliding with the side of Faus' face.

The man was thrown to the ground, the crunch of bone and rush of blood from his mouth indicating he'd been hurt badly. He lay there for a long moment as Clay stared down at him.

"Clay, don't hu–"

"Shut the fuck up!" Clay spat, turning on his heel. "You don't understand this world and I don't need your help to run my own kingdom!"

Tyler bit his tongue. He wanted to say something, anything to get Faus out of the room, even if it meant getting punched himself. But Clay had gone from relaxed to maniacal in the span of a few seconds and it sent fear flooding through his body. Even if he wanted to speak, his teeth were too tightly clenched together to get anything out.

"So, some whore thinks he can break into my room and steal my most prized possessions." He reached down and grabbed Faus by the neck, lifting him off the ground. "Tell me, what were you going to do? Sell it? Give it to the Sage?" He pulled him in close, Faus staring at him through the blood streaming across his face. "Are you working for him too?" He waited a moment, but only the sound of choking came from Faus' mouth. "You were trouble from the start. I hoped I could beat it out of you, but I should have known you'd never change."

A sudden flash of steel cut through the air and Tyler watched as Faus' belly opened up, his entrails spilling out onto the ground. He couldn't scream for the hand clamping his windpipe shut, but the look in his eyes as he glanced at Tyler told him everything. Clay threw the knife to the ground and reached his armored hand up into Faus' chest, tearing his heart free with a vicious yank. Immediately the man went limp, blood and viscera pouring out onto the floor as the heart beat one last time in Clay's hand before going still. With one last squeeze of his hand, crushing the dead man's windpipe completely, Clay threw him to the ground.

Tyler didn't have time to react as the bile rose in his throat. He turned away and emptied the contents of his stomach onto the stone floor, tearing streaming down his face.

TWENTY-FIVE

Tyler sat with his knees pressed against his chest as the first rays of sunlight came over the horizon. He was shivering, the dew on the grass having soaked through his pants. Burying his face further to block out the light he clenched his eyes shut. He'd been out in the garden all night, having fled Clay's room after watching him murder Faus in cold blood. He hadn't just been a servant, but a man who'd only been there at Tyler's request. A man he'd promised he'd keep safe in exchange for his help. He couldn't get the images of the blood and gore out of his head or the moment where the heart continued to beat in Clay's hand even after it had been ripped from Faus' chest. It was a horrifying image and he wasn't sure if he'd ever be able to bring himself to sleep again. His nights were still filled with images from the Fossar attack and now he knew they'd be nothing but Faus' face full of horror and fear for weeks to come.

Clay was a monster. The book had told him of his dealings over the past year and how he'd manipulated his way into the throne. At first, Tyler tried to give his friend the benefit of the doubt. Every story had two sides and he wanted to give Clay a chance to tell his own. But after watching him murder a man in the most gruesome way possible, he no longer felt like there was a safe way to talk to him. If he ever found out Tyler was the one who orchestrated the stealing of the book, he might meet the same sticky end and that wasn't something he wanted to test. Not to mention Clay had somehow managed to kidnap his mom and wipe her memory of him completely. Between his mom, Danny, and himself, he felt like there was no move he could make to confront Clay that would keep them all safe. Even playing along would only last for a short while. If the book was to be believed, even a vow of fealty wouldn't keep him at bay indefinitely.

Then there was the issue of the dragons and the Sage. The book had mentioned them both briefly, but in a way that Tyler didn't fully understand. Sections of the book had been wiped clean somehow, whole paragraphs removed from the pages. They seemed to happen mostly around the mention of the dragon attacks, but there wasn't enough to go on to figure it out. Knowing how paranoid Clay had become, he wondered if it had been wiped away to prevent it from being stolen by the Sage himself and giving him some unknown edge. Either way, there weren't any conclusions to be drawn from what he'd read. What was clear was that Tyler needed to talk to Danny and get both him and his mom out of the castle as soon as possible. He just had no idea how he was going to pull it off.

Lifting his head he glanced up over the stone garden wall draped in vines and flowers. He squinted as the sunlight hit his eyes again, forcing him to hold a hand up to block it. The sky was ablaze with pinks and reds as the last dredges of the night were driven away. He felt a lump rise in his throat, although he was too exhausted and dehydrated to cry anymore. Everything had gone so wrong and now his very life was in danger, more so than ever before.

All he'd wanted to do was give Danny one last gift before he got too sick and he was willing to admit it was a way for himself to escape his own decisions as well. A simple act of kindness had landed him in this mess and now he was trapped with no way out. The only thing he could do was try to survive. And if he by some miracle managed to escape, he had no idea where to go. Clay was the most powerful man in the world besides the Sage.

Tyler's attention snapped back to the castle. The Sage,

that was it. If he was the only man Clay feared, then that was who Tyler should go to for help. The enemy of my enemy is my friend. That's how the saying went, right? There was no reason for the Sage to be upset with Tyler and it was clear from the dragon attacks that he wanted Clay gone. If Tyler could convince him to just send all three of them home, all their problems would be solved. It was a simple plan that would spare them all, but he'd need help finding the Sage. The only person who knew anything about him was Koto and he was trapped in the castle dungeons. Breaking him out would be nearly impossible. He wasn't sure if he could even trust Koto not to kill him, much less lead them across Bramoria. But as he gazed up at the sky he realized he didn't have a choice. Maybe, if he had Danny's help, they just might be able to pull it off.

Tyler pushed himself up from the wet grass. As much as he didn't want to, it was time to start pulling the strings himself. For too long he'd been relying on others and it had landed him in a mess. Now it was his turn to take the reins and try to steer all of them in a better direction, even if it meant forcing Clay out of Bramoria and sending him back to an abusive home. There was more on the line than bruises and shouts. Their very lives were at stake.

An hour later with a fresh set of clothing, Tyler made his way through the palace to find Danny. He knew his room was near Clay's, but he wasn't sure if he'd already gone down to breakfast or not. It took him a few minutes to find it, but eventually, he came to Danny's door. Lifting a hand, he knocked quietly, trying not to draw too much attention to himself. There was a long pause and just as he was about to leave he heard a small click from the latch as the door swung open. Standing on the other side in the same thin gown was Ninsar, her eyes bloodshot and puffy.

Her gaze narrowed as she stared at him, her body language stiff. "What can I help you with, *sir*?"

Tyler knew she must have heard about Faus and it was clear she was doing everything in her power to hold back whatever she was feeling. "Is... Is Danny here?" he asked timidly.

"Sir Tiragan is *not* here, he went down to breakfast a few minutes ago with the king." Her face was caught somewhere between a forced smile and rage. "Can I help you with something?"

"Can I speak with you?" He looked up and down the hall. "Privately?"

Her body tensed, but she stepped aside, allowing him into the room and shutting the door behind him. For a long moment, he stood there awkwardly, wondering how to start the conversation. She kept her head bowed, not giving him any way to read her expressions. Finally, he took a deep breath, hoping for the best.

"Ninsar, I'm sorry about Faus."

Her body tensed even further as her eyes flashed upward, boring into his soul.

"When I asked him to steal the book I didn–"

Tyler's words were cut off as a fist collided with the side of his face. He was thrown into the wall and tumbled to the ground, his cheek on fire and his mouth filling with the metallic tang of blood. He looked back up to see Ninsar standing over him, her fist still raised in the air as if to strike again. She looked like she wanted to kill him.

"I knew it was *you*," she hissed, tears running down her face. "I knew Faus wasn't stupid enough to steal that book by himself. You *used* him in your own foolish game and got him killed!" She spat in his direction, the saliva landing on his shirt collar. "You're a murderer!"

"I... I didn't know," Tyler muttered back. "I thought I could protect him..."

"Then you're fucking stupid too," she snarled. Bending down she grabbed him by the shirt and hefted him up, her small form hiding more strength than he imagined. "If you come near me or *any* of my fellow servants again, I'll tell the king *myself* that it was you that stole the book. And then I'll laugh as he strings you up and guts you so the crows can feast on you while you're still alive to watch."

With that, she threw him back to the stone floor. Giving him one final kick she turned and stormed out of the room, leaving the door wide open. Tyler lay there for a few moments grappling with the fact that he could now be outed at any moment by a woman who thoroughly hated him with good reason. He could feel the fear rising in his chest as his thoughts began to race. Was he really a murderer? He hadn't thought to give himself that title, but now that it was in his head he couldn't shake it. Faus was dead and it was his fault, even though it had been an accident. Or at least that's what he had to tell himself to stop the anxiety from consuming him. He pushed it down as much as he could. He'd have to worry about that later. For now, there was too much at stake to let himself go to pieces. With Ninsar ready to turn him in at any moment, his plans had to be accelerated. He had to find Danny and fast.

Pushing himself up from the ground and ignoring the bruise forming on his cheek, Tyler left the room and closed the door behind him. Heading back to his own he made a quick stop to grab his sword and a set of leather armor that had been brought up for him at Clay's request. It took him a long time to get it all strapped together, but as he looked himself over in the mirror he hoped he'd done it right. It may be the only thing that saved him if he were discovered. The last piece to go on was his belt and the sword Koto had purchased him. He knew he was still no good with it, but at least he'd have a weapon if it came to blows. Knowing he'd never survive such a thing, he whispered a quick prayer under his breath to anyone who was listening.

"Just let me get through this day," he muttered. "I can take care of the rest after that."

A last thought crossed his mind as he jogged back to the desk in his room. He took the mage stone from the top drawer and slipped it into his pocket thinking the Sage could help him with it if he made it that far. Pulling out a quill and paper, he jotted down a quick note. Slipping it into his pocket he headed back to the door. With everything he could think of needing on his person, he left his room for the last time, working his way through the maze of hallways. He stopped for a moment at the end of a corridor, glancing back at the room he knew belonged to his mother. Once he had Danny and Koto on his side, he'd come back for her too. Together they'd be able to escape Clay's influence and get back to their own world. But he'd have to trick her if he was to get her out of the castle without being caught. He took a quick detour to her door and knelt down, slipping the handwritten note under the door. A chair slid across the floor inside, signaling it had been noticed, and Tyler quickly dashed away, not wanting her to know who left it behind.

At the bottom of the stairs, Tyler wound through the passages toward the great hall. More than once he dodged guards, knowing he'd been missing all night after seeing Faus' execution. He knew they weren't actively searching for him, but Clay may have ordered them to keep a closer eye on him for the time being. The last thing he wanted was to be followed. His trepidation was rewarded when he rounded a tight corner and nearly ran face-first into Danny.

"Woah there!" Danny said, a bright smile on his face as he grabbed Tyler by the shoulders to stop him. "Watch yourself, buddy."

"Man am I glad to see you," Tyler breathed, his heart still pounding from the surprise. He glanced around, making sure no one was watching them. "We need to talk. Now."

Danny's face twisted into one of concern. "What's wrong?" His eyes wandered over Tyler's armor. "Why are you dressed for battle?"

"Not here." Tyler grabbed him by the hand. "Follow me."

His brows furrowed in confusion, but he didn't resist as Tyler pulled him down the hallway. He didn't know where he was going, but he took as many turns as he could, trying to get as far away from the main areas of the castle as possible. At last, he found a small stained door leading to a tiny dining room with three tables shoved in close proximity to one another. It looked mostly unused and safe enough to speak freely in. Grabbing a torch from a nearby sconce, Tyler pulled Danny inside and shut the door behind them.

"Tyler, what's going on?"

"I need you to hear me out on this, alright?" Tyler began, placing the torch in a bracket near the door. "There's a lot to cover."

"Okay?" Danny tilted his head to the side but nodded. "I've never seen you this worked up."

"Come sit down." Tyler gestured for Danny to follow him to one of the tables. He took a seat in one of the moldy chairs and placed his elbows on the table.

"What's wrong, Tyler?"

"Something's wrong with Clay," he managed to say. "And I don't think it's something we can save him from."

TWENTY-SIX

Danny wore a perplexed and worrisome expression. "Are you sure?" He leaned across the table, the reality of their conversation sinking in. "Would Clay really do all that? He doesn't seem like the murdering type to me."

"Danny, I swear to you," Tyler replied, reaching up and placing a hand over his heart. "I saw it with my own eyes. And what I read in the book confirms it. Even Clay said the book couldn't be manipulated. It only tells the truth."

"I don't know Tyler..."

"Look, I don't think Clay's the bad guy here," Tyler interrupted, choosing his words carefully. He needed Danny on his side at any cost. "The book... it mentioned something... like a spell that Clay might be under." Lying wasn't his strongest suit, but he forced himself to focus. "I think... I think it might have been put on him by a great evil of some kind. It wasn't specific." He searched his mind for a single detail to make it more believable. "It has something to do with that armor he can't take off. Even he said it was cursed."

Danny's eyes lit up. Tyler knew turning their problem into a fantasy trope would get him excited. Anything that would put him on a hero's journey would win him over.

"The only way we can help him is by going to see the Sage." He held up his hands before Danny could reply. "I know Clay *thinks* the Sage is after him, but the book said differently. That's why the curse on him is so bad, it forces him to think the only person that can help him is his enemy."

"That's terrible..." Danny leaned forward, stroking the stubble on his chin. "So we need to journey across Bramoria and find the Sage to help him out, right?" He didn't miss a beat. "When are we leaving?"

"There's a couple of other things we have to take care of as well." This was the part of the story that was going to be hard to sell. "It looks like my mom is trapped here as well under a similar spell. We need to rescue her and get Koto."

"I'm sorry... your mom is here?"

"I don't know how either, but I saw her, even talked to her. She has no idea who I am."

Danny nodded. "We'll have to save her. But I'm not sold on Koto. Didn't he try to kill Clay?"

"No," Tyler said with confidence. "That is another piece of the curse. Koto is the only one who knows where the Sage is." His lies were getting deeper and deeper. "Clay had to lock him up to stop anyone from helping him."

A smile crept across Danny's face. "This is a complicated curse... and one I can't refuse to free Clay from, especially since I'm the hero of the story." He glanced around. "This castle is comfortable, but I prefer the life of an adventurer." He slapped his hand on the table, his excitement almost palpable. "I'm in! When do we leave?"

Tyler had to stop himself from commenting how easy it was. "Tonight. I'll meet you in your room at sundown. Remember, don't breathe a word of this or we might both find ourselves at the end of a rope."

"My lips are sealed," Danny smiled, making a locking motion with his fingers. "This is the kind of quest I've always dreamed of."

Tyler spent the entire day wandering through the castle doing everything he could to keep away from his room, the guards, and especially Clay. There were plenty of places to hide, although when he finally found the library with its multitude of nooks and shelves, he felt much safer. It reminded him of his room back home, private and dark. He was more homesick than he could express, but he was confident in his plan the more he thought about it. Koto would help them find the Sage and once there they would all be able to go home at last. Even if Danny and Clay hated him for it, he couldn't leave them in Bramoria. It was corrupting them both even if they were too blind to see it. Too much was at stake to care about their childish wants and Tyler knew he was doing the right thing even if it meant lying to Danny and kidnapping his own mother.

When the first hints of gold struck the library windows, Tyler pushed himself out of the stuffed chair in the hidden alcove and stretched. His heart was already pounding in his chest at the thought of what he was about to do but he ignored it. Over the past few days, it had become clear he was the only one of his friends with enough sanity to get them home. If it had to be through deceit, then so be it. For the first time since he set foot in that strange land, he didn't feel lost. He glanced up at the stained glass windows, the light of the sunset catching the bonding between the shards sparkling. It was time to go home.

Taking extra precautions, Tyler snuck out of the mostly abandoned library and through the corridors of the castle. Danny's room was close to Clay's, but he couldn't risk going back to his own. For some reason he had a sneaking suspicion that Clay would be looking for him and so keeping far away from there was his only choice. He knew with every passing moment that they couldn't find him, his absence became more suspicious. But he didn't have another choice. If Clay confronted him there was a good chance he wouldn't be able to lie convincingly enough, especially after watching Faus be murdered. The images of the previous night still haunted him. He'd spent the entire afternoon doing everything he could to not close his eyes despite the exhaustion from not yet having slept.

After several minutes of dodging guards and weaving his

way through the castle, Tyler finally found himself at Danny's door. He lifted his hand to knock, then thought better of it. Instead, he tested the latch and found it unlocked. As quietly as he could he slipped inside, closing the door behind him. He turned around and his heart dropped. Danny was standing in the center of the room with Ninsar held in his arms. Tyler's eyes wandered down her pale nude form, her dress in a pile around her feet. Danny stood beside her shirtless with his pants undone, held up only by the curve of his hips. Tyler immediately turned away, his face growing bright red. At the same time, fear leapt up into his throat. Ninsar was the second to last person he wanted to run into.

"You should knock next time, buddy," Danny laughed.

"S-Sorry. I didn't think–"

"It's fine," Danny said, cutting him off. Tyler could hear the pair of them pulling their clothes back on. "Actually I wanted to talk to you about our plan. I want to take Ninsar with us."

Tyler turned on his heel to stare at his friend, ignoring the nudity as they continued to dress. "What? Why?"

"She's a damsel in distress," Danny smiled. "I have to save her."

Tyler's eyes wandered to Ninsar as she pulled the last of her dress on. "I... She can't..." He tried to find some way to deny his request. "We don't know if she'll be safe!"

"I'll keep her safe, don't you worry." Danny pulled her in by the shoulder, leaning her body against his. From under his arm, Tyler could see the venomous glare of Ninsar piercing his soul. "Besides, she's a slave and it's our duty as heroes to free anybody who finds themselves entrapped by society's shortcomings."

"Are you sure about this?" he asked, ignoring the fear and distrust in his gut. "What if something happens to her? Everyone will be free if we pull this off and we can come back for her then."

"Tyler," Danny said seriously, gently removing Ninsar from his side and striding over. "This is what good people do. If we're going to save this world and Clay I want to do it the right way."

Staring up at Danny, Tyler realized he looked a little more tired than usual and his skin was less vibrant. The red spots on his face and shoulders were growing darker and more numerous. A heavy feeling settled in his stomach like a stone as he realized his illness was getting worse. As much as he didn't want to include unnecessary complications, he couldn't say no to Danny. This was the last adventure he'd ever go on.

"Okay," Tyler sighed, nodding his head. "But you need to get dressed! We should have been out of here already."

Danny placed a hand on his shoulder. "Thanks, buddy."

"Let's go!" Tyler said, shooing him away. "Don't forget your sword. You actually know how to use it."

Darting about the room, Danny scooped up his supplies. He strapped a set of well-fitted leather armor to himself with Ninsar's help, threw the sword sheath over his shoulders, and grabbed a spare thigh bag that looked like it had already been packed with a small amount of supplies. Tyler felt foolish for not grabbing a bag of his own. All he had was a pocket full of coins and his mage stone, however worthless it might be. At the last moment, Danny slid a hand under his pillow and pulled out a sheathed dagger on a thin leather strap. He tossed it to Ninsar.

"You know how to use that?" he asked, strapping the bag to his leg.

She nodded. "I wasn't always a servant girl, you know." Her eyes narrowed as she turned to Tyler, unsheathing the blade in his line of vision and checking it in the firelight. "It looks nice and sharp too."

Tyler swallowed hard. He didn't really want to bring an enemy on their trip, but whatever it took to get Danny out of the castle he'd work with.

"Are you ready, Danny?" Tyler asked, standing with his hand on the door handle.

"It's not Danny anymore," he replied with a grin. "It's Tiragan."

"Okay, well, whoever you are, let's get the hell out of here."

With one last nod from Danny, Tyler pulled the door open and the three of them crept out of the room, closing it softly behind them. He motioned for the other two to follow him and he'd only gone a few feet when Ninsar spoke up.

"You're going the wrong way," she hissed.

"Look, I know where I–"

"No, you don't," she snapped, cutting him off. "If you want to get into the dungeons without running into every guard in the castle you'll need to go through the servant's quarters."

Tyler stared at her for a long moment, wondering if she was trying to trick him into getting caught.

"Do you want to get your friend out or not?" she finally asked, her foot tapping impatiently on the ground.

"Yes."

"Then stop being a headstrong idiot and follow me."

She turned and walked away in the opposite direction, keeping close to the wall. Tyler glanced at Danny who had a hand over his mouth, trying to stifle his laughter.

"Shut the hell up," he muttered and followed after her.

TWENTY-SEVEN

Ninsar was true to her word. She led both of them through a series of doors and back stairwells down into the servant's quarters. There they were able to move about freely, the castle staff ignoring their movements completely. The halls were free of guards and by passing through the kitchens and dormitories they were able to make good time. After a series of small corridors and a flight of stairs, Ninsar stopped them at the top landing of another stairwell. The light was dim, the torches burning low in their brackets. A foul smell wafted up from the stairway that reminded Tyler of the gym lockers at his school mixed with feces and piss. He pulled his shirt up over his nose, trying to block it out.

"Where are we?" he asked through the linen fabric.

"This is the servant's entrance to the dungeons," Ninsar replied, keeping her voice low.

"Why would a dungeon have a servant's entrance?" he sniped back, believing she'd led them to the castle toilet.

She whipped around, her face only inches from his. "Who do you think cleans the cells? Feeds the inmates? Waits on the guards hand and foot?"

He didn't reply.

"That's right, servants. Did you think the king himself comes down here to wait on his victims?"

"No… I just didn't think–"

"Yes, that's the problem. You don't." She turned back

toward the stairs. "Keep quiet and follow me. The guards should be changing soon. We'll only have a moment to get your friend out."

"Lead the way," Danny said, gesturing toward the stairs with a smile.

She returned the smile before shooting Tyler another venomous glare. He was already regretting agreeing to bring her along. But then again, if he hadn't she would have just turned him in. It's not like he had much of a choice in the matter. Instead, he did his best to swallow his pride for the time being and let her lead the way.

At the bottom of the stairs they came to a dark wooden door slick with moisture and mold, a barred window fit into the top of it. Reaching to the edge, Ninsar hoisted herself up to look through the small window. She stared for a few moments before slowly lowering herself back down.

"There's only one guard on duty," she whispered. "If I can distract him you can sneak by and break your friend out." She glanced up at Danny. "At the end of the hall is a storage closet where they keep the items they confiscate from prisoners. You'll find all his things there if the guards didn't keep it themselves. He should be able to arm himself one way or another." Taking a deep breath she pulled the dagger from her belt and tucked it inside her dress. She turned back toward the door, her hand on the metallic ring. "I don't want to raise the alarm if we can help it, so be quick."

Before anyone could respond she pulled the door open and stepped through, leaving it standing wide enough behind her so they could slip through without disturbing it. Tyler and Danny hid on the other side out of sight, listening intently to what was going on inside. At first, all they could hear were her footsteps across the stone, then a rattling of armor as the guard noticed her.

"Good evening, sir," she said in her servant's tone.

"Mmm," the guard hummed like he was looking at a steak. Tyler could almost hear his eyes wandering over her thin dress.

"What's a pretty lady like you doing down here?"

"I apologize for the interruption, but I was sent down by the captain as a birthday gift for one of his best soldiers." She paused for a moment, waiting for him to take the bait.

"Well... it's uh... it's my birthday... so it must be me!" the man replied, his lie so obvious that Tyler rolled his eyes impulsively.

"Oh! Well happy birthday to you!" Ninsar giggled, her voice getting higher. Tyler and Danny peeked around the corner to watch her work. "You know," she said, leaning close to the soldier's face, her lips pouted in his direction, "you're just my type." She lifted a finger and ran it down his neck and armor stopping only when it reached the leather codpiece of his armor. "But this pesky armor... it just gets in the way of all the fun I want to have with you."

The man was out of his chair and pulling at the leather straps before she could finish her sentence.

"Calm down, soldier," she cooed, taking him by the face and planting a soft kiss on his lips. "I'm yours for the whole night."

He melted in her grasp. Tyler had to admit, she was good at what she did. Either that or all guys were suckers. He was inclined to believe the latter.

"Why don't you turn around so I can help you with these straps, huh?" She gave him another small kiss and pushed him to face the wall. "We'll make it a little game."

"Uh, okay!" he replied enthusiastically, placing his hands on the wall as Ninsar began to pull at the straps.

"Why don't we start with this belt." She reached around the man's waist and undid his belt slowly. With her free hand, she waved for them to come into the room. "You won't be needing this."

With a flick of her wrist, Ninsar managed to not only toss the belt to the floor along with the man's sword but also detach the keys and clutch them in her free hand. She held them out behind her as Tyler and Danny snuck down the hall. Danny reached out and took the keys silently, giving her a thumbs-up as he snuck by.

The soldier started to laugh and Tyler froze in place. "That tickles!" he exclaimed, grabbing at his waist where Ninsar's hand had worked under the leather plate. He began to turn back around.

"No peeking!" Ninsar laughed, pushing him back toward the wall forcefully. "You don't want to spoil the surprise, do you?"

"What's the surprise?"

He started to turn around again but before he could Ninsar grabbed his hand and pressed it to her chest. Immediately he relaxed and leaned forward, his face resting against the stone with a small sigh.

"Now if you're a good boy there'll be more of that as soon as I get this armor undone. Can you do that for me?"

"Yes ma'am," he cooed, relaxing into her touch.

With another scowl Ninsar looked at Tyler and mouthed the word 'go', pointing down the hallway after Danny. With a stiff nod, he hurried to catch up.

There were several cells lining the outer wall of the castle, each divided by a stone partition so that the prisoners could neither see nor touch one another. The majority of them were empty, but now and again Tyler would pass one with some long-forgotten prisoner sulking in its dark corners, their flesh sallow and eyes sunken. They looked less than human, wasting away in the cells completely cut off from everyone. One such man, who looked worse than the rest, had his back to the bars. For a moment Tyler suspected he was already dead, but the slow rise and fall of his chest gave him away even if his gray skin and shedding hair made him look like a corpse.

At the far end, Danny was standing in front of a set of iron bars. He looked up at Tyler and motioned him over. Even in the shadows, he was able to make out the tall cat-like ears and the swishing tail. It was Koto, although he looked a bit worse for wear. At the sound of their boots his ears perked up and he lifted his head. For a moment he stared, squinting as if he didn't believe what he was seeing.

"Ty?" he whispered, his voice raspy. "What... Why are you here?"

Tyler held up the keys. "We're here to get you out."

"But... why?"

"It's too much to explain right now," Tyler hushed him, gently unfolding the keys and slipping the first into the lock. It didn't work so he switched to another. "This place isn't safe for anyone. We have to go."

Koto grabbed the edge of the cot chained to the wall and hoisted himself up from the ground. His knees were shaky and judging by his slow movements, he was dangerously weak with hunger. Tyler tried the third key, then a fourth. On the fifth try, the lock finally clicked and the door swung inward, creaking slightly on its hinges.

"Give me the keys," Danny said, holding out his hand. "I'll grab his gear and you help him out." He pulled open his bag and traded Tyler an apple for the keys. "Get something in his stomach so he can walk."

Tyler nodded. "Be quick."

With a grin, Danny turned on his heel and rushed down the hall toward the heavy wooden door at the end where Ninsar said the prisoner's items would be stored. Stepping inside the stone and metal cage, Tyler reached out a hand to help Koto. He lifted an arm over his shoulder and helped the man take his first steps out of the cell.

"Koto..." he began, handing the man the apple. "I'm sorry. I didn't know they were going to teleport us here." The words were filling his head so fast he couldn't get them out coherently. "I didn't know Clay was... you were right... I should have listened... everything is messed up."

"Ty," Koto said, swallowing his first bite. "Why did you come back for me?"

Tyler's first inclination was to lie, to tell Koto how much he meant or what a great friend he was. But he was already lying to enough people, he couldn't handle another. "I… I need your help." He glanced up into Koto's green eyes. "I have to find the Sage."

Koto took another bite, too tired to react much to the confession. He stared at Tyler for a long moment, chewing and thinking. His brows furrowed together as if he was about to ask something, but he stopped. At last, he simply replied, "Okay."

Tyler breathed a sigh of relief. "Thank you."

"I think these are yours," Danny interjected, jogging over to them. He handed Koto a leather breastplate, a bow, quiver, a dagger, and a shortsword. "Or at least they are yours now." He turned to Tyler and held out a small bag with three leather straps. "Put this on, you'll need it once we're on the road." He patted his own bag strapped to his upper thigh.

Tyler nodded and began to put it on while Danny helped Koto slip on his armor. It took less than a minute for them to prepare, but with every second that ticked by Tyler knew they came closer to being found out. Despite himself, he was also worried about Ninsar and how long she could tease the guard before he lost his patience. His thoughts were answered by a sudden clattering of metal. All of their heads whipped back down the hall. It had gone completely silent. With a quiet nod, Danny pulled his sword and started back in the direction they'd come from. Tyler followed suit. Even Koto pulled the sword into his off-hand, the other still wounded from their fight with the Fossars. Together they crept down the hall, taking great pains to keep their boots silent on the stone.

Danny stopped at the corner and waited, his ear turned toward the table where the guard sat. It was still silent. He gave the others a signal to be ready. Gripping his weapon with both hands he leapt around the corner, Tyler and Koto dashing in behind him. Their eyes fell on a lump of metal on the floor, dark crimson blood slowly pooling over the stones. Ninsar stood over the fallen guard, a bloody dagger in her hand. She bent down and ripped a piece of his tunic off, cleaning her blade with the cloth.

"What took you guys so long?" she asked, wiping a bit

of blood from her cheek. She looked between them, her brows furrowing at their open-mouthed stares. "What? He was getting handsy." She turned her glare to Tyler. "I told you to be quick about it!"

"We need to go," Tyler said, still staring at the bloody mess. "As soon as someone sees this we're fucked."

"Agreed." Danny reached out a hand for Ninsar. "Milady? Get us out as fast as possible please."

"Through the walled gardens," Tyler cut in. "Someone is waiting there for us."

Ninsar lifted an eyebrow but didn't argue. She tucked the dagger back into her belt. "Follow me."

TWENTY-EIGHT

They were nearly past the kitchens when the horns finally sounded, blasting through the halls of the castle like foreboding fanfare. Someone had found the body of the dungeon guard. Tyler hoped it would have taken longer, but it was too late to worry about it now. Immediately the entire castle came alive and the pounding of boots and clanking of metal could be heard throughout every corner of the grounds. It was all Tyler could do to stop his heart from pounding straight out of his chest in fear. The others seemed less concerned or else they were good at hiding it, he wasn't sure. What was clear was that they needed to move fast or they'd find themselves in an early grave.

True to her word, Ninsar led them in the most direct path toward the walled garden. Once there Tyler figured they'd be able to easily slip through the rear gate of the grounds, but now that everyone was on high alert and Koto missing from his cell, the guard would surely be doubled at all the entrances. He had no idea how they were going to escape but they had to find a way. There was no going back.

Finally, the group came to the last door leading to the courtyard. All of them huddled around the doorframe, peering across the enclosed yard and through the gate to the garden. A group of soldiers to their left hustled down a covered hall then through a door into the castle itself. Tyler felt his hands shaking. If they wanted to make it across the courtyard and into the garden without being seen, they'd need to move fast.

"Through there," he said, pointing at the iron gate on the far side that stood open. "That's our way out."

"Is the back gate a good idea? Won't they be expecting that?" Koto asked, leaning forward to get a better look.

"We don't have to use the gate," Ninsar cut in. "There's another way out... but... it's gross."

Danny turned to her. "It's a sewer, isn't it?"

She nodded. "How did you know?"

"I read a lot. It's always a sewer."

"What? And it's full of giant rats or something? Isn't that how this goes?" Tyler asked, rolling his eyes. His video game back home had a level just like this. "Maybe there's a big slime at the end we have to fight?"

"What... What are you two talking about?" Ninsar wore an expression of complete confusion as she looked between the pair of them. "It's just a sewer. There's water and shit in it. It drains into the river."

"That's it? No demon horse? No evil bat queen?"

Ninsar narrowed her eyes at Tyler. "Are you making fun of me at a time like this?"

He held up his hands, worried she'd stab him right then and there. "No no!"

"He's not," Danny smiled, placing a hand on her tense shoulder. "We've just read a lot of books is all."

"Hmm," she hummed, shooting a sideways glare at Tyler. "I'll take your word for it." She turned back to the courtyard and held up a pale hand. "On my signal."

Just as she started to lower her hand a group of dragon-like men exited a passage nearby, coming into the courtyard. Tyler recognized their leader immediately. It was Liran, the bounty hunter that had nearly killed him the day he came to Bramoria. If he was in the castle, he was in league with Clay. He should have known.

"Be on the lookout! Kotolor has escaped!" Liran called out to his men. "He's already killed a soldier and he won't hesitate to kill more!" He stopped, pointing the men through another door near their hiding spot. "Search every room! Nobody rests until he's found!"

Tyler and the other three ducked behind the door as they passed by, thankfully not drawing any attention to themselves. Ninsar leaned back out as the last of them disappeared into the main castle, Liran giving one last look over his shoulder before he vanished.

"Now!" she whispered, her hand slicing through the air.

All four of them took off at a mad dash for the other side of the courtyard. Koto was the slowest from lack of food, but even at his slowest, he was nearly as fast as Tyler. Danny and Ninsar made it to the other side before he'd even gotten halfway. The voice of a soldier rose behind them and Tyler's heart nearly leapt out of his throat. He glanced over his shoulder to see a guard looking in their direction but before he could cry out again for backup, there was the twang of a bowstring and an arrow struck him in the throat. Koto hissed through his teeth, clutching at his still broken arm that he'd used to fire it. The soldier sank to his knees and fell onto the cobblestones, the blood visible even from the other side of the yard. Both Tyler and Koto dashed around the wall and stopped to catch their breaths.

"Thanks," Tyler huffed.

"Sure. Thanks for getting me out," Koto panted in reply. He winced as he slipped the bow back over his shoulders and cradled his arm to his chest. "I won't be able to do that again."

"Hopefully we won't need it." He turned to Ninsar. "Keep an eye out, the queen is meeting us here."

"The queen?!" both Ninsar and Danny said at once.

"I told you, Danny," he replied. "I can't leave my mother behind."

Danny stared at him for a long moment, his eyes searching. "Okay," he managed to let out. "And it's Tiragan."

Tyler nodded. He didn't have time to worry about made-up names. "Lead the way," he said, nodding to Ninsar. "And keep your eyes peeled."

Before she could reply another voice rose up behind them followed by another, then another. Fear streaked across all of their faces at once as their gazes fell to Tyler.

"Run!" he shouted and the four of them took off at a breakneck pace.

The roses and shrubs in full bloom whipped by as they ran through the walled gardens. Dodging behind hedges and topiaries, the group tried to stay out of sight for as long as possible. Ninsar led the charge while Tyler kept his eyes open for his mother. The note he'd slipped under her door told her to meet Clay after sunset in the gardens. He knew she would never show up if he'd signed it himself. She had no idea who he was. But she'd meet Clay who she seemed completely devoted to. Even if it meant kidnapping her, Tyler was going to get her out of harm's way.

As they came around the edge of a hedge Tyler saw a figure cloaked in white and he knew it was her. He called to the others and shifted their course toward her. Leaping over a rosebush he skidded to a halt, gasping for breath.

"You got my note," he huffed, grabbing her shoulder. "Come on, we need to go right now."

There was a long pause.

"Let's go!" Tyler urged, pulling at her again.

"So it was you. I should have known," a baritone voice replied. The figure turned around and whipped the cloak off. "You always run when things get the tiniest bit complicated."

Tyler took a step back. There, standing in the garden was Clay, the king of Bramoria. He wore dark metal armor, a rectangular obsidian stone set into the breastplate. Tyler knew immediately it was his mage stone. The others came to a halt behind him, each of them holding their weapons at the ready. Tyler wanted to speak but his voice was caught in his throat, trapped by the pounding of his heart and the terror that threatened to consume him. Clay looked up at the others calmly, his armored hand resting on the hilt of his sword. Slowly his gaze came to rest on Danny.

"Tiragan," he stated calmly. "I didn't expect this from you. I thought we were friends."

"We are friends, Clay," Danny replied, still clutching his blade. "But Tyler saw the book and he told me what's been going on."

"Is that so?" Clay's eyes shifted to Tyler. "So you were the one that convinced that whore to steal my book, were you?"

"Don't you call him that!" Ninsar growled, stepping forward with her dagger brandished. "He was a better man than you'll ever be!"

Clay ignored her and glanced at Koto. "And you've let my would-be assassin out of jail. I'm honestly impressed you managed to pull this off. You've never really struck me as much of *anything* if I'm honest."

"I... I know what you are Clay. What you did." He was trying his best to keep tears of frustration and fear from forming in his eyes. "You poisoned the king to take his place, you stole my mother away to be your own, and you've been enslaving your own people!"

"Yes, that's true."

"And Koto didn't try to kill you, he tried to turn you in!"

"Those are the same thing." He smiled at Tyler's confusion. "What? Do you think they would have just let me go after they found out I tried to kill the king? You can't be that naive."

Tyler swallowed hard. "You've got the academy under your thumb and you're using the Divinarae for something with the dragons, I just don't know what." He glanced back at Danny. "Somehow he managed to wipe away parts of the book to hide what he's up to."

"So much good detective work. I am really impressed."

The sound of clanking armor and shouts was drawing nearer, but Tyler didn't break eye contact with Clay. "Why are you doing this? You came all the way to a new world just to be an asshole? You're no better than your father!"

Clay's rapier was drawn and leveled at Tyler's neck before

he could even blink, the sharp tip digging into his skin. "Don't you *fucking* dare compare me to that man," he hissed through clenched teeth.

Tyler could see the vein twitching in his forehead, the tendons of his neck stretched taut. Apparently, he'd struck a nerve. "Tell me, how are you two any different? Taking advantage of those inferior to you to fulfill your own selfish desires? You want everyone to feel bad for you, but you just create all your own problems!"

"You know *nothing* about my life," Clay growled, the blade pressing harder against Tyler's throat. "You don't know what it was like, what he *did* to me. I spent every moment of the last six years living in absolute terror of what he'd do next. What I'd have to deal with when I got home." He cocked his head to the side. "And what did you do to help me? What did *anybody* do to help?!" He looked ready to burst. "NOTHING!"

Soldiers spilled into the garden around them, filling every available space. They pressed in, their weapons drawn, ready to take down everyone to protect the king. Tyler saw Liran and his men take a spot to the left, their eyes fixed on Koto.

"Back the fuck off!" Clay yelled, a burst of magical energy emanating from his body and blowing a few of the guards off their feet. The stone at his chest glowed with dull gray wisps floating around it. "I can handle this by myself!"

"What did you want me to do, Clay?" Tyler asked, his voice rising in anger. "I'm just a kid! Until a week ago I was still in high school! What was I supposed to do? Come rescue you? Buy you a house? A new life? Tell me what you want and I'll give it to you! Anything to stop you from doing all this horrible shit!"

Clay chuckled, his features darkening. "Oh no no no. It's far too late for that now." He drew the blade back slowly, sliding it into the sheath. "I'm finally in a position of power, in control of my own destiny with the world at my fingertips and you think you're going to buy me off with some paltry gift given when I no longer need it? No." He flexed his metallic fingers, reaching up and touching the stone at his chest. "Nobody will ever hold me down again."

"Clay," Tyler said, trying to soften his voice. "Please, just come with us and we'll go home. We'll get you out of your dad's place and help you get started in life. I know you don't want to be like this. This isn't you."

"You want me to go back?" He threw his head back and began to laugh. "To what? A world full of pollution, disease, poverty, and wage labor? You're a fucking fool to want to live in that shithole of a world you call home!" He held out his arms, gesturing to the gardens around him. "This world is beautiful, it's full of life, adventure, and," his smile widened, "it's all mine." He paused for a moment, waiting for a response, but none came. "You have nothing to offer me, Tyler Wilson. And now you've made yourself my enemy." Clay's attention turned to Danny. "But you haven't. Not yet, Tiragan."

Danny's troubled expression shifted to confusion as he looked up at Clay. "What do you mean?"

"Stay here with me," Clay said simply, his voice gentle. "I can give you anything you want. I have the book, the magic of the entire academy, and the whole world at my feet. Name it and you'll have it."

"Danny, don't li–"

A metal hand caught Tyler across the face and he tasted blood as he was lifted off his feet. His sword nearly fell from his grip as he crashed to the ground, toppling Ninsar and Koto at the same time. All three landed in a pile, a tangle of limbs. He reached up to touch his throbbing lip and his fingers came away crimson.

"Anything you want Tiragan," Clay repeated as if nothing had happened. "I can give you money, jewels, adventure." He looked Danny up and down. "I can even give you a *cure*."

Danny's sword dipped a few inches as his jaw fell open. "Is... Is that even possible?"

"I have every mage in the world at my disposal. With that amount of power and my own, *anything* is possible."

Tyler watched as Danny's entire demeanor shifted. His

sword fell to his side and he no longer looked concerned about Clay's actions. Instead, he looked tempted, like he was thinking it over.

"All you have to do is stay here with me and forget about *him*." Clay shot a glare at Tyler. "He doesn't care about you anyway. If he really cared he wouldn't be trying to force you to go home to die. He'd be looking for a way to save you, to save us both." Clay held out his metal hand. "I will do what he refuses to do. I *will* save you and give you everything you've ever dreamed of."

Danny's hand twitched at his side and Tyler could tell he was losing him. Clay's offer was too tempting, but Tyler knew it was a lie. If Clay could cure Danny, why hadn't he done it yet? They'd been there for a few days and already met all the mages in the city. Surely they would have performed the magic already if it was possible instead of making him needlessly suffer. No, Clay was lying just like he had been from the beginning but Danny couldn't see it. As Tyler looked up into his blue eyes all he saw was hope. For the first time in four years, he thought he had a chance to live. Tyler couldn't blame him for wanting it, but it wasn't real. He had to save his best friend, even if it wasn't what he thought he wanted. He just didn't know how.

A warmth on Tyler's thigh drew his attention away from the scene. He glanced down and saw a faintly glowing amber light emanating through the fabric of his pants. Digging his hand in his fingers wrapped around the rectangular mage stone he'd been carrying since he came to Bramoria. For the first time, it was no longer just a transparent rock. Instead, it was a dimly glowing amber crystal with arcs of energy crackling around it. As he stared, it grew brighter and brighter. He could feel the power within it coursing through his body, filling him up with a feeling of great potential. The feeling was intense and it nearly overwhelmed him as every inch of his body began to buzz. Glancing back up at Danny the idea came to him and he realized what he had to do. He just hoped his magic would be powerful enough to do it. As Danny lifted his hand to take Clay's, he knew he had no choice but to try.

"Grab hold of me!" Tyler shouted to Ninsar and Koto.

Both of them grabbed his shoulders as he gripped the stone in one hand and reached out for Danny with the other. His hand intercepted Danny's in mid-air, his finger wrapping over the red flecked skin and he gripped it tight. He thought back to the magic Gordanth had done a few days before and one word rang in his mind.

Teleport.

With a flash of blinding white light, Tyler felt himself yanked off the ground and into the void, Clay's cry of fury and rage cut off in an instant.

For a moment there was nothing but darkness, but in the blink of an eye, the world popped back into view as they reappeared. Confused by the sudden rush of magic, it took a moment for Tyler to realize he and his friends were falling, his guts lurching from the feeling. The wind filled his ears as he gathered speed, cutting off the cries of his friends. He looked down into the sky full of heavy gray clouds only to recognize he was upside down. Craning his neck in the opposite direction the wind whipped at his eyes. Through the tears, he was able to see the blue rushing up to meet them. He didn't even have time to wonder what he'd done wrong before he crashed into the icy-cold surface of the water.

Click here to continue the adventure in Book 2: The Sage and the Phoenix!

BOOKS BY THIS AUTHOR

Join The Newsletter

Sign up for Blake's monthly newsletter to receive news on upcoming releases, interact with the author, and hear about exclusive deals on his body of work!

The Crystalline Chronicles Series

The power of the ancient dragon lords has been unearthed. Can an escaped slave hope to control that power or will it ultimately destroy him?

Join Dusk and his companions in this complete epic fantasy series full of magic, dragons, monsters, and adventure!

Bone, Stone, And Wood Series

When Nox discovers a mysterious ring and a talking fox, he's chosen by the gods to save the world from unimaginable darkness. Will he rise to the challenge or perish on the road destiny has laid out before him?

The Tales Of Bramoria Trilogy

Transported to a magical fantasy world. Tyler's friends are losing their minds. Can he hope to save them or will their new world consume them?

ABOUT THE AUTHOR

Blake R. Wolfe

Blake spends most nights with his laptop pulled close, clacking away on the keyboard to get the next great idea written down. Surrounded by piles of notebooks, journals, and a cat of course, he does his best to keep his brain on the task at hand.  Blake has published across multiple genres, but prefers the fantasy realm to all others. He is a beach bum during the summer, a wannabe yogi, and an avid Muppets fan. Seriously.

You can find the rest of his work on his website at https://www.blakerwolfe.com

Printed in Great Britain
by Amazon

40262487R00129